COAUTHORED BOOKS

*The Money Shot***
(with Parnell Hall)

*Smooth Operator***
(with Parnell Hall)

Barely Legal††
(with Parnell Hall)

TRAVEL

A Romantic's Guide to the Country Inns of Britain and Ireland (1979)

MEMOIR

Blue Water, Green Skipper

*A Holly Barker Novel
†A Stone Barrington Novel
‡A Will Lee Novel

§An Ed Eagle Novel
**A Teddy Fay Novel
††A Herbie Fisher Novel

Stone Barrington is pulled along for the ride when a friend pursues a perilous course of vengeance in the newest novel from #1 *New York Times*–bestselling author Stuart Woods.

In the wake of a personal tragedy, former CIA operative Teddy Fay—now a successful Hollywood film producer known as Billy Barnett—takes a leave of absence to travel and grieve, and lands in Santa Fe in the company of his friends Stone Barrington and Ed Eagle. There, fate hands him an unexpected opportunity to exact quiet revenge for his recent loss, from a man who helped to cover up the crime.

But when his enemy wises up to Teddy's machinations, a discreet game of sabotage escalates to a potentially lethal battle. From the arid splendor of the New Mexico desert to the glamour of Hollywood's rolling hills, it will take all of Stone Barrington's diplomacy and skill to maneuver for Teddy's advantage while keeping innocents out of the crossfire.

Praise for Stuart Woods's Stone Barrington Novels

Quick & Dirty

"Suspenseful . . . The excitement builds."

—*Publishers Weekly*

Indecent Exposure

"[An] irresistible, luxury-soaked soap opera."

—*Publishers Weekly*

Fast & Loose

"Another entertaining episode in [a] soap opera about the rich and famous."   —Associated Press

Below the Belt

Compulsively readable . . . [An] easy-reading page-turner."

—*Booklist*

Sex, Lies & Serious Money

"Series fans will continue to enjoy this bird's-eye view of the high life." —*Booklist*

Dishonorable Intentions

"Diverting." —*Publishers Weekly*

Family Jewels

"A master of dialogue, action and atmosphere, the Key West resident has added one more jewel of a thriller-mystery to his ever-growing collection."
—Fort Myers *Florida Weekly*

Scandalous Behavior

"Woods offers another wild ride with his hero, bringing readers back into a world of action-packed adventure, murder and mayhem, steamy romance, and a twist you don't see coming." —*Booklist*

Foreign Affairs

"Purrs like a well-tuned dream machine . . . Enjoy this slick thriller by a thoroughly satisfying professional."
—*Florida Weekly*

Hot Pursuit

"Fans will enjoy the vicarious luxury ride."
—*Publishers Weekly*

Insatiable Appetites

"Multiple exciting storylines . . . Readers of the series will enjoy the return of the dangerous Dolce." —*Booklist*

Paris Match

"Plenty of fast-paced action and deluxe experiences that keep the pages turning. Woods is masterful with his use of dialogue and creates natural and vivid scenes for his readers to enjoy." —Myrtle Beach *Sun News*

Cut and Thrust

"Goes down as smoothly as a glass of Knob Creek."
—*Publishers Weekly*

Carnal Curiosity

"Stone Barrington shows he's one of the smoothest operators around."
—*Publishers Weekly*

Standup Guy

"Stuart Woods still owns an imagination that simply won't quit. . . . This is yet another edge-of-your-seat adventure."
—*Suspense Magazine*

Doing Hard Time

"High escapist suspense."
—*Mystery Scene*

Collateral Damage

"Undoubtedly a hit. It starts off strong and never lets up, building to an exciting showdown."
—*Booklist*

Severe Clear

"Stuart Woods has proven time and time again that he's a master of suspense who keeps his readers frantically turning the pages."
—Bookreporter.com

Unnatural Acts

"[It] makes you covet the fast-paced, charmed life of Woods's characters from the safety of your favorite chair."
—Code451.com

D.C. Dead

"Engaging . . . The story line is fast-paced."
—*Midwest Book Review*

Son of Stone

"Woods's vast and loyal audience will be thrilled with a second-generation Barrington charmer."
—*Booklist*

BOOKS BY STUART WOODS

FICTION

UNBOUND

A STONE BARRINGTON NOVEL

STUART WOODS

G. P. PUTNAM'S SONS • NEW YORK

PUTNAM

G. P. PUTNAM'S SONS
Publishers Since 1838
An imprint of Penguin Random House LLC
375 Hudson Street
New York, New York 10014

Copyright © 2018 by Stuart Woods
Excerpt from *Shoot First* copyright © 2018 by Stuart Woods

The Library of Congress has catalogued the G. P. Putnam's Sons hardcover edition as follows:

Library of Congress Cataloging-in-Publication Data

Names: Woods, Stuart, author.
Title: Unbound : a Stone Barrington novel / Stuart Woods.
Description: New York : G. P. Putnam's Sons, 2018.
Identifiers: LCCN 2017036717 | ISBN 9780735217171 (hardcover)
Subjects: | GSAFD: Mystery fiction. | Suspense fiction.
Classification: LCC PS3573.O642 U49 2018 | DDC 813/.54—dc23
LC record available at https://lccn.loc.gov/2017036717
p.   cm.

First G. P. Putnam's Sons hardcover edition / January 2018
First G. P. Putnam's Sons premium edition / August 2018
G. P. Putnam's Sons premium edition ISBN: 9780735217188

Printed in the United States of America
1 3 5 7 9 10 8 6 4 2

UNBOUND

1

TEDDY FAY STARED into the smog-filtered rising sun and set his speed control to seventy-five miles per hour. The road seemed for a moment to rise into the flaming ball, then, as he crested what passed for a hill, it fell back into its proper place. He reached into the center armrest, fumbled for his Ray-Bans and put them on. No need to drill a hole into his corneas.

Teddy, who for some time had been called Billy Barnett, had done all the right things. He had identified his wife's body in the morgue, though he had winced at her injuries. The instrument of her death had been a huge SUV, driven down Rodeo Drive at an incomprehensible speed by a woman who had, reportedly, just finished a three-cosmo lunch with some friends. His wife's only participation had been to go shopping and to cross with the light in her favor. She had been the definition of innocence, and her killer had been the definition of murderer. Apparently, as he'd been told by police, the woman was the wife of one of Hollywood's most famous producers, who specialized in the kind of mayhem inflicted by his spouse on that sunny, sunny L.A. day.

Teddy Fay had done the right thing. He had engaged an undertaker, sat through a well-attended memorial service, and scattered her ashes in the surf at Malibu Beach in front of their house, a place she had loved. He had asked Peter Barrington, for whom he worked, to be relieved of his duties on a film he was scheduled to produce, and had been told to take all the time he needed. She would be missed, he had been told, having been the heart and soul of the business side of the production company and a fixture at Centurion Studios.

Teddy had then packed a couple of bags, tossed them into the rear of his new Porsche Cayenne Turbo, which had, seemingly of its own accord, found its way onto I-40, pointed east, toward Oklahoma City. The car may have known the way, but Teddy had no idea where he was going.

An hour after sunrise, Teddy surprised himself by feeling hungry. He had not eaten for nearly two days. He got off the interstate and found a small-town diner—he didn't know which town—and ate a big breakfast. He gassed up and got back onto I-40. He passed exits to places with familiar names, but none of them had any life for him.

He spent the night in a motel and continued at dawn the next day. He was in the western outskirts of Albuquerque when he saw a sign for Santa Fe. The name resonated for Teddy; he had visited, even lived there when he had been on the run from most of the law and intelligence services in the United States. He took I-25 north. It might be a nicer place since he had been presidentially pardoned for his many sins—more than the President knew about, but all covered.

He was at five thousand feet of elevation at Albuquerque, the same as Denver, the Mile-High City, and as he drove north the landscape rose before him, until his GPS told him he was nearing seven thousand feet. He knew the name of a hotel there: the Inn of the Anasazi. He had always liked the name, and now he phoned ahead for accommodations. He noted several calls received on his iPhone, but the ringer had been off, and he didn't feel like returning them.

HE LAY STARING at the beamed ceiling for a long time before he fell asleep.

STONE BARRINGTON WAS at his desk in his home office in New York when Joan, his secretary, buzzed him. "Your son is on line one."

They normally talked once a week, and it had only been three or four days since their last conversation, so Stone was immediately worried. He picked up the phone. "Peter?"

"Hello, Dad."

"You sound sad. Is anything wrong?"

"It's Billy Barnett," Peter said.

"Is he ill?"

"No, his wife was run down and killed by a drunk driver in Beverly Hills a few days ago, and now he's missing."

"I'm very sorry to hear that. I liked her. What do you mean, 'missing'?"

"I'm sorry, I didn't mean to sound ominous. I just mean that he asked for some time off, and I haven't been able to reach him since. I went out to his house in Malibu this morning. His car was gone, and the place was locked up."

"Somehow, that doesn't surprise me," Stone said. "Billy was a loner before he married, so maybe he just wants to be alone again for a while."

"But Billy has become more gregarious over the past few years, in his quiet way, of course. I wouldn't have expected him to just walk away from everyone he knows here."

"Peter, people don't always do what you expect them to, even when you think you know them well. Give him a while, then try calling him again, or just send him a text saying that you're thinking about him and you hope to hear from him soon."

"You're right, that's what I should do."

"When you hear from him tell him he's in my thoughts, and if he finds his way to New York he's welcome at my house."

"I'll do that, Dad." They said goodbye and hung up.

*   *   *

TEDDY AWOKE LATE and had breakfast. As noon approached he thought he'd take a stroll around the Plaza, which was a few steps from the inn. He passed through the large group of Indian craftspeople selling their silver jewelry under the portico of the old Governor's Mansion and immediately thought of buying something for his wife but brought himself up short. He forced himself to walk on.

He was approaching some sort of commercial building when a familiar figure suddenly appeared a few yards ahead, leaving its front door. The figure was unmistakable, since he was something like six feet, eight inches tall and, further, wore a large Western hat that added another half a foot to his height. Teddy walked a little faster to catch up.

Then he saw a second man, and there was something furtive in his posture and movement. He had fallen into step behind the tall man, and there was something in his right hand, bumping against his leg.

"Ed!" Teddy shouted. Then louder, as he began to run. "Ed Eagle!"

Eagle turned and looked over his left shoulder but didn't stop, missing sight of the man, who was behind and to his right.

Teddy lunged at the man, striking him in the lower back with his forearm and knocking him to the ground. Teddy was climbing the man's back, reaching for the wrist of the hand that held the long blade, when Eagle turned around and, seeing what had happened, stomped on the wrist and kicked the knife away.

"Billy?" Eagle said. "Jesus Christ, what's going on?"

Teddy had the man's left arm behind his back, his wrist shoved up between his shoulder blades.

"I think you'd better ask this guy," he said to Eagle, "but maybe you'd better call a cop first."

2

T EDDY SAT AT the dining table in Ed Eagle's home, with Ed and his wife, the actress and writer Susannah Wilde, as well. The business on the sidewalk outside Eagle's offices had been handled with dispatch by the Santa Fe police, and both Ed and Teddy had given statements.

"I'm sorry to hear about your wife's death," Eagle said.

"Thank you, Ed," Teddy replied, "I was sorry to hear about it myself."

"Of course. What brings you to Santa Fe?"

"Four wheels and a wandering nature," Teddy replied. "For some reason I suddenly craved the open road."

"I'm glad it brought you our way," Ed said. "Otherwise, I might be on a slab down at the morgue."

"I didn't get a chance to ask you," Teddy said, "who was the guy, and what was his beef?"

"His name is Sanchez, and his beef was that I talked his brother into taking a plea bargain of thirty years, instead of what would almost certainly have been the death penalty. Now his brother will be out in fifteen years or so, and the other Mr. Sanchez, the one with the sword, will likely be serving life, since he opposes plea bargains."

"It was a sword?"

"A Roman sword, or a reasonable facsimile thereof. Last year Mr. Sanchez was an extra in a sword and sandal opus being shot somewhere out in the hills, and the company went back to L.A. one sword short. Except for you, they would have located it between my shoulder blades."

"I'm glad I was there," Teddy said.

"I'm glad you were, too," Susannah offered. "Mind you, I've occasionally been tempted to do much the same thing to Ed with a steak knife, but I must have a bit more personal restraint than Mr. Sanchez."

Everybody laughed.

"If I'd known you were here," Ed said, "you'd be occupying our guesthouse instead of the inn. It's not too late to make the move. We'd be delighted to have you."

"Thank you, Ed, but I think I'll move on in a day or two, so I won't trouble you."

"Do you have a destination in mind?" Ed said.

"Not yet."

"Do you intend to pursue justice with Mrs. Dax Baxter?"

"She's Dax Baxter's wife? I didn't know. In any case, I'll let the law have its way with her."

"I've made a couple of calls to L.A., and I'm afraid the law appears to have lost interest in Mrs. Baxter," Ed said. "She was unconscious when the police arrived at the scene and she was taken to a hospital. Before she could be admitted or even regained consciousness, she had been moved to a private clinic, where she had previously been treated for drug and alcohol abuse, and by the time the police got access, her bloodstream was clear of any substance. Mr. Baxter has hired a very competent attorney, one Rex Winston, to represent her, and I'm afraid that by the time the district attorney has completed his investigation, Mrs. Baxter will have been found to have had a small stroke while driving and was already unconscious at the time of the accident."

"So she will just walk away from killing another human being?" Teddy asked incredulously.

"That seems very likely," Ed said. "Dax Baxter is well acquainted with the wheels upon which his city rolls and knows how and which ones to lubricate."

"Then perhaps I should consider a civil suit?"

"Perhaps, but you should know that Mrs. Baxter, in her previous incarnation as Willa Mather, was a well-regarded actress, until her husband decided, given her history of substance abuse, that she should confine her career to red-carpet appearances in his company. She would probably regard taking the stand in her own defense as an opportunity for a comeback, and she would be a formidable witness."

Teddy nodded. "I remember her work, and I tend to agree with your opinion of her."

"I'm sorry I can't be more encouraging, Billy."

Susannah spoke up. "Or," she said, "you could just shoot them both in the head."

Ed smiled. "I'm afraid my wife, though she is a brilliant actress, a fine screenwriter, and an ace producer and director, would make a poor attorney. She lacks the patience."

"Tell me, Ed," Susannah said sweetly, "how would patience improve Billy's situation?"

Ed shrugged. "Improvement can be hard to come by, but patience is time, and time, though it may not heal all wounds, heals some of them and usually ameliorates the rest."

"My husband is so wise," Susannah said with a smile.

"I appreciate both your points of view," Teddy said, "though perhaps not equally."

THE FOLLOWING MORNING Ed Eagle made a phone call east, where it was two hours later.

"Stone Barrington."

"Hello, Stone, it's Ed Eagle."

"Ed! How are you?"

"I'm very well, thanks to a friend of yours."

"Who and why?"

"Billy Barnett, as he is now known, and he saved me from having a long piece of sharp steel driven into my back." Ed filled in the details.

"You are a very fortunate man to have *that* man come along at just the right moment."

"I am very aware of that," Ed said, "but I'm worried about Billy."

"I heard from Peter what happened to his wife."

"Perhaps you haven't heard what's happened since?"

"Please tell me."

Ed brought him up to date.

"Well," Stone said, "I tend to think that Billy would be more inclined to take Susannah's advice over yours."

"That had crossed my mind. Stone, it's been a while since you've visited me in Santa Fe. I think the news that you were coming might cause Billy to stay on for a bit, and perhaps together we might slow him down, or perhaps even keep him out of prison."

"Have I ever told you how Billy saved the lives of my son, Peter, and Dino's son, Ben?"

"No."

"Then I'll tell you over dinner tonight," Stone said. "Sit on Billy until I get there."

"Call me an hour out, and I'll meet you at the airport."

"See you then." Both men hung up.

STONE BUZZED JOAN.

"Yes, boss?"

"Please call Jet Aviation at Teterboro and ask them to have my airplane on the ramp in an hour, fueled to the gills, and cancel anything I might have on the books for the next week. And ask Fred to have the car out in fifteen minutes."

"May I ask where you're going?"

"To Santa Fe. A little vacation."

"Consider it done."

Stone hung up and went upstairs to pack.

3

AS STONE TOUCHED down at Santa Fe Airport and rolled out, he saw an unfamiliar SUV parked on the ramp. He taxied in and was directed to a parking spot near the car, where Ed Eagle was leaning against it.

Stone shut down, waited for chocks, then went down the boarding ladder and closed and locked the cabin door behind him.

Ed took Stone's hand in his more massive one. "I'm glad to see you," he said.

"What's this?" Stone asked, indicating the car.

"It's the new Bentley Bentayga," Ed replied. "First one in Santa Fe."

"What does Bentayga mean?"

"I've no idea. I'm not sure that Bentley does."

A lineman put Stone's luggage into the trunk, and both men got into the car.

"Very nice," Stone said, fondling the quilted leather upholstery.

"Lots of legroom," Ed replied. "A personal requirement." He started the car and was let out of the gate.

"How's Billy?"

"Placid, on the surface. Boiling underneath and deeply, deeply depressed."

"That's a dangerous combination with someone like Billy," Stone observed. "What can we do about it?"

"I don't know—a woman?"

"I think, at this stage, that would be both inappropriate and unadvisable."

"She can be yours, then."

"Who can be mine?"

"The friend of Susannah's who's invited to dinner tonight, name of Anastasia Bounine, said to be the great-great-granddaughter of Tsar Nicholas the Second and great-granddaughter of her namesake, the tsar's only surviving daughter."

"You're kidding me," Stone said.

"Maybe somebody up the line is kidding all of us, but that's the scuttlebutt on the lady. Story is, the original Anastasia took up with General Sergei Pavlovich Bounine, who squired her around Paris trying to get her accepted by the tsar's mother. They had a son, who had a son, et cetera, et cetera."

"I thought Anastasia's remains were found with the others in a well in Siberia, or someplace."

"It's said that one set of bones was missing, and the rest is history, sort of."

"So you've fixed me up with a Russian? I can't tell you the trouble I've had with Russians, Ed."

"I know all about that, but you can rest easy. Ana, as she's called, is third-generation French and came to this country as a small child. She's indistinguishable from an American—or from a Frenchwoman, or a Russian, if she feels like it. Swears like a sailor, when she's mad, and in three languages."

"What does she do with herself when she's not swearing?"

"She's the queen—or should I say tsarina—of Santa Fe real estate. Year in, year out, she's said to sell more houses than anybody else in town."

"So the first thing she's going to do is try to sell me a house."

"Ana is more subtle than that," Ed replied. "She'll wait for you to bring it up."

"She could grow old waiting for me to bring it up. Lately, I've been selling, not buying."

"I know, I handled the presidential sale, remember?"

"Of course." Stone had, in a complicated transaction, exchanged his Santa Fe house for the Presidents Lee's Georgetown house, then donated that to the State Department as a residence for the secretary of state, Holly Barker, who was his old friend and lover.

"I never asked," Ed said. "Why'd you do that deal?"

"When Kate Lee nominated Holly," Stone said, "she was living in an apartment over an antiques shop. It was unsuitable for a secretary of state, who has to entertain a lot."

Ed laughed. "I think you just wanted a comfortable place to screw a cabinet member."

"A particular cabinet member," Stone said.

"Why don't you just marry her? It'd be cheaper."

"Our lives are totally incompatible, except for short, intense periods when we find ourselves in the same city."

"Whatever you say." Ed pulled into his driveway, past a large stone eagle that identified the house, and a houseman in a white jacket came out and took Stone's luggage.

"You're in the big guest room," Ed said.

"Is Billy in the guesthouse?"

"No, he prefers to be at the Inn of the Anasazi. We didn't insist."

Susannah threw her arms around Stone and kissed him on the ear. "Too long!" she said.

"You should come to New York more often," Stone replied, kissing her back.

"Has Ed told you about your dinner partner this evening?"

"He has, and I'm terrified."

"Well, I could put you next to Theo Raven, who's in her eighties."

"She sounds safer."

"I didn't want Billy to feel threatened," Susannah said. "Come, let's get a drink."

*   *   *

THEY GOT A DRINK and watched the sky change colors as the day latened.

"Susannah," Stone said, "what are you doing with yourself?"

"Polishing a screenplay," she said. "I'll be shopping it around soon."

"In addition to writing and producing, will you direct and star?"

"Who else would hire me at my age?" Susannah was in her early forties. "Haven't you heard that Hollywood doesn't create desirable roles for women my age?"

"I have heard that, yes."

"What I'd like to do is steal Billy Barnett away from your son. He'd take a huge load off my hands."

"As he does for Peter," Stone replied. "I don't think Billy's looking to make a move. He's too well situated at Centurion. You'd better look farther afield."

"It wouldn't work," Ed said. "Susannah has trust issues. She wouldn't hire *me* to produce her pictures."

"I wouldn't hire you, my love, because you are ignorant of the process. I'm looking for someone with a track record, and yours is too much involved with getting guilty people off."

"None of my clients are guilty," Ed said, "just misunderstood."

They were still arguing about that when Teddy arrived.

4

SUSANNAH GOT TEDDY a drink, then went to check on dinner, leaving the men alone.

"How are you, Billy?" Stone said.

"I've been better, but I've been worse, too."

"I'm sorry for your trouble."

"Thank you, Stone. I'm looking for something to occupy my mind for a few weeks."

"What did you have in mind?" Ed asked.

"Revenge," Teddy said quietly.

Before Stone could explore that, Susannah returned with a beautiful woman, somewhat younger than her. Tall and with what, to Stone, appeared to be natural blond hair. He'd been fooled before.

"Stone," Susannah said, "this is our friend and neighbor Anastasia Bounine." Anastasia received a drink, and sat down next to Stone on a comfortable love seat. The size of the furniture guaranteed proximity. "Please call me Ana," she said.

"Ana it is."

"I've heard so much about you, Stone."

"Uh-oh," Stone replied.

"Your reputation precedes you."

"I was afraid of that."

"Don't worry, I've heard nothing but good. I understand that Santa Fe has you to thank for bringing the Presidents Lee to town in their retirement."

"I believe they're already here," Stone said, "though I'm not sure they're in town."

"They're not," Ed said, "or they'd be coming to dinner tonight. I hear their house is about finished, though, and they'll be coming soon to inspect the designer's work. Not that it needed a lot of work when you sold it."

"Or when I bought it," Stone said. "The previous owner had done a good job."

"Most of the work was done on the neighboring house," Ana said, "converting it to house the Secret Service. They had to add four bedrooms."

"Ana always knows exactly what's going on with Santa Fe real estate," Ed said. "It's her career."

"It's fun," Ana corrected him. "Much more than a career, a serious pastime. I know, for instance, that when Stone's predecessor owned the house, Stone was required to shoot a three-hundred-and-fifty-pound bear in her kitchen."

"I thought that was a closely held secret," Stone said.

"In Santa Fe?" she asked. "Surely you jest."

Theo Raven arrived, and shortly after that Susannah was seating them at her dinner table.

A GOOD THREE HOURS later Stone, Ed, and Teddy were once again alone together, this time in Ed's study.

"Billy," Stone said, "what was that about revenge?"

"I'm sure Ed has brought you up to date on the difficulties involved with seeking justice from the woman who killed my wife."

"He has."

"Have you thought of any legal avenue worth pursuing, Stone? I'm sure you've thought it over."

"I have, Billy, and I haven't come up with anything. Mr. Baxter has effectively cut off both the criminal and civil paths."

"That's what Ed had given me to understand, and I trust his judgment."

"Now, about that revenge, Billy," Stone said.

"Are you sure you want to know? Either of you?"

Ed looked at Stone. "I certainly want to know—though I emphasize that I don't want to know, if you take my meaning."

"I take your meaning," Stone said, "and I share it."

"All right," Teddy said. "Dax Baxter is coming to Santa Fe to shoot a film out at the movie ranch."

"And?" Ed asked.

"And the film company is hiring. They get a tax break from the state for using local people. It's said to be a four-week shoot here, before they return to L.A. to shoot interiors. I thought I might go out there and put in an application."

"For what job?" Stone asked.

"I can do, and have done, anything and everything on a film set. Baxter will be bringing his key people with him, but I thought I might go for something like an assistant production manager. Not too high up the tree, but useful. It would look good for the company to have a local in such a position."

"I'm sorry, Billy," Stone said, "but when did you get to be a local?"

"This afternoon," Teddy said.

"You became a local in an afternoon?"

"I've rented a little house, furnished. My story is, I just blew in from New York, where I worked in television and film. I have a couple of references there from people I've worked with in the past."

"You can't use your own name," Ed said.

"I've had a lot of identities in my time," Teddy said. "I'll dust one of them off."

"Billy," Stone said, "I hope you're not contemplating harming Baxter."

"Well, not in the sense that you might think, but there are lots of ways to get in the way of a man producing a film on location."

"What did you have in mind?" Ed asked.

"I'll improvise," Teddy said, shrugging. "Perhaps an opportunity will present itself."

The ladies joined them, and the conversation took a different turn.

ANA RESUMED HER SEAT next to Stone. "How long will you be in town?" she asked.

"I'm not sure," Stone replied. "Perhaps a day or two, perhaps longer."

"Will you come to my house for dinner tomorrow evening? I live just up the path to the left, through the trees."

"I'd like that," Stone replied.

"Do you eat beef?"

"With both hands."

"Then the menu is settled. Other things remain to be seen."

"I'll look forward to exploring them," Stone said.

"Exploration is fun, isn't it?"

"It certainly can be."

"Have you ever experienced the night sky in Santa Fe from a hot tub?" she asked.

"I have, but only once."

"Did you enjoy it?"

"It was a wonderful experience."

"Did you bring a swimsuit with you?" she asked.

"No."

"Oh, good."

5

STONE STARED UP at the wildly starred sky, the view made all the better because he was looking over Ana's shoulder as she faced him. The lights of Tesuque were just below and those of Santa Fe farther to the south. A sliver of moon did not challenge the Milky Way in its splendor, and the burble of the hot tub's jets added a sound track.

"Everything all right?" Ana whispered in his ear.

"I was just thinking I don't know how things could be better."

"Have you boiled long enough?" she asked.

"I believe I'm about medium done."

"Well, the one thing this spa doesn't have is a built-in bar, so why don't we go inside and see if we can locate a bottle of cognac?"

"A worthy notion, even if I have to move."

"I could bring you a snifter here," she said.

"You'd probably find me floating facedown when you returned, so why don't we select the first option?"

She disconnected herself from him, and he stood up, watching her shining body as she walked up the spa's steps to where they had left towels and robes. She handed him both as he emerged, and he toweled his hair, then got into the thick terry robe and his slippers and followed her into the master bedroom, where they had left their clothes.

"You stretch out and relax, and I'll get the brandy."

"What a good idea," he said, lying on the bed and using the remote control to raise his head a bit.

A jazz trio floated from the sound system and relaxed him even further. Ana returned a moment later with a bottle and two snifters and poured them both one before she got into bed beside him and adjusted the height to match his.

"How do you feel?" she asked.

"I believe I've somehow achieved an almost liquid state."

"The brandy should do the rest, then."

He took a sip. "I think you're right. Isn't this about the point where you should sell me a house?"

She laughed.

"I'd be helpless to refuse you anything."

"Well, I do have a couple of suitable things in mind.

The problem is, neither of them could match the house you've just sold the Presidents Lee."

"I try never to go backward," he replied.

"You live in New York?"

"I am a resident of that state and city, and I have the tax returns to prove it."

"Do you have a place anywhere else, where you can get away?"

"I have a place in Dark Harbor, Maine," he said.

"Is that all?"

"Well, there's a house in Paris and a small estate in the South of England."

"Anything else?" she snorted.

"Oh, and a place in Los Angeles."

"Where?"

"In L.A. at the Arrington, up Stone Canyon."

"You keep a room there?"

"Not exactly."

"Please explain to me how you come to have a house at the Arrington. I didn't know anybody did."

"Arrington Carter Calder, for whom the hotels are named, was my wife. My late wife."

"She was Vance Calder's widow, was she not?"

"Yes. She inherited a large parcel of land that he had accumulated over several decades, and where he had built his home. I inherited it from her, and with some friends as investors, we built the hotel, incorporating Vance's house as the reception area and main restaurant. When I sold the land to the group, I retained the right to build a house on the property, to be built at their expense and to my specifications. I use it, perhaps, half a dozen times a year, when I have business in L.A. Or pleasure."

"Why so many houses?"

"That's an odd question, coming from a Realtor."

"I suppose it is, but I'm curious."

"They just kept popping up, and they were each irresistible. I did sell a house last year, in Washington, Connecticut, and, of course, the place in Tesuque, so I'm not completely crazy."

"Ted Turner has—or maybe, had—ten houses," she said.

"I feel his pain."

"One of his places is said to have something like two hundred thousand acres of grassland."

"That's a lot of lawn to mow," Stone said. "Only two of my houses have lawns, and one of those is quite small, so I don't have to spend much time on a tractor."

"Who is this Billy Barnett fellow that you and Ed Eagle seem so fond of? I couldn't get a handle on him."

"Billy is a film producer who works with my son, Peter, at Centurion Studios. Billy recently lost his wife in an accident, and Ed and I are commiserating."

"Hang on, you have a son? With whom?"

"Arrington."

"I thought . . ."

"We knew each other before she met Vance Calder. Neither of us knew she was pregnant when they were married, nor did Vance, for that matter."

"You must be a very complicated man."

"No, I'm a simple man with a complicated life. I spend my days wrestling it into submission."

"I don't suppose Billy is house-hunting?"

Stone sighed. "Not in his present frame of mind."

"What's he doing in Santa Fe?"

"I can't talk about that."

"I understand."

"Ana, do you know anything about a man named Dax Baxter?"

"Ach!" she spat. "I hope he's not a friend of yours."

"I've never met the man, but it sounds as though you have."

"I spent half a day with him a few weeks ago, showing him grandiose houses, but I couldn't find one bad enough for him. Instead, I excused myself from duty and gave him the names of a couple of other real estate ladies whom I despise. He bought a house that I look upon as the ugliest and most overbearing in Santa Fe County."

"That sounds like a pretty good description of the Baxter I've heard about," Stone said. "Ugly and over-bearing."

"And arrogant. I think the villains in his movies are all autobiographical."

"How many have you seen?"

"About a third of one—that was enough. I've had enough of Dax Baxter, too. What made you bring up his name?"

"Someone I know hates him," Stone said. "Now I think I know why."

6

TEDDY SAT AT the dressing table in the bedroom of the little house he had rented, regarded himself in the mirror, and made some decisions about who he should become. He had always had a distinctly anonymous look about him, a face that lent itself to change, one that people had trouble remembering.

He had to keep it simple, since he would spend considerable time in this character, and he began with a thick, gray mustache with little handlebars. That one thing would establish him in the minds of others as Ted Shirley, the name he had chosen for himself, one easy to remember. He had already spent a couple of hours online, creating a structure for this identity—New York driver's license, Social Security number, union memberships, credit report, everything an employer would need to hire him.

He stared at the face in the mirror: it was already tan from his years in California, so no makeup was required. It needed one other distinguishing feature, though, one more thing. He fished around in his makeup box and found a pair of round, steel-rimmed eyeglasses; he wiped the lenses clean and put them on, securing them over his ears with the flexible stems. There: sort of a more youthful Wilford Brimley type.

He opened his Ted Shirley file and ran through his particulars again. He had to be this character completely, and he couldn't allow himself to stumble over facts, like the year he was born or the last four digits of his Social.

He got into some faded but clean jeans, a Western-flavored shirt, a pair of well-worn suede boots, and a belt with a silver buckle, then he put on a Western hat that he had bought in a custom hat shop on the Plaza and had decorated with some sweat stains made of mineral oil, then he consulted the image in the mirror once more. "How do you do, Ted Shirley?" The answer was, pretty damned satisfactory.

The Porsche Cayenne was in the garage, locked away for the duration. He had met a man in a bar the day before who owned a nicely restored old pickup truck and had rented it from him for a month for $1,000, which the fellow was glad to have.

He slipped into an old suede jacket and tucked an envelope into an inside pocket, which contained a copy of the carefully constructed employment application he had filed at the movie employment office in a downtown hotel. He tucked his Ted Shirley wallet into a hip pocket, got his truck keys, and headed south of Santa Fe, to the J. W. Eaves Movie Ranch, a few miles off I-25.

Once there, he parked in the public lot and walked into the nicely designed and constructed Western town, entering the saloon. A woman sat at a table on the front porch, and he tipped his hat to her. "Good morning," he said. "My name is Ted Shirley. I have an appointment just about now."

She gave him a dry smile and found his name on a list. "You're not an actor?"

"I can do just about anything."

"You're supposed to see Dan Waters, inside at table number three. Dan is our production manager."

He thanked her and went inside. There were four poker tables, each with a number. He walked up to number three. "Dan Waters?"

"That's me."

Teddy held out a hand. "I'm Ted Shirley."

"Oh, yeah," Waters replied, shuffling among some applications on the table. "Siddown. You've got an interesting sheet."

Teddy sat down. "Thank you."

"Let's see, theater, documentary films, a few TV shows. You've done a little of everything, haven't you?"

"I guess I have."

"I'd hire you as an actor if I didn't need technical people more. We've brought a skeleton crew from L.A., and our tax deal with the state film commission calls for us to hire locally, when we can. What would you like to do on this picture, Ted?"

"I think I'd like to work for you," Teddy replied.

Waters leaned back in his chair. "How long you been in Santa Fe?"

"A few weeks."

"Why'd you leave New York?"

"Twenty years in the big city was enough. I was looking for a change of scenery." He paused. "And maybe another wife. The last one didn't work out too well."

Waters smiled. "We've all been there. You got a place here?"

"I rent. I don't know the town well enough yet to buy."

"You ever done any casting?"

"Sure."

"We're gonna need about thirty actors with SAG cards, and maybe sixty extras. We've already nailed down the SAG people. Why don't we put you in charge of casting extras?"

"Sounds good."

Waters handed him a heavy cardboard box. "Here are head shots and CVs and a list of what we need. Most of these applicants have shown up in Western dress, and we'll favor them to save money on costumes, but if you run across good ones who need dressing, we can handle that. Oh, no weapons—we'll issue those."

Teddy stood and picked up the box. "Where do I work?"

"There's a number eight in the box. Pick a poker table, start interviewing, and bring me a list of your preferences, plus a dozen alternates, by the end of the day. Then maybe we'll find something else for you to do."

Teddy picked up the box, chose a table in a corner, and stuck the number on it. In short order, a line had formed before him, and he looked it over for a moment. Some of them looked ridiculous, but others, pretty good. He started to interview the first in line, a wiry fifty-year-old who looked at home in cowboy boots and hat. He was also wearing a six-shooter in a worn holster. Teddy took about three minutes to put him on the list to hire. "One thing," he said.

"Yessir?"

"Lose the weapon. Lock it in your car, or something. If a gun is called for, the armory will issue it to you."

"I'm kind of fond of my own," the man said.

"You can't work this picture with it. It's a liability thing."

He shrugged. "Whatever you say."

They broke for an hour for lunch, which was served from two actual chuck wagons: hamburgers and beans.

Teddy went back to work, and at three-thirty, he walked over to Dan Waters and handed him his preferred list and their photographs. "Here you go. I think this is a pretty good bunch."

Waters looked through the photos. "I think you're right. Now go send them over to Personnel, across the street in the general store, and they'll get formally hired, then come back and we'll see what else we can find for you to do."

Teddy felt someone approach from behind, and he turned to find a tall, heavily muscled man with a thick head of gray hair under a large, cocked-back Stetson.

"Ted, this is the boss," Waters said, "Dax Baxter."

Baxter regarded him coolly for a moment, then gave him a quick nod and turned to Waters to start a different conversation. He was followed by two equally tall, equally muscled men.

"Those are Dax's body men," Dan said, "Hank and Joe. We call 'em Hinky and Dinky when they're not listening."

Teddy nodded. He wanted to hurt Baxter, but he thought better of it.

TEDDY SPENT THE REST of the day with Dan Waters, evaluating costumes for the supporting cast. They quit at six o'clock.

"Ted," Waters said, "can I buy you a drink? Those bottles behind that bar over there contain the real thing, and this saloon is the crew and cast canteen after six."

"Sure," Teddy replied. "Bourbon and rocks, if they've got 'em."

Dan waved at a man dressed as a waiter. "Two bourbons, rocks," he said. The man left and Dan chuckled. "That guy's an actor, but he's a waiter in the evenings. There's an ice machine concealed behind the bar."

"Pretty neat, Dan," Teddy said. "Where are you from?"

"L.A., born and bred. You?"

"Born in Florida, then everywhere. Marine brat."

"When you left New York, why didn't you go to L.A.?" Dan asked. "Plenty of work for a guy like you."

"I didn't want to work all the time, and I like this town. I've had it with big cities. Tell me, who are Hinky and Dinky protecting Dax Baxter from?"

"Whatever rises in that paranoid brain of his," Dan said. "He doesn't like to be touched, so don't ever slap him on the back or you'll find Hink and Dink sitting on you."

"I'll keep that in mind. Sounds like you don't like him very much."

"*Nobody* likes him very much. Oh, he's got plenty of charm, if you're a studio exec or a movie star he wants for a picture or somebody he wants something else for. He does okay with the ladies, too."

"I thought he was married to Willa Mather, the actress," Ted said.

"Sort of an actress," Dan replied, with an eye roll. "He doesn't like her to work, and on top of that, she's got a drinking problem, so she doesn't get offers anymore. A few weeks ago she was driving through Beverly Hills, drunk, and ran down a pedestrian, killed her, but Dax got it hushed up. She's still in rehab, so she's not on our shoot."

"You sure make Dax sound like a sweet guy."

"Oh, you'll form your own opinions before we're done here. This is a twenty-six-day shoot. By the way, I need an assistant. The pay is five hundred a day. You want the job?"

"Sounds great."

"Do it well, and I'll get you a screen credit."

"That would look nice on my résumé."

"About Dax—he's not lovable, but he's a hell of a producer. He has an eye for what the public wants to see, and for a good script, and he knows how to deal with the studio."

"Does he have a production deal somewhere?" Teddy asked, already knowing the answer.

"Yeah, at SAC, Standard American Cinema, in Burbank. He's made them a lot of money, so he gets what he wants."

"I expect he does."

Their drinks arrived, along with some cheese and charcuterie.

"This is an example of what Dax gets from the studios," Dan said, picking up a slice of prosciutto from the plate. "The cast gets very nice trailers, and Dax has a double-wide that gets split up, towed, then put back together again on location. He likes Santa Fe, too. He's bought a big house here, and our production designer is decorating it for him, right out of the studio's warehouses. There'll be a wrap party when we're done. Save Dax some money here and there, and you'll get an engraved invitation."

"I'll see what I can do," Teddy said.

"Where's your place?"

"Out in Tesuque, on the north side of town. It's smaller than Dax's double-wide, but it'll do."

"Hey, Sally!" Dan yelled at a woman in tight jeans and a decorated cowgirl hat. "Join us." She sat down, and

Dan introduced them. "Ted, this is Sally Ryder. Sally, Ted Shirley."

"We've met," Sally said. She had been working the table on the porch when Teddy had presented himself that morning.

They shook hands. "I'm glad you've joined us," she said to Teddy. "You have an interesting résumé."

"Thanks, I'm glad, too. Nice not to be a tourist here all the time. I'm glad for the work."

"Ted's going to be my assistant on the shoot," Dan said.

"That's good. He'll work you hard, Ted, but you'll have fun, if you can steer clear of Dax."

"That's not a problem, Ted," Dan said. "Just let me do the talking when he has questions."

"I'm happy to be mute," Teddy said. "Are you from L.A., Sally?"

"Used to be, but now I live in Santa Fe. I work on just about every film that gets shot here, and it's enough to keep me in beans and bourbon."

"Who could want more?" Dan asked. "She could produce at any studio in L.A.," he said to Teddy, "but she likes it here, too, like you."

"Tell me about you, Ted," she said.

Teddy told her what he'd told Dan.

"I was an army brat," she said, "so you'll never have to tell me about your childhood."

"I'm thankful for that," Teddy replied.

"My dad did three tours in Germany."

"So you've got the language?"

"I know how to order a beer," she said.

Teddy liked her; she was trim and fit, pretty, and had blond hair, with some gray in it. He liked that she wasn't dyeing it.

"Did you get overseas?" she asked.

"No, we were mostly stateside. When my father built some rank we were in the D.C. area. I can order a beer in Georgetown."

She laughed, a very nice sound.

Then Dax Baxter was standing at their table. "A word, Dan?"

Dan started to rise, but Baxter sat down. "Have you had a look at the horses?" he asked.

"Yeah, I told the wrangler to replace eight of them with something better."

"Good, we don't want livestock dying on us."

"Dax, you met Ted Shirley, here, this morning. He's going to be my assistant on the shoot."

Baxter glanced at Teddy. "Is he qualified, or are you just queer for him?"

Waters managed a smile. "He's overqualified, and I got him cheap," he replied.

"That's a combination I like to hear," Baxter said, then he got up and left.

"He knows I'm not gay," Dan said to Teddy. "He just likes to put the needle in."

"With Dax, it's what passes for a sense of humor," Sally said. "You'll get used to it."

"I don't think so," Teddy said, "but I can ignore it."

8

AS SALLY AND TEDDY were walking back to the parking lot, it occurred to him that he was going to be looking at four walls all evening. "Would you like to have dinner?" he asked her. "There's a good restaurant in Tesuque, called El Nido."

"Sure," Sally replied. "Shall I follow you?"

"I'm in the old red pickup," Teddy said, pointing.

"Nice. Where'd you come by that?"

"I got it from a guy I met in a bar. It's in real good shape."

They got into their vehicles, and Teddy led her to Tesuque, which was a quick drive, fast highway all the way.

There were no tables available, so they sat at the bar, ordered margaritas, and were given menus.

"Do you live near here, Ted?" she asked.

"Just up the hill behind the restaurant," Teddy said. "El Nido and the Tesuque Market, next door, are the only restaurants I know here."

They ordered dinner and another margarita. When their food came Sally got quiet for a couple of minutes.

"What are you thinking about?" Teddy asked.

"Listen," Sally said, "I don't want you to think of this as hostile, but I know your name isn't Ted Shirley, it's Billy Barnett. I had a small part in a Peter Barrington film at Centurion a couple of years ago, and you were the line producer. How come that wasn't on your résumé, and how come the name change?"

Teddy took a deep breath and let it out. "Nailed," he said. "The story is complicated."

"All the best stories are," she said.

"Well, first of all, I'm not on the run from the law, or from anybody else, for that matter."

"That's good to know," she said. "Then why the fake name and the mustache?"

"The mustache is because I don't want to be recognized."

"A lot of good that did you," she laughed.

"So far, you're the only one who's twigged," Teddy said. "I saw two other people on the lot today who've worked around me, and they didn't."

"I have a good eye for faces and bodies," Sally said, "especially when it's an attractive man. Does this have something to do with Dan Waters or Dax Baxter?"

"Let's just say it has nothing to do with Dan Waters," Teddy said. "As for Dax Baxter, I never laid eyes on him until today."

"That's not the same as not hating his guts—almost everybody does."

"Then why do they work for him?"

"He runs a smooth production, he doesn't yell at anybody or create big scenes—ones that aren't in the script. The money's above average, if he likes your work, and the perks are nice, like the trailers for casts and the saloon set that's also cast and crew canteen. If he's aware that you're doing good work, you'll find a nice little bonus in your final paycheck."

"Then what is it about him that so puts people's teeth on edge?"

"He seems to want to be disliked. I don't know why."

"The man's a bully," Teddy said, "I can tell you that much."

"I guess a lot of people sense that. Mind you, if there's any bullying to be done, that's taken care of by Heckel and Jeckel."

Teddy laughed. "Dan calls them something else."

"My advice is to stick with Hank and Joe."

"Have they ever actually hurt anybody who gave Dax a hard time?"

"People have disappeared from shoots and turned up later in the local hospital—people who were stealing from Dax, that sort of thing."

"So, Dax doesn't bother with the cops or the sheriff?"

Sally shook her head slowly. "I think Dax is the kind

of guy who thinks a broken nose or maybe a couple of ribs makes a better point than a night in the pokey."

"Okay, I'll do my best not to make Dax mad."

"Always a good way to go," Sally said. "I mean, Dax is big enough and, I guess, mean enough to handle that sort of thing himself, but if he did that, he could end up in jail, and that's not good for business. If somebody displeases him, they just disappear from the set for the rest of the shoot. Everybody notices they've gone, and they always turn up later, maybe with a slightly different face, or some new dental work."

They both took big bites of their food and were quiet while they chewed. The waiter came and refreshed their glasses.

"There's a story going around the shoot," Sally said, "that Dax's wife killed somebody in a traffic accident, and that Dax got it hushed up."

"I heard that from Dan today," Teddy said.

"Does your being here have anything to do with that?"

"Ask me no questions and I'll tell you no lies," he replied.

"You've already told me a bunch of lies about your name and your background, and it's part of my job to check out people who may have inflated their résumés."

"As you have seen, I have *de*flated, not inflated, my résumé, in order not to call undue attention to myself. It was nothing personal, and I'd appreciate your letting it slide. After all, being exposed might mean a visit from Heckel and Jeckel, and you wouldn't want to put me into a hospital bed, would you?"

"Well, not a *hospital* bed," she said with a little leer.

"I'll take that as a compliment."

"You should. As a rule, I don't believe in paying men compliments—they tend to go to their heads."

"I can't deny that," Teddy said. "Come on, what's it going to take to keep you quiet and me healthy?"

"How about oral sex?"

Teddy broke up, and dropped his fork. A waiter appeared with a clean one.

"How often?" he managed to say.

"Often, but it doesn't have to be just oral—you can mix it up, if you want to."

"I think I'd enjoy mixing it up," Teddy said.

"So would I."

"I must say, this is a new kind of blackmail."

"I'm glad you like the idea."

"I like it very much," Teddy said. "When do we start?"

"Let's skip dessert," Sally replied.

9

SHORTLY AFTER SUNRISE, Stone and Ed Eagle, on horseback, walked slowly along a trail through the trees above Ed's house.

"Susannah noticed your bed wasn't slept in last night," Ed said with a wry smile.

"Is sleeping in one's own bed a requirement in the Eagles' household?"

"Not at all. She was just amused, and so was I. We wondered how long it would take Ana to get you into the sack."

"Well, Ana didn't meet with a lot of resistance," Stone replied. "I've been seeing somebody in New York, but it has sort of petered out—so to speak."

"That tends to happen with Ana, too," Eagle said. "She wears them out pretty quickly."

"This is the first time we've ever ridden together, Ed, and the first time I've used Western tack in years."

"Ah, a change of subject," Ed said. "Western gives you something to hang on to when a rattlesnake spooks your mount."

"Is that why we're out here? Rattlesnake hunting?"

"We're out here because I want to talk to you about Teddy Fay, or whatever he's calling himself this week. Billy Barnett?"

"That was last week," Stone said. "This week it's Ted Shirley, and he got a job on Dax Baxter's movie."

"Whatever," Ed said. "I'm just worried that Teddy is going to off the guy, and if he does, I'd like to be separated from him by a good distance."

"Isn't Tesuque far enough away?"

"I guess. I also didn't want Susannah to hear us talking about him."

"Are you afraid her tender nature would be bruised?"

"Stone, I'm afraid Susannah would hold Teddy's hat while he beat Baxter to death with a baseball bat."

Stone laughed. "Sometimes I forget what a tough nut Susannah can be. Now that I think of it, I know of two men she's shot."

"But not without good cause," Ed said, "and not illegally. I don't expect Teddy would do such a thing without good cause, but I'm not so sure about the legal part."

"I can understand your concern, Ed, but what I know about Teddy makes me think that he's a very careful man.

He wouldn't have been on the loose for as long as he was, if he weren't careful."

"He reminds me of somebody out of the Old West," Ed said, "except he's not a Westerner."

"That's not an outrageous comparison," Stone agreed.

"What do you think he's up to, if it's not murder?"

"Justice, I should think."

"And how would Teddy define justice?"

"That's a tricky question, and one I wouldn't hazard a guess on."

"If he's thinking about wrecking that movie production, then we have a different problem altogether," Ed said. "There's a chunk of state money tied up in that shoot, because of a bill that I had a lot to do with getting through the legislature, not to mention the reputation of Santa Fe as hospitable to the film community. If something terrible happened, film production could dry up around here, and a lot of locals would be thrown out of work."

"You want me to have a word with Teddy?"

"While you're here I'd appreciate it if you'd stay as far away from him as you can. You're known locally as a friend of mine."

"Then what do you want me to do?"

"Shit, if I knew that I'd do it myself."

"Do you know anybody connected with the film commission or the production?"

"Sure I do. You think I oughta sidle up to somebody at a dinner and say, 'Hey, if anything awful happens on that Baxter shoot, let me know and I'll see what I can do about it'?"

"I guess that would be none too subtle," Stone admitted.

"I guess not."

"So what do you plan to do, Ed?"

"Well, our little early-morning conversation has cleared that up for me," Ed said. "I think the best thing I can do is nothing, and that's something I'm not very good at."

"There's nothing like clarity of mind, is there?"

DOWN IN TESUQUE the first rays of sun through the blinds woke Teddy. There was a bare arm thrown across his chest, a leg over his own, and a head on his shoulder, and he had no feeling in the fingers on one hand. He kissed the head on the forehead.

"Oh, God," she muttered, "not again—I'll expire."

"To the best of my recollection," he said, "it was you who jumped me."

"Three times," she said. "You up for a fourth?"

"If we attempt that, we're going to be late for work, and I, for one, don't want to call attention to myself—or, for that matter, to you." He retrieved his arm and massaged the fingers.

"There could be talk," she admitted.

"Can I scramble you some eggs?"

"No, I can't show up to work in these clothes, so I'll make myself some coffee at home while I shower and beat you to the set. Don't you dare get there before me."

"I'll restrain myself," Teddy said.

"I'm going to have to remember not to call you Billy," she said, sitting up in bed and searching for her underwear. She found her thong and got into it.

"If you make that mistake, I'll have to ignore you."

"Well, we wouldn't want that, would we?" she asked, hooking her bra. She stepped into her jeans, pulled them up, then lay back on the bed and sucked in her belly so she could zip them.

"Well done," Teddy said.

"Well practiced," she replied, pulling on her sweater, then tugging at her boots. She picked up her jacket and looked around. "I think that's everything I came with, except my virtue."

"I'll take good care of it," Teddy said, accepting a goodbye kiss.

"How about I fix you some dinner at my house tonight?"

"A man's gotta eat."

"I expect Dan Waters will have found somebody to screw by now," she said. "Shall I ask them to join us?"

"As long as they don't stay too late."

"Bring a change of clothes," she said. "It'll save you having to drive back to Tesuque before work tomorrow."

"You think of everything."

"We've got four setups to get through today," she said. "We're likely to be a little tired by six o'clock. I wouldn't want you to drive home drunk and exhausted."

"Tonight," he said, "can we begin at the count of four? I don't think I could survive starting all over."

"We'll work something out," she said, then ran for the door. He heard her Jeep start and gravel scatter.

10

THEY SPENT THE MORNING rehearsing a single-camera, single-take shot in the saloon with a Steadicam, which stabilized the camera during movement. When they were ready to go, Dax Baxter called the director, the assistant director, and the cinematographer over to him, and they stood, their backs to the camera, while Baxter pointed out a couple of things.

Teddy walked between them and the camera and, after being sure that no one was watching him, drew a knuckle across the lens as he passed the equipment.

"Let's shoot it," Baxter said, and everyone assumed their positions. The plan was: the Steadicam would pick up the protagonist as he dismounted his horse in front of the saloon, then follow him inside as he fended off swings from several people, returned some punches, and, finally, outdrew two men and shot them both. The take lasted about fifty seconds, and the director yelled, "Cut! Print! Absolutely perfect!"

"Let's look at it," Baxter said, and the group huddled around a monitor and watched the take.

The cameraman spoke up. "What's that smudge across the screen?" he asked.

"I don't see it," Baxter said.

"Neither do I," echoed the director.

"Watch it again," the cameraman said, and they all did.

"I see it," the director said. "Shit! Doesn't anybody know how to clean a lens around here?"

"I cleaned it about three minutes before the take," an assistant said.

"There it is," the cameraman said, inspecting the lens. "We'll have to do another take."

There ensued a comedy of errors as they screwed up take after take, and they finally got it right on the eighth.

"Anybody know what those retakes cost me?" Baxter asked nobody in particular.

Nobody in particular answered.

"All for a dirty lens?" he added, unnecessarily.

"It won't happen again, Dax," the cameraman said, glaring at his assistant, who could only look at the floor.

"Break for lunch!" the assistant director said.

It was quiet around the chuck wagons while everyone ate.

Teddy enjoyed his burger and tried to look glum, like everybody else.

Sally sidled up to him with her plate and sat down beside him. "What happened in there this morning?" she asked. "Everybody looks like death warmed over."

"Somebody screwed up on a perfect first take of an extended shot, and it took seven more to get it right."

"What was the problem?"

"A smudged lens."

"Does our cinematographer still have a job?"

"It was just one of those things, I think, nobody's fault," Teddy replied.

"Everything is somebody's fault," she said, "and it's easy to see Dax is pissed off."

"That's life," Teddy said.

"Don't you ever say that to Dax."

"I wouldn't."

THAT AFTERNOON, another three scenes required multiple takes, and for no good reason. Teddy walked past Baxter's double-wide and heard the male star yelling, "What the fuck is wrong with this production? I don't appreciate having to do everything half a dozen times because of some fuckup! I had expected better of you, Dax."

"Jake, we just had a bad day," Baxter replied soothingly. "It happens sometimes, in spite of everybody's best efforts."

"Well, it better stop happening," the actor said. "I signed up to do one movie, not seven or eight. I'll have trouble sleeping tonight, and that's not good for the production."

"I'll send the nurse over with some Ambien," Dax said.

*   *   *

THAT EVENING, at Sally's house up in the hills, the four of them met for dinner. Dan had brought the makeup artist's assistant, Mara, who seemed bright as well as pretty.

Dan raised his glass. "To fewer days like today," he said.

"Hear, hear," Teddy said.

"Did you notice that Dax ordered the cameraman to stop moving the camera during scenes? He had to throw away the storyboards for practically every one."

"Everybody was pretty rattled," Mara said. "I could hardly get the cast to hold still for makeup, they were all so fidgety."

"Dax was worse than fidgety," Sally said. "He was practically volcanic. I heard our leading man, our Jake, nearly walked."

"That would scare Dax shitless," Dan said. "He hates to be in a position where he's not perfectly in control. He had to pay Jake Preston more than his usual fee, because Jake thought the part was beneath him."

Sally grilled steaks and baked potatoes, and Teddy had picked up an especially good cabernet. Everybody relaxed after the first bottle, and they began to have a good time. Then Dan's cell phone went off.

Dan looked at it. "It's Dax. I'm going to have to take this." He grabbed the phone, walked across the room, and flopped down on the sofa. "Yes, Dax?" For the next ten minutes Dan sat and gave monosyllabic answers to nearly every question. Finally he was able to hang up and come back to the table.

"It's worse than we thought," he said. "He wasn't able to get Jake to say he would continue, so he's been on the phone all evening with agents, trying to scare up a new leading man, just in case. In the end, he had to pay Darth Kramer half a salary just to stand by, if Jake walks."

"Well, doing nothing for half a star's salary ain't too bad," Sally said.

"I've never heard of anything like that," Teddy said. "I mean, in the old days, when the studio was king, they'd have half a dozen actors under contract who could step up in a case like that."

"Them days is gone," Dan said.

AFTER DINNER, the girls did the dishes while Teddy and Dan sat on the front porch with a brandy and gazed down at the lights of Santa Fe.

"What do you think is going to happen, Dan?" Teddy asked.

"Well, we've got two possibilities," Dan replied. "One, things will continue to go badly, and Jake Preston, who has a loose grip on reality anyway, will get on his jet and go home to L.A., then we'll start the production over with Darth Kramer in the part. On the other hand, things could smooth out, Jake could calm down, and we'd add a day or two to the shoot, because he'd demand a lot of vanity retakes and close-ups, knowing that Dax was worried. I'm not sure which would be worse for us."

Teddy thought he had an idea which would be worse for Dax Baxter.

When the guests had gone, Teddy said, "What say we start again at square one?"

"It ain't gonna be square," Sally said, getting out of her clothes.

11

ON SUNDAY MORNING, Teddy got a call. "Hello?"

"Billy," Stone said, "it's Stone Barrington. You free for lunch?"

"Sure, Stone."

"Let's meet at the Tesuque Market at noon, if that's okay."

"It's right in my backyard," Teddy said.

"YOU LOOK FIT and well rested, Billy," Stone said after they had gotten a table and a menu.

"I feel a lot better than I'd hoped to," Teddy said. He looked a little embarrassed. "I've even got a girl."

"Good for you!"

"I would never have thought it could happen this fast, but I've no complaints at all. She's a lovely person, works on the shoot, name of Sally Ryder."

"I hope to meet her one of these days," Stone said.

"She's picking me up here at one o'clock. We're taking a hike up in the hills, so you'll meet her."

"I'll look forward to that," Stone said. "Tell me, how's the shoot going?"

Teddy pulled a mock frown. "Not as well as could be expected," he said. "Lots of small problems are slowing us down and costing Mr. Baxter money of his own. He has a contract price with the studio, as it turns out, and any delays or reshoots come out of his own pocket."

"That must hurt," Stone said.

"Not only that, but we could lose our leading man and have to start over, since he's in practically every scene we've shot. Baxter is paying another actor half his usual salary, just to have him standing by."

"Can the leading man get away with just walking off the movie?"

"I expect there'll be litigation, or the threat of it," Teddy said. "But who knows?"

"In the meantime, Baxter loses everything he's shot and everything he's already paid the leading man?"

Teddy nodded. "I hear it could cost Baxter upwards of two million dollars, when you add in the extra shooting days. He has to pay the whole crew for those."

"And what sorts of things are causing these problems?"

"Tiny things that seem to just come out of the wood-work," Teddy said. "If it keeps up, it could cost Baxter his fee for producing the film. Of course, he'd still have his profit participation, but I hear Dax is a big spender, lives close to the edge. He's already bought a big house in Santa Fe, and found a way to redo it at the studio's expense, and they somehow found out about it and are demanding their money back. Word is, he's borrowing against the contract for his next production to make ends meet."

"And how long do you expect this to go on, Billy?"

"Me? I have no expectations, I just do my job every day, and my boss is real happy with me."

"You're probably better at it than your boss," Stone said.

"I'm better at it than Dax Baxter," Teddy replied. "If I weren't so happy with Peter and Ben, I'd probably go independent, like Baxter, and make a fortune. My tastes aren't as expensive as his."

"What's with the pickup truck you're driving, Billy?"

"Oh, I rented that from a fellow I met. I think a new Cayenne might cause some talk among the crew. It's safely garaged."

"Billy, don't you think you may have taken enough out of Dax Baxter's hide?"

"Oh, I just go with the flow, do what I can. I'm not pressing myself."

"Ed Eagle and I are both concerned that this whole thing might blow up into something bigger than you'd counted on. Ed's worried about the effect a production disaster could have on the state film commission, and the money they've got tied up in it. He was instrumental in getting the commission established and funded by the state legislature, and a lot of people's jobs could be affected if the film were shut down. It would make it more difficult to attract new productions if the town seemed jinxed for moviemakers."

"Well, Dax seems to have a gift for pulling back from the edge just before disaster strikes," Teddy said, "and I expect he'll manage that in this case—maybe even get a good picture out of it."

"But it'll cost him?"

"That would be my best guess," Teddy said. "Oh, here comes Sally."

Stone looked up to see a trim, mostly blond woman approaching. "You've done well, Billy," he said.

"Sally," Teddy said, rising, "this is an old friend, Stone Barrington. We knew each other in New York."

Sally offered him a hand. "Hello, Stone."

"How do you do?" Stone asked, taking the hand. "Will you join us for a minute? Before your hike?"

"Sure."

Stone pulled up a chair for her. "Margarita?"

"They're too big here—I might fall off a mountain."

"I'm staying sober, too," Teddy said, sipping his diet soda.

"Where are you hiking?" Stone asked.

"I thought I'd show Ted the Bandelier National Monument, up Los Alamos way."

"I've heard good things about it," Stone said. "Refresh my memory."

"Upwards of thirty thousand acres, dwelling ruins going back eleven thousand years, plenty of wildlife, gorgeous scenery. Why don't you join us?"

"Thanks, I'm not dressed for it, and I have to fly to L.A. on business in a little while."

"Another time, then."

"Maybe, who knows?"

The two of them excused themselves and went on their way.

Stone drove back to the Eagles' house and packed his things, then went to say goodbye to his hosts. Ed was alone in his study.

"Did you put the fear of God into Teddy?" he asked.

"I don't think anything could put the fear of God into Teddy," Stone replied. "Still, I managed to convey that there might be unintended consequences for others, if he goes too far."

"Do you think he'll do that?"

"No, I don't. So far he's managed to put Dax Baxter into a world of trouble by doing small things to slow him down. Apparently, his contract calls for Baxter to personally pick up costs over and above the agreed budget, and Teddy is bleeding him in small ways."

"As long as he doesn't hurt anybody," Eagle said.

"I don't think Teddy gets mad," Stone said. "He just gets even."

12

STONE DROVE THE HUNDRED YARDS up the mountain and turned into Anastasia Bounine's driveway. She was just locking the door to her house, and a suitcase and a train case stood next to her.

"Good afternoon," Stone said with a kiss. "Ready to go?"

"Always," she replied.

He stowed her luggage, and they drove to the airport and through the security gate. Stone's CJ3 Plus awaited, and he put their luggage on board. "Last chance for the powder room," he said to Ana. She walked into the FBO, and he did a thorough preflight inspection.

"Would you like to be comfortable in the rear?" he asked when she returned.

"Where are you sitting?"

"In the pilot's seat."

Her eyes opened a little wider. "Somehow I was under the impression that two gentlemen in those cute uniforms would be occupying the front seats."

"I prefer doing it myself. Would you like to be copilot?"

Ana raised an eyebrow. "I think that would terrify me, but I'll do it anyway, just to be near you."

Stone closed and locked the cabin door, then got her settled and strapped in and adjusted her headset so they could hear each other over the intercom. "The microphone should be close enough to your lips so that you can kiss it," he said.

She kissed the microphone. "There, dear," she said.

"Is your seat belt comfortable?"

"It's a little like being in a straitjacket, isn't it?" she said.

"It's called a five-point restraint, to keep you secure. The FAA requires it." Stone handed her the checklist. "It would be a help if you read me the items one by one." He pointed at the first.

She began reading, and he began replying with "Check" after accomplishing each task. After a little while, he said, "Now we're ready to start engines." He talked her through the procedure as he accomplished it, and soon both engines were running smoothly and the air-conditioning was on.

Stone called the tower for his clearance and permission to taxi, and he turned the airplane and taxied to runway 20. A moment later they were given an initial altitude and cleared for takeoff. The winds were light, so there was no turbulence. He steered the airplane onto the runway center line, then moved the throttles smoothly to the max. The light jet began to roll, and a moment later he eased back the yoke, and the aircraft rose into the clean, clear high desert air.

"It's very powerful, isn't it?" Ana said.

"For its size, yes." He switched on the autopilot and the airplane turned toward its first assigned waypoint.

"Why don't you have your hands on the thing, there?" she asked, pointing at the yoke.

"The autopilot is flying the airplane, now, and it's a better pilot than I. It will continue to fly us until we're ready to land."

An hour and a half later Stone set down the airplane gently at Santa Monica Airport.

"I'm surprised," Ana said, "that was actually fun."

"I always enjoy flying myself rather than being flown. It gives me a sense of accomplishment all out of proportion to what I've actually done." He steered the airplane onto the Atlantic Aviation ramp, ran through his checklist, and shut everything down. A Bentley with the Hotel Arrington insignia on the door pulled up to the airplane; Stone unlocked the luggage compartment, and the driver moved their bags to the car. Then they were gone.

TWENTY MINUTES LATER they were waved through the security gate at the Arrington, and the driver deposited them at Stone's house, where the butler took charge of their things.

"You keep a butler, even when you're not here?"

"No, the hotel provides a cook, a maid, and a butler when I'm in residence. It's very convenient." While their bags were taken upstairs he gave her a tour of the house. "Oh, your own pool?" she asked, looking out a window.

"Ours alone."

"Does one need a swimsuit?"

"One does not."

In no time they were in the water, and after a bit of frolicking, Stone handed her a robe and a towel and called the house for a pitcher of sangria. They occupied a double lounge and relaxed.

"Usually, Sundays are a big workday for me," Ana said. "It's nice to be off." She let her hand wander under his robe, and shortly, she was on top of him.

TEDDY AND SALLY arrived back at her house, dusty and tired. "Let's go straight into the hot tub," she said, starting to strip.

"I didn't even know you had a hot tub," Teddy replied.

"You haven't seen my back garden." She took him by the hand and led him out the back door into a beautifully planted garden, then uncovered the tub and set the temperature. It was getting dark.

"This is lovely," Teddy said, getting out of his clothes.

"It's my pride and joy. I don't mind if there's time between jobs—I use it here." Her cell phone rang, and she looked at the caller's name before answering. "Excuse me," she said, "it's my assistant, Jenny." She walked away and talked for a moment, then returned.

"You look concerned," Teddy said.

"It's our leading man, Jake. He and Dax had a big argument in the bar at La Fonda, and now he's there alone, drinking."

"I hope he makes work tomorrow."

"There seems to be some doubt about that. Jenny thinks he may have quit the film, and Heckel and Jeckel are lurking nearby, apparently waiting for Jake to leave."

Teddy started to get dressed. "Is Jenny with Jake?"

"She's been trying to talk to him, but he's not very communicative."

"Tell her to keep him at the bar, whatever she has to do," Teddy said, buttoning his shirt.

"Where are you going?" Sally asked, alarmed.

"I think I'll have a drink at La Fonda and see that Jake gets to his suite unmolested."

"I'm coming with you," Sally said.

"I don't need help for this," Teddy said.

"Jake likes me. I can talk him out of there. I don't want you mixing with those two apes, though."

"Come on, then." They drove the few blocks to the big hotel, and Teddy parked the pickup in the indoor lot. They walked into the hotel and down the hallway toward the bar. Teddy stopped at a shop in the little mall, where there was a basket of umbrellas outside the door, seeking buyers. He bought a golf umbrella with a thick, curved handle.

"Ted, it's not raining," Sally said, as they hurried toward the bar.

"It could get wet," Teddy replied.

13

JAKE WAS HALF SLUMPED on his bar stool, while Jenny stood next to him, pushing his drink away. Teddy looked up and saw Heckel and Jeckel at the far end of the bar, watching them intently.

"Hi, Jake," Teddy said. "I'm Ted Shirley, assistant to Dan Waters, the production manager."

"Hey, Ted," Jake mumbled.

"I think we'd better get you to your suite," Teddy said. "You're not looking well."

"Okay," Jake said.

Teddy and Sally got him off the bar stool and onto his feet, and the three of them headed slowly toward the hallway. Teddy looked over his shoulder and saw that Heckel and Jeckel were moving their way.

The elevator door was open and waiting and Teddy, Sally, Jenny, and Jake got aboard. "Which floor?" Teddy asked.

"The top," Jake replied.

Teddy pressed the button and the door closed just as the two muscle guys reached it. They rode up, but it was very slow. When the door opened, Jake said, "That way," pointing to his right.

They were halfway to the suite when Teddy heard the fire stairs door open and close behind them. "Hey!" a voice said. "We'll take care of Jake."

"I'll need your key card, Jake," Teddy said, but he didn't stop moving. At the door to the suite, Jake was still fumbling in his pocket when Heckel and Jeckel arrived. Heckel, the larger of the two, hooked his fingers in Jake's belt. "We'll take care of this," he said to Teddy. "Now get lost."

Teddy brought the thick umbrella handle down sharply on Heckel's wrist, and the man let go of Jake's belt with a yelp. Jeckel came to his rescue, but Teddy rammed the umbrella handle into his solar plexus, and the man made a loud noise and sat down on the floor.

Jake came up with the key card, and Sally let them into the suite. Teddy backed in to be sure they weren't followed, but the fight had gone out of the two men. "I think my wrist is broken," Heckel said as the door closed.

Teddy turned and walked down a short hall to the living room, which was large and handsomely furnished.

"I need a drink," Jake said.

"That's the last thing you need, Jake," Sally replied,

and she and Jenny hustled him into the bedroom and onto the bed.

Teddy sat down and found a leather-bound copy of their script, with Jake's name stamped on it in gold. He picked it up and flipped through the pages.

Sally came back into the room and sat down next to him on the sofa. "Whew, that was close," she said. "I expect Heckel and Jeckel are on their way to report to Dax."

"I expect they're on their way to the emergency room," Teddy replied.

Teddy found the marked page in the script that indicated how much they had shot. He continued leafing through the script to the end. "Sally," he said, "can you call Dan Waters and ask him to come over here?"

"Do you really think he wants to know about this?"

"I think he will want to know."

Jenny came into the room. "Jake is finally asleep," she said. "He did manage to say that he had told Dax he was quitting the film."

"Let him sleep it off," Teddy said. "In the meantime, I think we're stuck here until he wakes up."

A FEW MINUTES LATER there was a knock on the door, and Jenny let in Dan Waters.

"What's going on?" he asked.

Teddy told him what had transpired.

"You took on Heckel and Jeckel?" Dan asked, amazed.

"It had to be done," Teddy replied.

"Jake says he told Dax he's leaving the picture," Jenny said.

"Oh, shit!" Dan said. "This is a nightmare. We'll have to reshoot everything, and we'll be on this picture forever."

"Maybe not," Teddy said. "I've been looking through the script."

"We're nearly three-quarters through it," Dan said.

"Jake has eight scenes left to shoot," Teddy said. "I've read them, and I think his stand-in could do all the long shots, and, of course, the stunt double would be doing the climactic fight scene."

"Which leaves what?" Dan asked.

"Ten two-shots and close-ups that require Jake's participation—about seven minutes of actual screen time, maybe less."

"What, you're saying that Jake has only seven minutes of work left on the picture? The stand-in and stunt double could do the rest?"

"You heard me correctly." Teddy handed him the script. "I've marked the places. Read it and see if you agree."

Dan read the pages quickly. "You're right. If we can calm both Jake and Dax down, we can have Jake on the way back to L.A. the day after tomorrow, and we can finish the shoot without him."

"What time does Dax get up in the morning?" Teddy asked.

"Early—his car comes for him at seven AM."

"Do we have any idea what time Jake told Dax he was quitting?" Teddy asked.

"I think I heard about it pretty quick," Jenny said, "so maybe two hours ago."

"Do you think Dax has already called our stand-by star?" Teddy asked Dan.

"I happen to know that our man, Kramer, weekends up in the Sierras somewhere, and there's no cell service."

"Okay, then," Teddy said. "We've got two jobs to do. Dan, you tell Dax about our plan and get him to hold off on calling the stand-by star. When Jake wakes up, I'll try to talk him into working two more days."

"I'll be there when Dax wakes up," Dan said.

"Oh, and you'd better get the director to meet you at Dax's place. He's the guy who has to make this work."

"I'll call you," Dan said.

TEDDY, SALLY, AND JENNY poured themselves a drink from Jake's well-stocked bar and settled down to wait for him to regain something like consciousness.

"Hey, good morning!" somebody yelled.

Teddy sat up, blinking. Jake was standing in front of him, looking remarkably human.

"Ted, thanks for last night," Jake said. "I remember some of it."

"Jake," Teddy said, "do you remember an argument with Dax?"

"I remember telling him to go fuck himself," Jake replied. "Hey, I've got to call my pilot and get my airplane to Santa Fe. I'm off the picture."

"Jake," Teddy said, "why don't you order some breakfast sent up, and let me tell you why you might not want to quit just yet."

* * *

THE FOUR OF THEM were having breakfast.

"Let me get this straight," Jake said. "If I do seven minutes of two-shots and close-ups, I'll be done and home in L.A. for dinner Tuesday?"

"That's right," Teddy said, "and you'll get your whole paycheck and avoid a very expensive lawsuit from Dax, which could have an unfavorable impact on your career."

Jake took a sip of coffee. "Well, shit," he said, "I guess I can put up with the fucker for another seven minutes. I'm in."

Teddy's cell phone rang. "Dan?"

"I'm with Dax. He buys it, and I got him to agree not to be on the set when Jake is working."

"Jake's on board, too," Teddy said, "and he'll be real glad to hear that news."

14

TEDDY RODE TO WORK with Jake in his studio car. When they arrived at the location for the first setup, he got out of the car and looked carefully at the waiting faces. Dax was nowhere in sight.

"Okay, Jake," Teddy said, "you're on. Got your script?"

"Sure, but I've already learned my lines," Jake said.

They were in a forested area near a small waterfall, ending in a creek. Dan introduced Teddy to the director, Troy Small.

"Dan told me what you did," Small said to Teddy. "I want to thank you, and I want to thank you both for keeping Dax off the set while we shoot these setups."

"You're welcome," Teddy said, "but I think we've got a problem here."

Both Small and Dan were immediately attentive. "What now?" Dan asked.

"The waterfall," Teddy said. "That's going to read on the soundtrack, and it's the sort of thing that could require some looping back at the studio."

"Oh, fuck, you're right," Small said. "Jake's not going to show up for looping, is he?"

"Doubtful," Teddy said.

Small conferred with his sound man while an assistant miked Jake. He came back to Teddy and Dan. "My guy thinks he can pull it off by using two mikes, one for Jake and one for the water, then reduce the water sound in the editing room."

"That could work," Dan said, "but maybe not, and we're not going to find out until we're in the editing room."

"It's worth a try," Teddy said. "If it doesn't, you can always hire another actor who's a good mimic to do the looping."

"I know just the guy," Small said. "He's a comedian and he can do *anybody*."

"Then let's shoot," Dan said.

Teddy got an extra headset from the sound man and plugged it into the equipment.

"I need levels," the sound man said.

"Jake, give me a quick reading for a level," Small said.

Jake counted to ten.

"Shit, that was perfect," the sound man said. "Good for me."

"Let's do one for real," Small said, and the other actor in the scene stepped in. They did two quick takes, and everybody was happy.

"All right," Dan said, "that's a minute and a half in the can. Let's do the close-up."

They set up for the close-up, and while the other actor read his lines, Jake spoke his part exactly as in the two-shot.

"The guy's a pro," Teddy said to Dan.

"Okay, next setup," Small called out, and everybody started moving equipment.

Dan took a cell call, then came over to Teddy. "Dax wants to see you in his double-wide," he said.

"What about?"

"He brushed me off when I asked, but he wasn't shouting."

"That's good," Teddy said.

"Maybe, but he was very quiet," Dan replied, "and he gets that way when he's most deeply upset. Jake's driver will take you there, then come back for Jake. Watch your ass."

Teddy got into the car, and they moved out. Halfway to the double-wide, his cell rang. "Yes?"

"It's Dan. Dax's assistant called me and said that Dax has found something wrong with your background."

"Any idea what?" Teddy asked, trying to sound baffled.

"No, but I say again, watch your ass."

The car pulled up, and Teddy got out and knocked on the door. Dax's assistant opened it, showed Teddy in, then she got out.

"Have a seat, Ted," Dax said. His voice was very quiet.

Teddy sat down. "What can I do for you?"

"Is Ted your real name?" Dax asked.

Teddy kept it conversational. "It's Theodore, but I've always been called Ted."

"I happened to speak to a friend of mine in New York an hour ago. He was a producer on the documentary film you listed as a credit on your résumé, and he says there was nobody named Ted Shirley on the crew."

Teddy's mind was racing now; the documentary had been filmed three years ago; he steamed straight ahead. "Who's your friend?"

"Jason Cohen, he's a partner in the company."

"I never met him," Teddy said. "I was called in the night before to replace somebody who had a medical emergency. Tell Mr. Cohen to check the call sheets for the last four days of the shoot, which were done on location at the Central Park Zoo." Teddy had seen the film, and he remembered those scenes. He reran the film credits in his mind. "The guy I replaced was Robert Swain. He got the assistant director screen credit." Teddy remembered something else about Swain: he was dead of a heart attack before the film hit the theaters.

Dax was less certain now. "Were you a friend of Swain's?"

"No, I didn't know him."

"How'd you happen to get the call?"

"They called the union in a panic for a replacement, since the rules didn't allow shooting without an AD, and somebody there gave them my name."

"That's a strange way to replace a key crew member," Dax said.

"I heard they tried two other people, who weren't available. It was late in the evening and the shoot was for dawn, before the zoo opened. What would you have done in the circumstances?" You would have called the union, Teddy thought: say it.

Dax didn't say it, but he thought about it. "What was Swain's medical emergency?"

"Heart problem, I heard on the set."

Dax turned to his computer and typed something.

He's Googling Robert Swain, Teddy thought. I hope.

Dax read something on the screen, then turned back to Teddy. "You broke my guy's wrist last night."

"He was threatening me," Teddy said, "and he's a lot bigger than I am."

"What did you hit him with?"

"An umbrella."

"An *umbrella*? You took those two guys down with an umbrella?"

"It was a big umbrella," Teddy said.

"What were you doing with an umbrella?"

"It looked like rain. I keep an umbrella in my truck."

Now Dax was trying to remember if it had rained the night before, but he gave up. "Okay, get out of here."

Teddy got up and headed for the door.

"Shirley?" Dax said.

Teddy turned back. "Yessir?"

"Dan told me how you solved our problem. I appreciate it."

"You're welcome."

"There'll be something extra in your paycheck when we wrap," Dax said.

"Thanks very much," Teddy said, then he got out of there.

15

TEDDY FOUND THE CREW shooting another setup in the hills. As he got out of the car, Dan Waters came striding over.

"Don't worry," Teddy said, "it went just fine."

Dan pulled him aside out of earshot of everybody else. "It didn't go as fine as you think."

"He asked me some questions, I answered him, and as I was leaving he thanked me for my suggestion about Jake and said there'd be a bonus in my final paycheck."

"I got a call from his assistant after you left. She said Dax was back on the phone, making calls about you."

"I don't know what his problem is," Teddy said.

"Dax thinks you're a danger to him."

"How could he think that? I just saved his shoot and a couple of million dollars that would have come right out of his pocket."

"He doesn't think you're a danger to his wallet, he thinks you're a threat to him, personally."

"Personally? What does that mean?"

"He thinks you're working for somebody who wants him taken out—a guy at Centurion named Billy Barnett—something about his wife."

That stopped Teddy in his tracks. "Dan, can I confide in you?"

"Sure."

"This can't go any further, or I'll go down fighting Heckel and Jeckel."

"Ted, come on, give."

"I'm not Ted Shirley, I'm Billy Barnett."

Dan froze, then looked at him closely to see if he was kidding. "You're kidding, aren't you?"

"I'm not kidding. I'm a producer at Centurion for Peter Barrington's production company."

"Holy shit! Dax thinks you've hired yourself to knock him off?"

"It sounds that way."

Dan started pacing, looking at the ground.

"What's the matter, Dan?"

"We've got to get you out of here, and you can't go back to the production center."

"Actually, I'm not that worried about Heckel and Jeckel. Heckel has a broken wrist, and Jeckel is scared of me."

"I'm not worried about them, either, but that doesn't mean there's nothing to worry about."

"What should I be worried about?"

"Dax has sent for a guy from L.A., and he's due in this afternoon."

"A guy? What kind of guy?"

"The kind of guy who makes people disappear. It sounds like he's coming for you, first, then for Billy Barnett."

Teddy couldn't help laughing. "He's going to kill me twice?"

"That's the idea."

"Who is this guy?"

"He's a Russian. His name is Dimitri Kasov."

"I've heard that name, never met him."

"If you'd met him, you wouldn't be here. We've got to get you out. Let me see if the chopper is free. They could pick you up here and take you straight to the airport."

"No, no, don't do that. Dax would know about it immediately."

Dan looked at his watch. "I think you've got, maybe, three or four hours."

"Then I'll be here when he arrives. He can come looking for me."

"Are you crazy? Don't you understand what I'm telling you?"

"Dan, if I'm here, at least I can see the guy coming. If I leave, he'll hunt me down and take me out when I least expect it."

"Ted . . . ah, Billy . . ."

"Keep calling me Ted."

"Ted, you're beginning to sound like you've had some experience at this sort of thing."

"Some," Teddy admitted.

"How can I help?"

"Do you know what this Kasov looks like?"

"Not big, maybe five-eight, a hundred and sixty pounds, all muscle and gristle."

"Does he dress in any particular way?"

"He dresses to blend in. Look around you, he'll look like one of us."

"I think I'd better shave," Teddy said. He peeled off his mustache. "Can we swap hats?" Teddy handed him his Stetson and took Dan's baseball cap.

"You look completely different," Dan said.

"That's the idea, isn't it? It may not work for long, but it'll give me a little edge."

"Listen, Ted," Dan said, "I've got a gun in my room. I don't know why I carry the thing, but you're welcome to it."

"I don't think guns will be involved," Teddy said. "Kasov is more likely to use a knife or an ice pick."

"I'm getting really scared," Dan said.

"Don't be. Kasov's not coming for you."

"I mean, scared for you. This guy's a pro, and from what I've heard, he's pretty much unstoppable."

"Nobody is unstoppable," Teddy said. "Everybody bleeds."

"Jesus," Dan sighed.

"Who knows where I live?" Teddy asked.

"Did you put your address on your employment application?"

"I used a P.O. box number in Tesuque."

"Then he'll know you're in Tesuque. It's a small place, it won't take long to track you down. Has Sally been there?"

"Yes."

"Then she's probably the only one on the shoot who knows." Dan raised his hands in a defensive gesture. "I don't want to know."

"Does anybody know Sally and I have been seeing each other?"

"Just me. Oh, and the makeup girl, Mala, remember?"

"Can you reach her?"

"I've got her cell number."

"Please call her and find out if she's mentioned Sally and me to anyone."

"Okay."

"And if she hasn't told anybody, tell her to keep quiet."

"Okay. What are you going to do?"

Teddy gave him the keys to his truck. "This is parked in the lot at La Fonda Hotel. The ticket's under the sun visor. Can you get somebody to get it out of there and return it to its owner?"

"Who's that?"

"His name and address are on a piece of paper in the glove compartment. Tell him I won't be needing it anymore."

"What are you going to do for wheels?"

"I've got wheels."

"You didn't tell me what you're going to do, Ted."

"I think I'm going to pay Dax another visit."

"Oh, shit."

16

WHEN JAKE HAD FINISHED his setups he went to his car, where Teddy caught up with him. "Jake, can I get a ride to Production with you?"

"I'm not going anywhere near Dax, but I'll drop you off at the main gate."

"Thanks."

Jake looked closely at him. "What happened to your face?"

Teddy took the mustache from his shirt pocket and glued it back on. "Is that better?"

"It's more familiar," Jake said. "Your hat is missing, too."

"Don't worry about it," Teddy said.

"Ted, I want to thank you again for the way you handled Heckel and Jeckel."

"Think nothing of it."

"I've seen those guys in action, and it didn't turn out well for their victim." Jake looked out the window. "You know, I'm a movie star, but that doesn't mean I can't take care of myself."

"I'm sure you can, Jake."

"I mean, if I'm not as drunk as I was last night."

Teddy nodded.

"Not many people know that I trained as a Navy SEAL."

Teddy looked at him anew. "Really?"

"I didn't say I graduated the course, but I did all the training, and I excelled. The night our training ended I got drunk and took a swing at a chief petty officer. I found myself on a bus the next morning."

"That's unfortunate," Teddy said.

"It's not that I couldn't handle the sergeant, I was just drunk, and that doesn't work unless the other guy is as drunk as you are."

"Good point."

"After I heard that he'd bounced me, I invited him outside for a chat, and I cleaned his clock. After that, he was all the more anxious to see me go."

"How'd you get from the navy to the movies?"

"I met a girl in a bar near where I was stationed, and we ended up in bed. Turned out she was an assistant to a movie producer at SAC, and they were making a Navy SEAL movie, and she thought I might get a small role. I went to Burbank, in uniform, to audition, and they were impressed. It was a supporting role, but I lent some authenticity to the shoot, and after that, it was more and better movies. I kept the SEAL stuff from the PR people at the studio, because I was embarrassed about being bounced."

"I can understand that," Teddy said.

"Here you go," Jake said. They had arrived at the gate. "You watch your back, now."

Teddy shook his hand and got out of the car. He walked down to Dax's double-wide and rapped on the door. Dax's assistant opened it. "What is it, Ted?"

"I need to speak to Dax again."

"Just a minute." She closed the door and came back shortly. "He's in his office."

"Siddown, Ted," Dax said. "What can I do you for?"

"I've heard a disturbing rumor, Dax, and I thought it might be better to address the issue directly."

Dax blinked rapidly. "What kind of rumor?"

"I've heard that you've called in a sort of specialist to deal with me, and I've heard that you think I'm working for a guy at Centurion named Billy Barnett. Anything to that?"

"Are you working for Barnett?"

"I am not. I work for nobody but me, and for the moment, you. I know who Barnett is, but I've never so much as shaken his hand."

"No?" Dax tried not to look surprised.

"No. What has Barnett got against you?"

"It's complicated."

"Well, I'm not a complication," Teddy said. "I'm just

a working stiff here to do the best job I can and to make a living."

"And you're doing a very good job, Ted."

"Then why this Russian guy?"

"He's somebody I call on—on rare occasions—when I need somebody to watch my back."

"I'm not at your back, Dax."

Dax regarded him calmly. "Then you're going to have to go on proving that to me."

"For how long?"

"Until we're done."

"We wrap tomorrow night," Teddy said. "I'm not involved in post-production."

"Would you like to be?" Dax asked.

"Doing what?"

"I can think of half a dozen jobs you could handle back in L.A."

"I don't want to work in L.A. I want to stay in Santa Fe."

"Everybody wants to work in L.A., Ted," Dax replied.

"I appreciate the offer. If you've got anything for me here, I'd sure consider that."

"Let me see what I can do. By the way, the wrap party is at my new house tomorrow night. I hope you can come."

"Sure, I'd be delighted. How're we dressing?"

Dax handed him a printed invitation. "Here's the address. Dress however you'd like."

"Is this Russian guy going to be there?"

"No. I'll make a call."

"Thanks, I'll see you tomorrow night."

They shook hands, and Teddy left. Dan Waters drove up, and Teddy flagged him down.

"Did you see Dax?" Dan asked.

"Yeah, and I think we cleared the air."

"That doesn't sound like Dax," he said.

"He even invited me to the wrap party tomorrow night."

"You were on the list to get an invitation, anyway. What are you going to do about the Russian?"

"Dax says he'll call him off."

"He admitted hiring him?"

"He did."

"I don't know if you ought to go to the party, Ted."

"I don't want to be unsociable, and I especially don't want to seem afraid to be there."

"Maybe you should be."

"Don't worry about it, Dan. Have you sent somebody for my truck?"

"Not yet."

"Then just give me back the keys. I'll get a ride into town with Sally."

Dan produced the keys. "Why don't you take my gun with you?"

"That won't be necessary," Teddy replied. "I'll see you tomorrow." He took back his Stetson and gave Dan his baseball cap.

Dan waved and drove off. Teddy went to Sally's office.

"Hey, there," she said. "I was just closing up shop for the day."

"Can you give me a lift to my truck?"

She smiled. "I'll give you a lift to my place," she said.

17

THEY PASSED SOME SHOPS near her house. "Drop me here," Teddy said. "I've got some shopping to do. I'll be with you in half an hour."

"Anything I can help with?" she asked.

"Nope." Teddy got out of the car and walked to a shop that advertised guns, knives, and outdoor equipment.

"Yes, sir?" a clerk said.

"Knives," Teddy replied.

"Hunting? Utility?"

"Self-defense," Teddy said. "Concealable."

"You're on shaky ground here, my friend," the man said. "I can't know about it if you plan to use a weapon."

"Far from it. I want to avoid such a situation."

"Over here," the man said, leading the way. "My advice would be to get something with a blade under six inches."

"Good advice," Teddy said, looking over the goods. "How about the switchblade there, second from the left."

"We call that an automatic opening knife," the man said, handing him the weapon. Teddy flicked it open and examined the blade. "Needs sharpening."

"I've got something used, here, that somebody has already honed." He presented another knife with a black handle and a stained blade, but Teddy felt he could shave with it. "That'll do," he said.

"That's eighty dollars. You want a scabbard?" the clerk asked.

"I'd settle for a thick rubber band," Teddy replied, reaching for his cash, while the man rummaged in a drawer and came up with a rubber band. "This do?"

"Ideal," Teddy said. He paid the man and pocketed the knife and band.

"DAX OFFERED ME a job in L.A.," Teddy said to Sally over dinner.

"Are you going to take it?"

"No, I already have a job. The day after Dax's wrap party, I need to drive back to L.A."

"Oh." She looked disappointed.

"And I'd like you to come with me."

"Wait a minute, here," Sally said. "What's this all about?"

"It's about two people who're fond of each other spending some time together."

"How much time are we talking about?"

"I don't want to pile too much on you all at once," he said. "How about a year, to start, then we'll figure out the future."

"You mean, just pack up and go?"

"You don't even have to pack. I'll take you shopping when we get there. If there's something you can't do without, and we can't get it in my car, then we'll ship it."

"And what would I do with my time in L.A.?"

"Whatever you like. I've got a very nice house on Malibu Beach. You can lie on the deck all day and get fat, if you like."

"I don't like. I'm accustomed to being busy."

"Then I'll hire you as an associate producer at Centurion."

"In the Barrington group?"

"If you like—in another group, if you don't. Peter's partner, Ben Bacchetti, is now head of production, and we're close. You have a good background, so it won't be a problem. Or, I expect, you could go to work for Dax."

"No, thank you!" she said. "By tomorrow night, I'll have had all I want of Dax."

"Same here. So, what's it going to be? Will you take a chance with Billy Barnett?"

"I'll have to get used to calling you that."

"Shouldn't be a problem."

"Does it bother you that we've only known each other for a couple of weeks? And that you're coming off a great personal loss?"

"About that—there's a cold hard place in the middle of me that I'd almost forgotten about. It comes to the fore when I've been damaged. It doesn't make me a better human being, but it helps me survive as one. I've closed a door, and you've opened a new one for me."

"I'm going to have to digest this," she said. "My idea was to make you happy enough to keep you in Santa Fe for a while."

"That's a good plan, and one I like, but I have a life and a career at Centurion that's important to me. I'd hate to leave Peter—he's done a lot for me."

"So I couldn't have persuaded you to stay?"

"No. It would have hurt a lot to leave you, though."

"Well, that's honest."

"I could never be anything but honest with you," Teddy said. "Except for the part about lying about who I am and why I'm here. Oh, and my past, which I haven't lied about to you, but I probably will, just to protect you."

"Protect me from what?"

"My life, my mistakes. Oh, I'm clean. I'm not a criminal."

Sally grabbed his arm. "If anybody comes at you, he's going to have to deal with me first."

"Well, if you're going to watch my back, you'll have to do it in Malibu and L.A."

"Yes," she said, "I will do that."

18

ED EAGLE AND HIS WIFE, Susannah, were having an after-work drink.

"We got a hand-delivered invitation this afternoon," she said, handing it to him.

Ed read it. "Let me get this straight," he said, "you despise Dax Baxter. Is that right?"

"That is absolutely right," she replied.

"Then why do you want to go to his wrap party?"

"I don't want to go to his wrap party," Susannah said.

"Then what are we talking about?"

"I want to see his house."

"You don't want to see Baxter, but you want to see his house?"

"That is correct."

"I'm baffled here."

"He bought that barn of a place on a hilltop out at the very end of Tano Road, and I hear the production designer on his film has done it up in a remarkable way."

"I remember that house," Ed said. "We went to some charity event there a couple of years ago."

"That's right, and it was awful. But the place had good bones, and I want to see what they did with it."

Ed sighed.

"I want to see the PD's work. I might want to use him sometime."

"I understand."

"There'll be people there we know, from the business," she said, "and if we get bored, we can just leave."

"If we think we're going to be bored, then we might as well not go."

"But then we couldn't see the house. Anyway, it's a wrap party, so some crew member who no longer has anything to lose might take a swing at Dax. That would be fun, no?"

"That would be fun, yes," Ed replied. "Okay, we'll go, but if I tug my earlobe, like this"—he tugged his earlobe—"then we get the hell out of there, agreed?"

"Agreed."

"And if we're going to the party, you don't have to cook dinner," he said.

"That had crossed my mind," she admitted.

* * *

BESIDE THE POOL at the Arrington, in Los Angeles, Stone's phone rang. "Hello?"

"Stone, it's Ed Eagle."

"Hi, Ed."

"Are you in L.A.?"

"Yes, Ana and I are having a drink out by the pool. Why don't you and Susannah join us?"

"I can't think of anything I'd like better. I'll mention it to her. Tonight, however, she's committed us to go to Dax Baxter's wrap party for his film crew, studio people, and other hangers-on."

"Oh, well, that's one evening shot."

"I know. Susannah wants to see his new house, which, rumor has it, has been redone by his production designer at studio expense."

"I suppose that could be interesting."

"I'm worried about it getting too interesting," Ed replied.

"How's that?"

"It occurs to me that Teddy Fay, as a member of Dax's crew, was probably invited and might be there."

"Those are reasonable assumptions, I suppose."

"And as a result, there might be trouble."

"My knowledge of Teddy is that, when he causes trouble, he does so in a quiet, almost unnoticeable way."

"You mean that if he offs Dax, nobody will notice?"

"I don't think Teddy is inclined to off Dax," Stone replied, "but if he were and did, I think no one would notice, at least until Teddy was well out of it."

"I wonder why that isn't comforting," Ed said.

"There's a solution to your anxiety about this, Ed."

"What's that?"

"Don't go to the party. Read about it tomorrow in the *Santa Fe New Mexican*. I'm sure they'll be covering it."

"I'm afraid that's not an option."

"Why not?"

"Well, I've already told Susannah we'll go, and such a statement cannot easily be withdrawn, unless I suddenly have an attack of appendicitis, and I'm not that good an actor."

"Ed, my advice, for what it's worth, is to go to the party, thereby placating Susannah, then stay the hell away from Dax Baxter, lest he splatters when attacked."

"That's not the sort of advice I had in mind," Ed said, "but I guess I asked for it."

"You did. Go to the party. Nothing will happen. Teddy will not off Dax. Dax will not splatter, and if you keep the room between you and Dax, you will not be a party to or a witness of anything that might occur. But should Dax somehow expire, you can dine out on the story for months to come."

Ed sighed. "Are you sure Susannah didn't speak to you earlier?"

"Not since I left your house."

"Do you think I should go there armed?"

"Ed, do you feel that going to this party might put your life in danger?"

"No, I don't."

"Then I would go unarmed. In my experience, people who go to parties armed are just looking for an excuse to shoot somebody. If you don't go armed, then you will be spared that urge."

"I guess so."

"Let me propose an alternative," Stone said.

"Of course."

"Is there a fireplace in Dax's living room?"

"I expect so. Every Santa Fe house has a few fireplaces."

"In that case," Stone said, "there will be fireplace tools near the fireplace."

"I suppose so."

"And among them will be a poker."

"Undoubtedly."

"Then stay close enough to the fireplace so that, if trouble starts, you will be able to reach the poker and use it to defend yourself and your gorgeous wife."

"Got it," Ed said drily. "Take care."

"Oh, Ed?"

"Yes, Stone?"

"Should trouble start at the party, make me your first call. I'll want to hear the gory details."

"Of course you will, Stone." Ed hung up.

Susannah came into the room.

"Are we ready to go?" Ed asked her.

"I just have to put on my lipstick," Susannah replied, digging into her handbag.

Ed knew this to be a ten-minute exercise. "I'll get the car out of the garage," he said.

"You do that," she replied, gazing into the hall mirror.

19

TEDDY FAY (or Billy Barnett or Ted Shirley, take your pick) regarded himself in the mirror. He wanted to be immediately identifiable to anyone on the crew who had known him for the past weeks, and yet he wanted to disappear into the crowd, if that became necessary. First, he shaved closely, then reapplied his handlebar mustache; then he dressed in faded but starched jeans and a matching denim jacket decorated with a little southwestern silver trim. His shirt was vaguely Western-flavored, open at the throat.

Then he unwrapped his very sharp, auto-release (switchblade) knife and secured it to his right ankle with the heavy rubber band the seller had given him. He pulled on his boots, then made sure the knife was accessible without being visible. He topped it all off with a very expensive new hat from the O'Farrell Hat Company in Santa Fe, well suited to the shape of his head and blocked to perfection, with a curled brim. He checked the mirror again: he was presentable.

Sally called from the bathroom. "You're taking longer to dress than I am," she said, "and I'm doing makeup."

"I'm done," he said, "are you?"

"Nearly."

"Nearly doesn't cut it."

She stepped out of the bathroom wearing a fringed suede jacket and matching skirt.

"Dale Evans, as I live and breathe!" Teddy said.

"All I need is her horse," she replied. "What was its name?"

"Buttermilk."

"I don't know how you remember all that stuff from old movies."

"I had a misspent youth," he replied. "I spent most of it at the movies, later at the pool hall."

"I like you better without the mustache," she said.

"What is it the French say, 'A kiss without a mustache is like a day without sunshine.'"

"The French don't say that."

"They do. They also say the same thing about cheese."

"A kiss without cheese?"

"A meal without cheese."

"Oh."

"But don't worry, the mustache goes when we leave Santa Fe."

"You're taking a lot for granted, aren't you?" she asked.

"Well, you're coming with me, aren't you?"

"What would you do if I didn't?"

"I'd throw a sack over your head and lock you in the trunk of the car."

She laughed. "Well," she said, "I guess I don't have a choice." She kissed him. "Maybe the French have got something there."

ED AND SUSANNAH EAGLE pulled up in front of Dax Baxter's new house and gave their car to a valet parker. "Well," Ed said, regarding the house, "the lighting guy did a good job."

The house stood out against the landscape, which was burned red by the setting sun.

"He did, didn't he?" Susannah said. "Let's go check out the inside."

"After that can we leave?" Ed asked plaintively.

"We'll see," she replied. She took his hand and towed him in through a very large set of weathered antique doors. The sounds of a mariachi band came from a corner of the enormous living room.

"The band was predictable, wasn't it?" Ed asked.

"Shut up and look at this place," Susannah said.

An enormous fireplace hosted a pile of burning piñon logs, sending out their pungent scent.

"Fit for a medieval castle," Ed muttered.

"But right in scale with the room," Susannah said. "It must be thirty by fifty feet."

"Come to think of it," Ed said, "I've never seen this many sofas in one place, outside a hotel lobby."

The room was half filled with people in Western outfits and more were arriving.

"They must be casting a musical number in a Roy Rogers movie," Ed said, looking over the crowd.

They passed through the living room, pausing to shake the hand of an acquaintance here and there.

"There," Susannah said, pointing to a clot of people surrounding a short, balding man crammed into a cowboy outfit. "That's Drake Shelbourne, the production designer," she said. "I have to speak to him."

Ed allowed himself to be maneuvered through the crowd.

"Susannah!" Shelbourne cried, as if she had come to rescue him.

"Hello, Drake," Susannah said, leaning down and allowing herself to be kissed on both cheeks. "This place looks fabulous! It's the only reason we're here."

Shelbourne broke up. "Me, too!" Susannah introduced him to her husband.

"I picked him out of the crowd," Shelbourne said, reaching up to shake his hand. "He's what, seven feet tall?"

"Only six-foot-eight," Susannah replied.

Ed sighed and shook the man's hand. "It was the only way I could get a college basketball scholarship. Nice job on the house, Drake. It was dreadful, before you came along."

"That's the God's truth," Shelbourne said. "I stripped it to the plaster everywhere. Now it at least looks as if a human being lives here—or maybe a dozen human beings. Check out the patio." He pointed to another set of double doors across the room.

They moved in that direction, stopping at the bar to acquire refreshments. The patio was large, with a pile of rocks making a water feature, a jazz trio playing, and, in one corner, one of Dan Ostermiller's wonderful bear sculptures, a bronze of a full-sized animal climbing a tree.

"I saw that at Nedra Matteucci's gallery," Ed said, "and I wanted it, but it cost more than my car."

"You can probably buy it from Dax Baxter for half that after the party. The word is, he's strapped for cash, and I have a feeling that everything here will be for sale tomorrow."

TEDDY AND SALLY made their entrance to the party a few minutes later and had much the same reaction to the house as had the Eagles.

"This place is the size of a sound stage," Teddy commented.

"I was going to say a high school gymnasium," Sally replied, "but I'll buy sound stage."

They had been there for less than a minute when Teddy spotted the Russian.

20

DIMITRI KASOV STOOD, immobile, scanning the crowd. He had apparently not spotted Teddy yet.

Teddy stepped behind Sally.

"Are you about to pinch my ass?" she asked.

"A good idea," he replied, "but not at the moment. I'm using you for cover."

"Cover from what?"

"Do you see the short, thickset guy standing by the fireplace in a black hat?"

"Yes, what about him?"

"The black hat is appropriate. He's a Russian from L.A. called Dimitri Kasov. There was a rumor going around this afternoon that Dax had sent for him."

"I didn't hear the rumor. Is he some sort of post-production expert? Who is he and what does he do?"

"As Dan put it to me, he makes people disappear."

"So he's a magician, here for the floor show?"

"Not exactly."

"Then what do you mean, he makes people disappear?"

Teddy didn't answer that. "Let's move to our left, out to the patio, and keep yourself between me and the Russian."

"Ted, ah, Billy, what's going on?"

"I'll explain it on the patio." They maneuvered outside, and the air was cool and crisp.

"You're starting to alarm me," Sally said.

"I don't mean to, I'm just being cautious."

"Good evening, Ted," a deep voice behind them said.

Teddy turned to find Dax Baxter standing there, wearing a buckskin suit, like Buffalo Bill, and a ten-gallon Stetson.

"Good evening, Dax," Teddy said. "Wonderful party, and the house is beautiful."

"I'm glad you think so," Dax said.

"Did you really get this done in just a few days?"

"I'm an impatient person, so I got it done in a hurry."

"Beautiful job," Sally said.

"Thank you, Sally," Dax replied. "You did a good job for me. You'll find my gratitude expressed in your final paycheck."

"Thank you, I appreciate that."

"Excuse me," Dax said. "I have to speak to someone." He went back into the house.

"No need to hide from the Russian now," Teddy said.

"What's changed?" Sally asked.

"Dax is telling him where I am right now. I guess this

is as good a place as any," he said, looking around the patio. "Sally, I'd appreciate it very much if, instead of asking questions, you'd just go and get into the truck."

"I'm not going anywhere until you tell me what's going on," she said.

"All right. Dax has hired the Russian to either kill me or hurt me very badly. He's on the way out here to do one of those things right now."

"I'll wait in the truck," she said, "unless you'd like me to throw myself between you."

"No, I wouldn't like that. Please go now. I'll be there in a few minutes."

"I'm going to call the cops," she said.

"If you do, they'll arrest me, instead of the Russian," Teddy said. "Now get out of here." He slapped her on the ass, propelling her toward the front of the house.

Teddy looked around. Ed and Susannah Eagle, who had been looking at a bronze bear, were on their way back into the house, leaving him alone on the patio. He went and stood by the tree the bear was climbing.

Dimitri Kasov appeared in the doorway, stopped, and had a look around.

Teddy bent down and retrieved the switchblade from his ankle. "I believe you're looking for me," he said across the expanse of the patio.

"Ah," Kasov said. "You've heard."

"Everybody has heard, Mr. Kasov. When we're done here, one of us will leave in an ambulance, the other with the police. You get to choose which one you want to be."

Kasov's right hand went behind him to the small of his back.

Teddy hoped it wouldn't come out holding a gun; a knife, he had reason to know, wasn't much use in a gunfight.

Kasov's hand emerged holding a straight knife with about an eight-inch blade. "You were expecting a gun, maybe?"

"No." Teddy flicked open the switchblade but kept it at his side.

"It won't hurt much," Kasov said, taking a step forward. Then, instead of using the knife, he aimed a kick at Teddy's head.

Teddy moved his head enough for the kick to miss, then grabbed Kasov by the ankle and made a swift cut through his jeans and the back of his calf. Then he shoved Kasov backward while holding onto his ankle. Kasov fell to the stone floor.

"You were wrong," Teddy said. "It hurts, doesn't it?"

Kasov crawled out of reach, spider-like. He took off his belt and wrapped it around his thigh above the knee, then jerked it tight. "If you're going to kill me, do it at the throat," he said.

"I haven't decided," Teddy said, "but I'll tell you this for a fact. If I ever see you again, I'll kill you. Now, your best move is to get yourself to your car, drive back to highway 284, then to St. Francis Drive and follow the signs to the hospital. Do you think you can manage that without causing a disturbance?"

"I can manage," Kasov said, getting awkwardly to his feet and hobbling toward the outdoor exit from the patio, while holding tightly to the end of his belt.

Teddy watched him go, then he wiped his blade with a tissue, folded it, and stuck it back into his boot.

Kasov stopped at the edge of the patio. "If I see you again," he called back, "you won't see me until it's too late."

Teddy watched him disappear around the corner of the house, then he walked back into the living room where Dax stood, talking to some men in suits. He walked over. "Excuse me, Dax," he said, "I'm leaving now, and I wanted to thank you for your kind invitation. It's an impressive house." He turned to leave, then stopped. "Oh, your Russian friend wasn't feeling well, and I think he's on the way to the hospital now. Good night."

Dax blinked rapidly. "What?"

Teddy walked out of the house without answering, and before he could give his ticket to the valet, Sally drove up in the truck, and he got in.

"I saw the Russian leave the house, limping badly," she said. "He got into a car and left."

"I'm glad to hear it," Teddy replied.

"Did you have anything to do with that?" she asked.

"I guess you could say I helped," Teddy replied.

"I'm hungry," she said.

"How about a bite at El Nido, then my place?"

"Sounds good to me." She put the truck in gear and drove away from the house.

"Tomorrow, we'll get an early start," Teddy said. "We'll stop for the night in Phoenix, then make L.A. the following day."

"Does the Russian live in L.A.?"

"We won't be seeing him again," Teddy replied.

21

TEDDY DROVE DOWN the Pacific Coast Highway and, just before the turn to Malibu Colony, turned into his short drive and opened the garage door with his clicker. His wife's Mercedes station wagon was parked next to him.

"Whose car?" Sally asked sleepily. It had been a long drive from Phoenix.

"Yours," he said. He reached into the glove box, extracted a plain key ring and handed it to her. "That's the key and the house key. The garage door works on a button at the bottom of the rearview mirror."

He opened the trunk and emptied it of their things, then unlocked the door to the house and ushered her in.

They walked into the living room and she stopped, staring at the broad view of the spectacular sunset over the Pacific. "And I thought we had great sunsets in Santa Fe," she said.

Teddy led her upstairs and put her suitcase in what had been his wife's dressing room. The housekeeper had, on his instructions, removed her clothes and belongings from the dressing room, bedroom, and her bathroom, and she had done a good job. Her jewelry was in the safe in his dressing room.

"My goodness," Sally said, "all this for one suitcase of jeans and shirts?"

"The shopping is very good in Malibu Village, and when you tire of them there's always Rodeo Drive." He went to his bedside table and found two pieces of mail— an envelope from his bank and another from American Express. He removed the Amex and Visa cards from the envelopes and handed them to her with a pen. "Sign the backs," he said.

"Let me get this straight," Sally said, "you're turning me loose on Rodeo Drive with credit cards?"

"Use mine, not yours."

"I only have a Mastercard, and I owe about two hundred bucks on it."

"We'll get a checking account working for you tomorrow, and you can pay that off and any other bills you may have outstanding. Do you have a mortgage on your house?"

"Yes, about ninety thousand."

"Call the mortgage company, get the exact payoff amount, and send them a check, then you won't have to worry about making payments."

Sally sat down on the bed. "Whew! This is all happening very fast."

"You'll get used to it," Teddy said, kissing her on the ear.

"What if I miss Santa Fe?"

"You can go back and visit anytime, and stay for as long as you like. Permanently, if you're unhappy with me."

"You're very smart, Billy. The best way to keep me is to leave the door open."

"Then I always will," he said. "Have you thought any more about what you'd like to do out here?"

"Well, I want a job, if that's what you mean. I'd go nuts sunning myself on the deck every day, though it's a very nice deck."

"Just remember it's the Pacific out there, and it's colder than it looks. Don't go swimming without me."

"Fear not."

"Are you exhausted? If so, I'll make us an omelet. We'll go out, if you feel up to it."

"Give me an hour's nap and I'll be ready to go out. Which is my side of the bed?"

"The one you're sitting on. Excuse me, I have to unpack." He grabbed his bags and went into his dressing room.

Sally stretched out on the bed and was asleep in seconds.

STONE'S PHONE RANG, and he picked it up. "Hello?"

"A Mr. and Mrs. Eagle at the front gate, in a hotel car," a security guard said.

"Please send them up to the house." Stone hung up and went to the bathroom door, where Ana was showering. "Ed and Susannah have landed, and they're on their way to the house."

"Sure you won't join me in here?" she asked.

"Joining you would be fun, but later. They're going to want a drink. We'll see you downstairs when you're dry." He closed the door and went downstairs to greet his guests. Their driver and the butler took their cases upstairs, while Stone took Ed and Susannah into his study and poured everyone a drink. "Ana will be down shortly," he said. "Well, maybe not shortly. I'm not yet accustomed to how long she takes to get presentable."

"Not long," Ana said from the doorway. "Can I have a drink, too?"

"Sit you down, and it will appear."

Stone sat down opposite the Eagles. "Good flight?" He and Ed flew the same airplane.

"Very good," Ed replied. "I'm going to miss Santa Monica Airport, if the fanatics ever actually get it closed."

"They're talking about shortening the runway to thirty-five hundred feet," Stone said, "just to keep you and me out of there." The Santa Monica City Council had been trying for years to close the airport.

"I can handle thirty-five hundred feet," Ed said.

"Yeah, but if they do that, soon they won't be selling jet fuel."

"You have a point. I guess it'll be Burbank if they win."

"You know," Stone said, "I could never understand why somebody would buy a house at the end of a runway, then complain about the noise."

"Go figure," Ed said. He shifted in his chair and changed the subject. "Have you heard about Teddy?" he asked.

"What is there to hear?"

"A couple of nights ago, Dax Baxter threw his wrap party for the cast and crew of his film, and Teddy showed up there."

"And why not?" Stone asked.

"The rumor is, Dax thought Teddy was trying to kill him, so he brought in a heavyweight from L.A., a Russian named Kasov."

"Never heard of him," Stone said, "but I've had my own problems with Russians out here, though not for a couple of years."

"Well, anyway, Susannah and I were out on the patio, admiring an Ostermiller bear, when Teddy came out with his girlfriend, just as we were going back inside. We saw this guy in a black hat go outside as we were entering the living room."

"The Russian?"

"One and the same. Next thing you know, there was some sort of commotion out there, and Dax's people blocked the doors to keep everybody inside. We heard later that Teddy had injured the guy, then left."

"Then the Russian must have attacked him, and Teddy was prepared. He wouldn't act without reason."

"In any case, the guy ended up in surgery to repair the damage from a big cut to his leg."

"Then he won't be bothering Teddy for a while."

"Not ever, if he's smart."

"Do you think Dax is done now?"

"Good question," Ed said. "I guess we'll have to wait and see."

22

TEDDY AND SALLY finished a good dinner at a Mexican restaurant in Malibu Village and drove back to the house. He let them in and showed her how the burglar alarm worked.

Sally pointed at a piece of paper just inside the door. "A message for you?" she asked.

"Looks like someone shoved it under the door." He picked it up and read it. It was typed in all caps:

I APOLOGIZE FOR THE CRUDITY OF THE ATTACK IN SANTA FE. NEXT TIME, I'LL SEE THAT IT IS CONDUCTED IN A SMOOTHER AND LESS PREDICTABLE MANNER.

It was unsigned.

Sally read it over his shoulder. "That sounds ominous," she said. "You never told me—what did you do to the Russian?"

"He tried to kick me in the head before knifing me, but I was a little quicker."

"Did you have a weapon?"

"I had taken precautions. I cut his leg in a way that demanded immediate medical attention, and he took my advice about getting to a hospital."

"Would he have known where the Santa Fe hospital is?"

"A professional assassin always knows where the nearest hospital is," Teddy replied. "I did give him directions, though."

"How badly was he injured?"

"Enough so that he would have bled to death without emergency treatment. He knew enough to apply a tourniquet, but he would still have needed immediate surgery to repair the damage, and he will be off that leg for some time while healing. He won't be coming after me anytime soon, if at all."

"You know, I used to have a boyfriend who went looking for bar fights, which he usually won, but he would come home from time to time with wounds I'd have to stitch up."

"And where did you acquire that skill?"

"In school. I'm a registered nurse."

"Well, then, you'd be handy to have around in certain circumstances. I've had to stitch myself up a couple of times, and it wasn't much fun."

"And you, sir—where did you acquire that skill?"

He poured them both a brandy, and they took it out to the deck, where the moon illuminated the sea. "All right, I'm going to tell you everything—or almost everything—so you'll know that I trust you."

"I already trust you," she replied.

"I know, but you make me feel the need to share."

"All right, share."

"I grew up in Virginia, small town, and I graduated from UVA, then got a master's in political science. Late in my last year of grad school a professor—a mentor, really—introduced me to a man over dinner, a very interesting fellow. He asked me a lot of questions, and I began to suspect that he was an officer of the Central Intelligence Agency. I was right. He called me a week later and invited me to a small dinner party at his home in Georgetown, specifying that I should come alone. The other guests, men and women, seemed to know him and each other very well. As it turned out, they were all CIA. The next day, the man turned up at my apartment in Charlottesville and invited me to join the Agency."

"And you took him up on it?"

"After a long conversation about my background, interests, and skills, he suggested that I attend a training course at a place called The Farm—actually Camp Peary, technically a naval installation, but occupied by the CIA, near Williamsburg. Before I even met the gentleman I had been very thoroughly vetted and found to be a candidate for the operations side of the Agency.

"I took all the usual courses—lock picking, use of radios, hand-to-hand combat—I even learned to fly at the airstrip there. I was particularly adept in the urban survival courses and in various technical classes, and after about nine months there—longer than the usual course—I was taken to Langley to visit the Technical Services department, the function of which is to provide agents with communications equipment, clothing, disguises, firearms, as well as other weapons—in short, everything necessary to help an agent survive and successfully complete his mission.

"I loved what I saw happening there, and I was taken on in the department as a trainee. After twenty years there I was deputy director of Technical Services. I was offered the director's job, but that was mostly an administrative position, which didn't appeal to me.

"I retired from the Agency soon after, took my pension. I also 'borrowed,' over the years, a lot of specialized equipment and weapons, enough to stock a very nice private workshop. For some years after retiring I was something of an outlaw—I won't go into the details of all that, since I broke the law in numerous ways. But I became the subject of a big search by my former employer, which was getting pretty hot. At that point, I encountered two young men in the Arizona desert who were unknowingly being pursued by some Russian gentlemen who meant them no good. I managed to extricate them from that situation, and in gratitude, the father of one of them, who had connections in high places, managed to obtain a presidential pardon for me.

"That was about six years ago, and I joined the two young men at Centurion Studios. They are Peter Barrington, the director, and his partner, Ben Bacchetti, who is now head of production at Centurion and who will probably eventually run the studio. After that, I lived happily ever after, until I lost my wife, but then I was fortunate enough to find you."

"My God, what a story," Sally said.

"It doesn't matter if you don't believe it. I got it off my chest."

"Oh, I believe every word of it," she replied. "I don't think you would ever lie to me."

"I thank you for that," Teddy said, then he took her to bed.

DAX BAXTER SAT in the study of his home in Bel-Air and regarded the two gentlemen who sat across the desk from him. "All right," he said, "you've been on the case for, what, thirty-six hours?"

"That is correct," the heavyset, balding man across from him said. His name was Grovitch. His companion was Medov—tall and lean, with thick black hair.

"Where is he, and what is he doing?"

"He has returned to his home on Malibu Beach," the man said, "in the company of the woman, Sally, from Santa Fe."

"So she took up with him?"

"Apparently," Grovitch said. "We don't know yet what are her intentions, to stay or go soon. If she stays it might be of usefulness to take her first, as a lure for neutralizing him."

"Not just yet," Dax said. "What is his correct name?"

Grovitch consulted a notebook: "Billy Barnett," he

replied. "He is employed at Centurion Studios, in the group of Peter Barrington."

"I know who Billy Barnett is," Dax said, "just didn't know that Ted Shirley was Billy Barnett."

"He is," Grovitch replied. "This is definite."

"That changes things," Dax replied.

23

TEDDY SAT AT a table on the executive side of the Centurion Commissary, across from Peter Barrington.

"It's good to see you, Billy," Peter said. "Are you ready to go back to work?"

"Not just yet, Peter. Perhaps in another week."

"How have you been feeling? We all know how much you must miss Betsy."

"I do, every day. But in fact, I've met someone who has helped me readjust, and faster than I would have believed possible."

"Who is she?"

"Her name is Sally Ryder."

"Tell me about her. Where did you meet?"

"In Santa Fe. I took some temporary work on a film there, and she was an assistant production manager. We just connected, somehow."

"I'm happy for you, Billy. Did you leave her in Santa Fe?"

"No, I brought her back with me. She's shopping in Malibu Village right now. I'm hoping to find her some work at Centurion. She's done just about everything on a movie set, and she's very, very good."

"That's high praise, coming from you," Peter said.

"It occurred to me that she might be good in Betsy's old job."

"You think she's *that* good?"

"I do."

"Well, there's a problem there. Right after you left for your break, Ben sent over a woman from the executive offices, on a temporary basis, and she's settled into Betsy's job very quickly. I hired her permanently yesterday."

"I see," Teddy said, disappointed.

"However," Peter said, "my number-two production assistant has found herself pregnant, so she's leaving soon and giving up her job in favor of full-time motherhood. Perhaps I could have a talk with Sally about that job."

"What a good idea," Teddy said.

"Are you in love with Sally, Billy?"

"Yes, I am."

"Well, that didn't interfere with either your work or Betsy's, so I don't see why it should be any different with Sally."

"I'm relieved you think that," Teddy said. "Shall I have her call your secretary?"

"Just tell her to show up at my office at ten tomorrow morning and to bring her résumé."

Teddy took an envelope from his pocket. "Here's her résumé," he said. "She'll be there at ten."

TEDDY WAS HAVING a drink on the deck when Sally arrived with half a dozen shopping bags. She dumped the shopping bags, poured herself a drink, and joined him. "Well, Billy, you're a poorer man by a couple of thousand dollars, and you have only yourself to blame, turning me loose with two credit cards."

"I'll survive," Teddy said. "You'll spend more as time goes by. You'll fill that dressing room, if I'm any judge of character."

"You are an embarrassingly good judge of character," Sally said, raising her glass. "Cheers."

"Anyway, I may have found you some work to keep you busy, instead of shopping."

"What, are you putting me on the street?"

Teddy laughed. "No, but the movie business isn't all that different."

"What would I be doing, sweeping up?"

"A bit more than that. You have a ten o'clock meeting tomorrow morning with Peter Barrington at Centurion, to discuss the possibility of becoming his number-two production assistant."

"You're kidding me!"

"I kid you not."

"Number two, huh? How many production assistants does he have?"

"Two, and number two is with child and thus changing careers."

"She's not coming back after maternity leave?"

"Nope, she's ascending to the nobility of full-time motherhood."

"Well, bless her heart! What would I be doing for Peter?"

"Whatever he asks you to do."

"What does it pay?"

"Whatever he offers you."

"Does it include being chased around a desk?"

"Peter is happily married."

"Aren't they all?"

"Are you speaking from experience?" he asked.

"God, yes. Movie people are the horniest people in the world, and they don't easily take no for an answer."

"Well, I gave him your résumé. I hope it says something about taking no for an answer."

"If I put that on my résumé, I'd never be interviewed."

"You have a point, but believe me, you have nothing to fear from Peter, except maybe being overworked from time to time."

"What makes you think I can do this job?"

"I've seen you in action. Also, Dan thought so, and apparently so did Dax Baxter."

"Well, he did offer me a job in L.A., didn't he?"

"There, you're fully qualified."

"What's Peter like?"

"Handsome, charming, smart—no, brilliant. Have you seen any of his films?"

"All six of them."

"Did you like any of them?"

"Each one more than the last."

"Then it couldn't hurt to tell him so. Peter has an ego, just like everybody else. Don't overdo it, though."

"I'll try not to actually slaver."

"Good idea. Are any of the clothes you bought appropriate for a job interview?" he asked.

"They all are, if he likes really, really tight jeans."

"I'm sure he does, but maybe you'd better run back to the Village before the shops close."

"Well, there is a very nice little dress that's appropriate for absolutely anything."

"Wear that."

"I thought I might."

"And maybe you should invest in a few more outfits in that category."

"I'll see what the other women in the office are wearing."

"That would be effective reconnaissance."

"Does Peter know that you and I are fucking *all* the time?"

"He'll guess that when he sees you, but it won't be a problem, unless we're doing it at the office."

"We can't fuck at the office?"

"We'll have to wait until we get home."

"Awwwwww!"

24

PETER BARRINGTON REGARDED the woman who sat across the desk from him. She was bright, sounded willing, had a good résumé, and was quite attractive. Billy, he thought, had very good judgment. "Sally, the job pays fifteen hundred a week to start—that's seventy-eight thousand. Is that satisfactory?"

It was a third more than Sally had ever made in a year. "It is," she replied.

"Can you start Monday?"

"Yes, I can."

"Good," Peter said. "Your predecessor is at a doctor's appointment right now, but she'll be here for your first week—two, if you need it—to get you up to speed." He stood up and offered her his hand. "Welcome aboard," he said.

She shook his hand and smiled. "Thank you, Mr. Barrington."

"I'm Peter to everybody around here," he said.

"Peter, it is."

"See you Monday morning." Sally left, and Peter turned to his schedule on one of his computer screens. He was meeting his father at the studio commissary for lunch in half an hour, and he was bringing a woman.

SALLY SAT IN HER CAR and phoned Teddy.

"Did you get it?" he asked, without saying hello.

"I got it. I start Monday."

"That's wonderful!"

"You don't think it will be odd for us to be working in the same office?" she asked.

"Certainly not. You'll hardly ever see me, anyway. I spend more than half my time on sound stages or locations."

"I'll be home in half an hour. Buy me lunch?"

"I'll make you lunch," he said. "And you're dessert."

"Promises, promises."

PETER PARKED HIS GOLF CART in a reserved spot outside the commissary and walked in to find his father and a very attractive woman at a table with his partner and the studio's head of production, Ben Bacchetti. He took a seat. "Are you joining us, Ben?"

"No, I've got a lunch date. I just wanted to say hello to your dad and ask about my dad."

"Your dad is as ever," Stone said.

Ben stood. "It's good to see you, Stone, and to meet you, Ana."

"I haven't met Ana," Peter said, as Ben departed. He shook her hand.

"You didn't tell me he was so handsome," Ana said to Stone.

"Is he?" Stone asked. "Ana is in Santa Fe real estate," he said to Peter. "She has to flatter everybody."

Ana's phone rang, and she stood. "I'm sorry, I have to take this." She walked away from the table.

"Dad," Peter said, "before Ana returns, I've been hearing rumors about some sort of incident at Dax Baxter's house in Santa Fe, something involving Billy. Do you know anything about that?"

"I do," Stone said. "I spent a few days with Ed and Susannah Eagle, and I saw Billy there at dinner. What do you know about Dax Baxter?"

"Able producer, miserable excuse for a human being, from all I've heard."

"Apparently he's also a paranoiac," Stone said.

"Only one of his charms," Peter replied.

"Somehow he got the idea that Billy had been sent by some enemy of his to kill him, and he promptly sent for a pro out of L.A. to eliminate his problem."

"That's insane. How does Baxter even know Billy?"

"Billy took a temporary job on a Baxter shoot at a movie ranch in Santa Fe. Didn't use his own name. Billy and his girl went to a wrap party at Baxter's new place there, and the pro, a Russian, came after him with a knife outside the house. The Russian got the worst of it. Billy put him in the hospital."

"Have there been any legal ramifications?"

"No. Baxter wasn't about to call the police."

"Billy's back in town, now, and I've just hired his new girlfriend, Sally Ryder, as one of my production assistants. I'm glad he's met somebody. I think he was in a pretty bad way after Betsy's death."

"How could you tell? The man has the most consistently calm mien of anyone I've ever met."

"I agree," Peter said. "He can be hard to read, but there was this sadness evident in him. Is this thing over with Baxter?"

"I don't know, and from what I've heard about Baxter, he may not know either."

"He has a reputation around town for being mercurial, to put it politely. I'm told he has to pay higher than usual salaries to get crew to work for him, and even then, there's a lot of turnover among his people. He'd probably be in jail or a padded room somewhere if he didn't make so much money for his studio."

"Keep an ear to the ground, and let me know what's going on with Billy, will you?" Stone asked.

Ana returned to the table. "Sorry about that. There was a problem with a closing in Santa Fe, but I got it sorted out."

"Funny I should meet you," Peter said. "My wife, Hattie, and I have been talking about getting a place for weekends and vacations, and Santa Fe keeps coming up."

"What a delightful son you have, Stone," she said, pro-

ducing a business card out of thin air and handing it to
Peter. "Do give me a call if you'd like to come out for a
weekend and look around. I'll put you and your wife up
in my guesthouse."

"Perhaps we'll do that," Peter replied, tucking the card
away.

"Hooked," Stone said.

Ana laughed. "Your father managed to sell his Santa Fe
house without an agent," Ana said, "which is against God's
law. What sort of place did you have in mind, Peter? Acre-
age? Horses? Sunset views?"

"Well, Hattie and I used to ride, but not much lately.
It might be fun to keep horses."

"Now you're talking about staff, Peter," Stone said.
"Careful."

"Not much staff," Ana said. "All you need is a groom,
who can double as a caretaker, and the phone number of
a good vet. I can get you both—all part of the service. Do
you have any kids?"

"Not yet," Peter said. "Neither of us seems much inclined that way."

"Fewer bedrooms, then," Ana replied.

For most of the rest of their lunch the two of them
talked houses, while Stone looked on, amazed.

25

BEN BACCHETTI LET himself into one of the commissary's private dining rooms, where his guest sat, waiting. "I'm sorry to be late," Ben said, checking his watch.

"Quite all right," the man said, rising and extending his hand. "I'm Dax Baxter." He was taller and heavier than Ben and was neatly dressed in a jacket, no tie.

"Mr. Baxter," Ben replied, shaking the hand.

"Dax, please."

"And I'm Ben." He sat down and spread the linen napkin over his lap. "Would you like a drink, Dax? Some wine, perhaps?"

"No, thank you, I'm fine with the mineral water." He tapped his glass. "I've been hearing good things about your takeover of production," Baxter said.

"Thank you, I think it's gone pretty well, so far."

"I especially like your productions with Peter Barrington."

"Peter is the genius in that partnership. I just try to clear the way for him." Ben took a sip of his water then found a button under the table and pressed it with his toe. "I'm continually impressed with your grosses," he said.

"Thank you, I try to keep them up."

A waiter entered the room and set two bowls of soup on their table.

"I've taken the liberty of ordering for us both," Ben said. "The commissary's daily special. If there's something you'd rather have, we can probably find it in the kitchen."

"I'm fond of gazpacho," Baxter said, tasting his soup.

"I was surprised to get your call," Ben said. "What can I do for you?"

"I like a man who cuts to the chase," Baxter said.

Ben didn't reply; he didn't get an answer to his question, though he thought he knew what it was.

"How would you like to add a few hundred million to your annual grosses?" Baxter asked, finally.

"It wouldn't give me a heart attack," Ben replied.

"I can do that for you," Baxter replied. "My last two pictures have grossed better than half a billion dollars worldwide, and I have a release about every eighteen months to two years."

"That's very productive of you," Ben said, "especially considering the complexity of your productions."

"I have good people, and I demand the best work of all of them."

"I've heard you're demanding," Ben said.

Baxter smiled. "And you've no doubt heard that I have occasional turnovers among my crews."

"And that you have to pay a premium to attract people."

"I like to pay well," Baxter replied. "Why not spread the wealth?"

"A good policy," Ben said.

"My contract with Standard ends after my current production," Baxter said. "They want to make a new deal, but before I do that I thought I'd look around a bit."

"And where are you looking?" Ben asked.

"Centurion is the first studio I've spoken to."

Ben pressed the button again and two waiters appeared: one took away the soup dishes, and the other set a pasta dish before them.

"The service is very quick here," Baxter commented.

"Like you, we like to get the best from our people," Ben replied. "Why Centurion?"

"Because if I decided to come here I'd be the only producer on the lot making the kind of films I make—not to mention that I'd immediately be your studio's highest grosser. I'd bring A-list stars and directors, as well."

"And writers?" Ben asked. He thought he noticed a tiny wince from Baxter.

"My writers write to my orders," he said.

"And to your formula?"

"If you want to call it that. I try and make each picture as different as I can, within certain boundaries of plot and action."

"What would you require of your next studio?" Ben asked.

Baxter leaned forward. "Twenty thousand square feet of office space, designed by my architect and built to my specifications. How many sound stages do you have?"

He probably already knew, Ben thought, but he told him anyway. "We have six, and there are two under construction. We're expanding in a planned way."

"I'd want one of the old stages and one of the new," Baxter said.

"Entirely to yourself?" Ben asked.

"Entirely. Believe me, I'll keep them busy."

"I'm sure you would."

"If you're thinking that might be a strain on a studio of your size, you're right," Baxter said, "but I'm worth the trouble. You'd be building more stages before you know it, and the banks would look very favorably on you."

"We don't do a lot of borrowing from banks," Ben said. "What else do you want?"

"Final script, final cut, fifteen percent of the gross from the first dollar, and very large promotion budgets."

"High production costs, too, I expect," Ben said.

"If you want to make the big bucks, you have to invest big," Baxter replied smoothly.

"I wonder, with your costs and your cut, what might be left over for us?" Ben said. He pressed the button, and the waiters performed their ballet again, depositing a slice of apple pie à la mode before each of them.

"There'd be plenty to go around," Baxter said. "Don't worry about that."

Ben cut and ingested a chunk of pie, then chewed

thoughtfully before he replied. "It's my job to worry about everything," he said, "and I worry about whether you would be happy at Centurion."

Baxter spread his hands. "I'm in the happiness business," he said. "You let me take care of that."

"And I worry about how you might fit in at Centurion."

"Fit in? I don't fit in. I build my own world, and I make it work. All you have to bother with is the cash register."

"We encourage individuality here, but we also like a team effort," Ben said.

"I don't play on teams," Baxter said. "I'm the coach and general manager."

"My very point," Ben said. "Whatever would I do with *my* time?"

"I don't much care what you do with it," Baxter said, and he wasn't trying as hard to be charming.

"Mr. Baxter—"

"Dax."

"Dax, of course. I don't want to be disrespectful, so I'll pay you the compliment of candor. Your way of working, your films, and your attitude toward others are not appealing to me. I regard this business as collaborative, which sometimes helps it rise to the level of art, and there is no art in you or your methods. You lack social skills. The people who work for you all too often despise you, and if you worked on this lot our people would soon come to despise us for collaborating with you. Finally, so you will have the complete picture, I am reliably informed that you hired a professional killer to take the life of one of our most valued producers. That it didn't work is beside the point. The point is that, should you ever set foot on this lot again, I will have you prosecuted for trespassing."

Ben rose. "Now, Mr. Baxter, I bid you good day. The door leading to your car is right over there." He pointed, then he turned and walked out the door he had entered. He strolled over to Peter Barrington's table. "Peter," he said, "I thought you might like to know that I've just had a very brief lunch with Dax Baxter, who thought he'd like to move onto the Centurion lot and make himself at home."

The sound of a car door slamming very hard came into the room.

"Ah," Ben said, "there he goes now."

Ben managed a small smile.

26

DAX BAXTER SLAMMED his Porsche 969 into gear, pointed it at the Centurion main gate and floored it. The car's 600-horsepower engine had it through sixty mph in two and a half seconds, and the guard only barely got the barrier up in time.

His boss came out of the glass booth. "What the fuck was that?" he demanded.

"That was Dax Baxter," his friend said weakly.

His boss picked up the phone in his office and dialed 911.

"This is nine-one-one. What is your emergency?"

"This is the gate guard at Centurion Studios. A sports car has just left our lot at a high rate of speed and turned

left toward the Valley. The license plate number is DAX—
Delta Alpha X-ray. He's gotta be traveling at more than a
hundred miles an hour on city streets."

"We're on it," the operator said.

BAXTER WAS WEAVING in and out of three lanes of traffic,
narrowly missing other vehicles and pedestrians, one of
whom was a Beverly Hills nanny pushing a baby carriage.
He blew through a light just turning red and made a hard
left turn against the oncoming traffic. In his rearview mirror, at a distance, blue lights began to flash, and some tiny
part of his brain registered a whooping noise. He made a
hard right turn, went to the middle of the block, slammed
on his brakes and turned into a car wash, skirting a line of
waiting cars and coming to a stop just as the conveyor
belt began to move the vehicle into the sprayer.

He got out, walked into the cashier's office, and threw a
hundred-dollar bill onto the counter. "The works for the
Porsche, and keep the change," he said, taking his cell phone
from its holster on his belt. He pressed a speed dial button,
and a voice answered. "Send somebody to pick me up," he
said, and gave the address. "Then get a flatbed truck and a
car cover here, pick up my Porsche, take it to the studio, and
garage it." He hung up and turned to the cashier. "I've got
a problem with my Porsche," he said, "and the dealer is
sending a flatbed to pick it up. The keys are in it."

"Yessir," the young man said, pocketing the hundred
and ringing up sixty dollars.

Dax sat down in a waiting room chair and dialed 911.
"I'd like to report a stolen car," he said, speaking slowly and

coherently. When he had made the report he picked up a magazine and pretended to read it. He was seething inside, and it wasn't going away soon. Fifteen minutes later his Bentley Mulsanne with his driver at the wheel pulled up outside. He watched the car wash crew push the Porsche around a corner, then went and sat in the Bentley until a flatbed truck pulled in and began to load it. When the cover was on the car and the truck had left, he spoke to his driver, giving him an address in the Hollywood Hills. "Take me there and obey the speed limits all the way."

He pressed the button that raised the soundproof glass panel between the front and rear seats, then took another cell phone from the armrest compartment and made a call.

A man with a thick Russian accent answered.

"Do you know who this is?" Dax asked.

"Yessir, I do," the man replied.

"I'll be at the last place where we met in half an hour. You be there, too." He hung up without waiting for a reply.

The cell phone in his pocket rang. "Hello?"

"Is that Mr. Dax Baxter?" a male voice asked.

"It is. Who's this, and how did you get this number?"

"This is Sergeant Rivera, with the car theft squad at the Beverly Hills Police Department. We've got everybody's number."

"How can I help you?"

"Did you report a stolen car a few minutes ago?"

"I did."

"A Porsche 969?"

"Yes."

"What is a 969? Is that like a 911?"

"Faster and much, much more expensive."

"Did you see the car taken?"

"I did. I had lunch at Centurion Studios, and as I came out of the commissary I saw the car drive away very fast. I didn't get a look at the driver. I could hear the car turn onto the city streets—it has a very distinctive sound—and then I called nine-one-one and reported it stolen."

"What is the value of the car?"

"Eight hundred thousand dollars, give or take."

"Did you say, *eight hundred thousand dollars*?"

"I did. I told you it was very, very expensive."

"What color is it?"

"Silver."

"Any other distinguishing signs?"

"Google it, you'll see a very good photograph." Baxter hung up.

TWENTY-FIVE MINUTES LATER the Mulsanne turned into a driveway in the Hollywood Hills. The driver opened the garage door remotely and pulled inside, then closed the door. Dax pressed the button to retract the glass panel, then got out. "Wait here," he said to the driver, "and open the other garage door. Another car will come in."

Dax went inside the house. It was still furnished as he had left it seven years before, and it had been regularly cleaned and restocked. He used it for meetings where he didn't want to be seen. He went to the bar, got some ice from the machine, and poured himself a stiff Macallan 18, a single-malt scotch whiskey, then went and took a chair before the fireplace. His hands were trembling, and he took a big swig of the whiskey.

Shortly, he heard a door open and an irregular foot-step. He turned to see the Russian swing into the room on crutches.

"You want a drink?" Dax asked.

"I already had drink," the man replied, lowering himself into the facing chair.

"So, when are you going to be walking without crutches?"

"Some few days, doctor says."

"I want you to finish the job you started in Santa Fe."

The man shook his head vehemently. "I will be off crutches, but it will be long time before I can deal with him."

"I figured that, so I want you to hire some help, whatever you need."

"What kind of help?"

"That sex maniac friend of yours—the one my lawyer got off the charges?"

"Bear."

"That's right, Igor. I want you to take the woman and give her to Bear. I want you to take the man, too, and make him watch."

"What you want Bear to do?"

"Whatever takes his fancy," Dax said. "And I want it to hurt. When he's done, kill them both."

"How fast you want this?"

"Take enough time to do it carefully. Follow them, establish their routine, then when you're ready, call me, and I'll give you the go-ahead. Then take them somewhere. Here would do, in the garage. Clean up after yourself."

"I got it," the Russian said.

27

SERGEANT CARLOS RIVERA entered the partitioned-off area of the squad room that contained the desks of the five officers of the car theft unit, hung up his suit jacket, and eased into his office chair, being careful of his back.

"Where you been?" Rossi, the old guy in the group (he was fifty-one) asked.

"Hollywood."

"We don't work Hollywood," Rossi said.

"Not the neighborhood, the world of Hollywood."

"Where?"

"Standard Studios, out in the Valley."

"Did Hollywood report a car stolen?"

"You might say that. A character named Dax Baxter did—a Porsche 969, yet."

"Is that like a Porsche 911?"

"It's set apart from the 911 by a figure of about six hundred and fifty thousand dollars."

Rossi ran the numbers in his head, his lips moving. "Are we talking about an eight-hundred-thousand-dollar car? There is no such thing."

"There is such a thing," Rivera said. "Google it."

Rossi did so on his desktop. "Holy shit," he muttered. "What makes it cost eight hundred grand?"

"I don't know, exactly, probably the fact that there are people out there who will buy it, just because it costs eight hundred grand."

"I mean, it only has four wheels and two doors," Rossi pointed out.

"Are we going to argue about this? That's what they get for the thing—it's not my fault."

"Who paid that much?"

"I told you, a guy named Dax Baxter."

"The movie producer? *Dead Man's Tale* and the whole *Dead Man* series? I seen them all."

"Then you helped pay for an eight-hundred-grand car," Rivera said.

"Now it's my fault?"

"You and all the schmucks who bought tickets to that trash."

"So this eight-hundred-grand Porsche is in a chop shop somewhere? Or on a ship to Hong Kong?"

"No, it was returned to its owner."

"*Returned*? I been working car theft for eight years, and I never heard of one being returned."

"It was returned. I saw it in the parking lot outside Baxter's office." He produced his iPhone, pressed some buttons, and handed it to Rossi. "I took pictures."

Rossi regarded the car with reverence. "So that's what eight hundred grand looks like?"

"That's it. The thief washed and waxed it, too. It was clean as a hound's tooth."

Rossi laughed. "Now I've heard it all. A car is stolen, and the thief returns it cleaner than it was?"

"It wasn't stolen," Rivera said.

"Run me through that."

"It went like this, as best as I can figure it out. Baxter drives the car out of Centurion Studios, where he had just had lunch, and he's running with the pedal to the metal. The gate guard at Centurion calls nine-one-one and reports a dangerous driver with a tag that reads 'DAX.' Baxter drives around town at a hundred miles an hour for a few minutes, then, when he realizes patrol cars are going to be looking for the car, he turns into a car wash, leaves it there, and takes a cab back to his office, while somebody collects the car for him. By the time I get to the studio, the car is in the parking lot."

"Did Baxter admit to any of that?"

"Of course not. He said he left the keys in the car and didn't see the thief."

"I believe that's what they used to call at the Academy an 'improbable explanation.' "

"Fucking outrageous," Rivera said, "and I had to drive out to the Valley to listen to it. Pisses me off."

"Well, what are ya going to do?" Rossi sighed.

"Something," Rivera said. "I don't know what, yet."

"I'll tell you what you should do," Rossi said. "You should take a look at the newly reported thefts, pick one, and run it down. Then do another one."

"That's your prescription, is it?"

"What are you going to do, break his taillight, then arrest him and beat him up? If that guy can pay eight hundred grand for a fucking car, he could spare a little more to hire a lawyer and make your life hell. People like that guy know people—you know?"

"What you say makes perfect sense, Joe," Rivera said, "but life doesn't always make sense. I mean, an Alka-Seltzer ain't going to make the feeling in my gut go away. This guy does this outrageous thing, then lies about it and wastes my time while he's lying. Just because he thinks he can get away with it."

"He *can* get away with it, Carlos," Rossi replied, "and he will, and you'll be left holding a bag with your stripes in it, if not your badge and gun. Forget about it and go find cars stolen in Beverly Hills. That's what you get paid for."

"Yeah, I know," Rivera said. But he knew he was going to do something about it; he just wasn't sure what.

28

TEDDY AND SALLY drove to work together on her first day, and as soon as they left the house something yellow appeared in his rearview mirror and stayed there. Not too close, but always within sight. It appeared to be an older model muscle car, but he never got a good enough look to nail the type.

The yellow disappeared as Teddy turned into the main gate at Centurion and got a salute from the captain in charge. He paused to say good morning to the man.

"How you doing, Billy?" the captain asked.

"Not bad, Jerry."

"You hear about our bit of bother on Friday?"

"Nope."

"Somebody in a souped-up Porsche was drag racing with himself on the lot, and nearly blew my gate away. I called the cops, but I hear the guy got away with it."

"They didn't catch him?"

"They caught the car, but the guy had reported it stolen. It had a license plate that said DAX. That ring a bell?"

"Dax Baxter?"

"That's what I hear. I know a cop named Rivera who runs the stolen vehicle unit at the Beverly Hills PD."

"That's very interesting, Jerry," Teddy said. "Gotta go to work." Teddy drove to the Barrington bungalow, parked his car, and escorted Sally into the building. "Right that way, sweetheart," he said, giving her a little push on the tush. "Knock 'em dead."

Sally pushed her way through the glass doors and disappeared into executive-office land.

CARLOS RIVERA SPOKE to his buddy Jerry at the gate, was given a pass, and found his way to the executive office building, where the studio's top brass worked.

Ben Bacchetti didn't keep him waiting long. He shook his guest's hand and motioned him to a chair across his desk. "What can I do for the Beverly Hills Police Department this morning, Sergeant?"

"I appreciate your taking the time to see me, Mr. Bacchetti. I just have a few questions. I understand that you had lunch on your lot last Friday with a Mr. Dax Baxter."

"That is correct," Ben replied. "It was a pretty brief

lunch. Turned out that Mr. Baxter and I really didn't have anything to say to each other."

"Do you remember what sort of mood Mr. Baxter was in when he left your lunch?"

"Actually, it was I who left the lunch, but I guess I would say that Baxter was in a foul mood."

"What did he say to indicate that?"

"He didn't say anything. I showed him where to exit, then I left the room. A minute later I heard a car door outside slam shut, just about as hard as anybody could slam a car door, then there was a roaring noise and some rubber burned."

"Did you actually see the car depart?"

"No, I just heard it. I expect just about everybody on the lot heard it."

"But you think it was Baxter?"

"I can't think of anybody who works here who would leave the lot in that manner."

"How well do you know Mr. Baxter, Mr. Bacchetti?"

"I had never met him before Friday, but his reputation preceded him."

"And what is his reputation?"

"You want rumors? I learned by watching *Dragnet* reruns as a kid that the cops want only the facts."

"Let's call it background information."

"All right. I hear the guy is a gold-plated asshole who doesn't give a damn for anybody but himself, and I'm told he has a stable of ex-wives who can confirm that."

"Do you know the names of any of his ex-wives?"

"Nobody on our lot. Google him."

Rivera stood up. "Thank you, Mr. Bacchetti," he said. "I'm grateful for your time."

Ben stood up and shook his hand. "Always glad to help. Tell me, did Baxter hurt anybody?"

"By some miracle, nobody. He reported his car stolen, weaseling out of any action we could take, in the absence of witnesses who could place him in the car."

Ben began walking his guest to the door. "There is something else," he said, "and I have this from a good source. One of our employees took some time off and went to Santa Fe, where he worked briefly on a Baxter film on location there. Baxter, who's apparently pretty paranoid, somehow got the impression that our man was there to do him harm, and he called in a professional from L.A. to rid him of the menace."

"Do you mean to eliminate him?"

"I don't know what his intentions were, but the pro attacked our man, who defended himself and put the man in the hospital."

"So there's some unresolved animus there?"

"I don't know. I just mention it as background, as you put it."

"May I have your employee's name?"

"Billy Barnett. He works as a producer in the Barrington unit on our lot. Would you like to speak to him?"

"Thank you, sir, yes."

Ben opened his office door and spoke to his secretary. "Marsha, would you call Billy and see if he has time to speak to Sergeant Rivera, here? He'll need directions to the bungalow."

*   *   *

RIVERA PARKED HIS CAR and walked into a bungalow with the name "Barrington" on a placard outside. A moment later he found himself sitting across the desk of a man, apparently in his fifties, but fit-looking.

"Ben Bacchetti's secretary called," Barnett said. "What can I do for you?"

"I spoke with Mr. Bacchetti for a few minutes about events following his lunch with a Mr. Dax Baxter last Friday."

"Yes, the gate guard captain told me about that. Apparently Mr. Baxter departed the lot in something of a hurry."

"That is my information," Rivera said. "Mr. Bacchetti also told me about an encounter you had with an associate of Mr. Baxter's in Santa Fe that resulted in the man's being hospitalized."

"Mr. Bacchetti told you that?"

"Yes."

"I believe I have some recollection of such an event. Is the fellow bringing charges against me?"

"Oh, no, sir, nothing like that. I asked Mr. Bacchetti for background information on Mr. Baxter, and he told me that story."

"Ah."

"During your time in Santa Fe, did you spend any time with Mr. Baxter?"

"Very little," Teddy replied. "Mr. Baxter's wife caused the death of my wife, Betsy, in an accident. He seemed to believe that I bore a grudge because of that and had come there to harm him in some way."

"And how did he get that impression?"

"His paranoia whispered it in his ear, I expect. I had no such intention and told him so."

"But he didn't believe you?"

"Apparently not. I was at Mr. Baxter's house at a wrap party, and the man approached me outside, holding a knife. He introduced himself by trying to kick me in the head."

"And what was the nature of the injury that put him in the hospital?"

"A knife wound to the back of a leg, his right, I believe, that required surgery to repair."

"Was it your intention to wound him in such a manner?"

"If I'd been trying to kill him, he would be dead," Teddy replied calmly. "Now, if you don't have any more questions, Sergeant, I don't think I should incriminate myself further." He smiled a little.

Rivera got to his feet and handed the man his business card. "Sounds like self-defense to me, Mr. Barnett. If you should come across any other relevant information about Mr. Baxter, I'd appreciate a call, and don't worry about incriminating yourself."

THEY SHOOK HANDS, and the policeman left. Teddy looked at the card and saw that the sergeant's assignment was to the vehicle theft unit, which puzzled him.

29

I T WAS NEARLY six o'clock when Sally came into Teddy's office. "I'm done for the day," she said.

"How did it go?"

"Very well, I think. Peter seemed pleased. I'm a quick study."

Teddy closed a couple of computer files and got his jacket on. "Then let's get out of here," he said. They went out to the parking lot and got into the Cayenne. At the front gate Teddy got out of the car and went to the glass booth where the captain sat.

"How are you, Billy?"

"Very well, thanks, Jerry."

"Your first day back go well?"

"Very well. There's something I'd like your help on though."

"Anything I can do," Jerry replied.

"This morning, driving in from Malibu, I saw a bright yellow vehicle in my rearview mirror, very well back, but persistent. It disappeared about the time I got here."

"I didn't see such a vehicle," Jerry replied.

"I think it was some sort of eighties muscle car, but I didn't get a good enough look at it to figure out which one. I'm going to leave the lot now, and I'd appreciate it if you'd observe from here and see if you see such a vehicle following me."

"Be glad to."

"I'd like to know the type of car and the plate number, if you see it."

Jerry picked up his binoculars. "I'm on it."

"You've got my cell number," Teddy said. "Call me if you see the car." He went back to the car and drove off the lot, keeping an eye on his rearview mirror. He saw nothing yellow there, just the usual mishmash of car colors. A few blocks away, his cell rang. "Yes?"

"It's Jerry. I kept an eagle eye on you until you were out of sight, but I didn't see anything yellow following you."

"Thank you, Jerry, I appreciate your help." He hung up.

Sally, who had heard the conversation on the car's speaker, said, "What's up?"

"I thought I saw a bright yellow car following us from Malibu this morning, and I asked Jerry to watch for it. He saw nothing."

"Well, that's a relief," Sally said.

"How about dinner in Malibu Village?"

"You're on," she replied.

CARLOS RIVERA, back at his desk, thought about what he'd heard at Centurion Studios, and he had a feeling he was getting involved in something beyond stolen cars. As he thought about that, Lieutenant Bart Goodwin, who headed up the violent crimes unit, passed his office door walking in the direction of the office of Captain Tom Fitzhugh, who commanded the station. He got up and followed.

Bart Goodwin was standing in the captain's office doorway, chatting with his boss, as Rivera approached.

"Afternoon, Carlos," the lieutenant said.

"Lieutenant, Captain," Rivera replied. "I wonder if I could speak with you both for a moment?"

"Come in, Carlos," the captain said, "and take a seat."

Rivera did so, and so did Goodwin. "On Friday we had a report of a very expensive sports car, a Porsche 969, being stolen."

"Is that anything like a 911?" the captain asked.

"Yes, sir, but it's a lot more expensive—eight hundred grand."

The captain made a small noise. "Did you recover the car?"

"It was returned to its owner—or so he says."

"I'm not following," the captain replied.

"The car belongs to a big-time movie producer named Dax Baxter. Its plate number is DAX. I interviewed Mr. Baxter and he gave me an implausible explanation of the return of the car." Rivera ran through Baxter's story.

"Well," the captain said, "that's a weird one, but what is your concern now?"

Rivera told him of his interview with Ben Bacchetti at Centurion.

"Baxter hired a hit man to kill somebody he thought might be trying to kill him?"

"That seems to be it."

"But this Barnett fellow took out the hired killer?"

"Put him in the hospital."

"This sounds like something out of one of Baxter's movies."

"Yes, sir, it does, but it's not Baxter's story. It was confirmed by Barnett, himself."

"I believe I'm getting the picture," Bart Goodwin said.

"Oh, good," the captain replied, "maybe you can explain it to me."

"I think Carlos believes that Baxter may not be done with Mr. Barnett, and he wants the case."

"What case?" the captain asked. "There isn't any case. Maybe Santa Fe has one, but we don't."

"But Baxter is back in L.A., Captain," Rivera said, "and if he continues with this, it will certainly be our problem. I'd rather deal with it before it's a homicide, instead of afterward."

"Carlos has a point, Captain," Goodwin said. "While, strictly speaking, my unit isn't in the homicide prevention business, we would be obliged to act if we heard someone was planning a murder. But right now, we're pursuing four active homicide cases, and we're stretched pretty thin. If you want to assign Carlos to this, I have no objection."

The captain regarded Rivera with interest. "Your unit, Carlos, or just you?"

"Me and a partner," Rivera said. "We don't usually work in teams in vehicle theft, but I'd like Joe Rossi on this."

"How big a case backlog do you have right now, Carlos?" the captain asked.

"We're all caught up, Captain. It seems that more Angelenos are buying their cars at the moment, instead of stealing them."

"All right, Carlos, take a few days, say a week, and check out Mr. Baxter's homicidal tendencies, but I don't want to see anything in the media about this. If it looks like it's going that way, you come back to me and I'll assign somebody in Media Relations to work with you. I don't like celebrity arrests unless we know we can make 'em stick."

"I understand, Captain," Carlos said. "We'll work quietly, don't worry."

"You've got a week," the captain said. "Get out of here."

"Thank you, sir, thank you, Lieutenant."

Carlos went back to his desk and found Joe Rossi playing a computer game on his iPhone. "Joe, I see you're underworked," he said.

"Aw come on, Carlos, it's not my fault people are returning stolen cars, instead of chopping them."

"Joe, did you ever work Homicide?"

"In my youth," Rossi replied. "I had a tour on the squad, but it was thought by my betters that I wasn't gifted in that area."

"How would you like to work on a homicide that hasn't happened yet?" Carlos asked.

30

THE RUSSIAN WAS sitting in his trailer at the park overlooking the Pacific Coast Highway, when there was a heavy knock on his door. He opened his desk drawer and put his hand on the snub-nosed .38 there. "Yeah?" he called.

"It's the Bear," a voice said.

"It's unlocked."

A large man in a short-sleeved shirt with a thick, short beard entered the trailer. "Okay," he said, "I followed them from the movie studio back to Malibu, where they're eating dinner right now at a Mexican joint in the Village."

The Russian gazed at Bear's thickly forested arms. "Bear," he said, "you ought not to wear short-sleeved shirts."

"It's hot," Bear said petulantly. "What do you want, that I should get a wax job?"

He didn't want to think about that. "What are you doing back here?"

"You want I should sit in the parking lot for a couple hours, doing nothing?"

"That was the idea."

"They're going to eat then go back to their house. I'm not stupid."

The Russian started to speak but thought better of it.

"I like the girl," Bear said. "I'd like to do stuff to her."

"All in good time, Bear. I'll let you know when the boss says it's okay."

"I'd like to make a movie with her, so I could look at it later," Bear said. Bear had the reputation in the world of porno for the biggest equipment in California, maybe the country. His sobriquet, for billing purposes, was "The Log."

"That's not going to happen," the Russian said, "but you might get to snuff her."

"That would be nice," Bear said.

"It's not like she could go free once she's seen your schlong. She could identify you in a lineup, no problem."

"A girl tried that one time. She didn't show up for trial."

"Yeah, that's the one that Dax's lawyer got you out of, right?"

"Right. I didn't think he had the guts to off her, but

like I said, she didn't show up for trial, and since I was in lockup at the time, I walked."

"You're a lucky guy," the Russian said. "What were you driving today?"

"The Malibu, the brown one."

"Drive something else tomorrow."

"Okay. Can I drive your GTO?"

"No, not that. Take the Crown Vic."

"Okay."

"Now, go back to the restaurant, wait for them, then follow them home, and note the times."

"Okay."

"And Bear?"

"Yeah?"

"Don't touch the girl until I tell you to."

"Oh, all right."

CARLOS RIVERA AND JOE ROSSI were having a drink at Cuffs, a cop bar, while Carlos told his partner everything he knew about what they were working on.

When Carlos had finished, Joe was quiet for a bit.

"So," Carlos asked, "what do you think?"

"What do I think about what?"

"How should we proceed, Joe? I'm counting on your experience and your brains." Joe, he knew, was very smart. Not many of the guys at the station knew that.

"I don't know," Joe said. "What do you think we should do?"

"I don't know."

"I was afraid of that."

"Yeah, well. I was intrigued with what's going on here. Problem is . . ."

"Nothing's going on," Joe said. "How do we stop something that hasn't happened yet, that we have no evidence is going to happen?"

"We've got Dax's previous behavior," Carlos said.

"I don't know," Joe replied. "If I were Dax Baxter, and I sent a pro out to do a guy and my pro came back crippled, I'd think again about proceeding, wouldn't you?"

"Yeah, that's what you and I might do, but not Dax Baxter. This is a guy who hasn't heard the word 'no,' from anybody, for a long time. Who's going to have the balls to give him advice? I mean, if he offed the head of the studio, they'd check his grosses before telling him he was a bad boy. Money is all those people care about."

"Yeah," Joe said. "Money is the only thing that's more powerful than love."

"You're a cynic, Joe."

"You said it yourself—I'm experienced."

Carlos looked up and saw a beautiful Latina enter the bar. He was transfixed, as he had been the first time he'd seen her.

"I think your mind just left the problem," Joe said, glancing at the girl.

"Nope," Carlos said, "she could be part of the solution."

"You lost me, amigo."

"She works in Dax Baxter's office. I saw her when I was there a couple of days ago."

She was joined by another, older woman Carlos had seen there, too. "The other one works there, too."

"I guess you're smarter than I thought," Joe said. "How'd you know they were going to turn up here?"

"I'd like to take the credit, but this one is just dumb luck."

"A coincidence?"

"If you like."

"I hate coincidence," Joe said.

Carlos got up and approached the two women, who had taken a booth near the bar. "Good evening, ladies," he said. "I believe I almost made your acquaintance at Standard Studios recently."

They looked up at him. "I remember you," said the younger one. "You're a cop."

Carlos laughed. "And I was trying so hard not to look like one."

"You need to work on your impression of a civilian," she said.

"Would you two ladies like to join a couple of Beverly Hills's finest for a drink?"

"Beverly Hills cops? Wasn't that a movie?"

"It would make a great one," Carlos replied.

"We've got the booth," she said. "Why don't you two join us?"

Carlos looked over at Joe and jerked his head a little.

Joe pointed his thumb at himself and mouthed, "Who, me?"

Carlos slid into the seat next to the younger one as Joe made his way across the room.

31

TEDDY AND SALLY left the restaurant and got into the Cayenne. As Teddy backed out of the parking place he saw taillights come on behind him as another car backed out.

"Billy?" Sally said.

Teddy was concentrating on getting a fix on the make and model as it passed under a streetlamp.

"Billy!"

"Oh, sorry."

"Are you getting paranoid on me?"

"No."

"Then what is it with pursuing vehicles?"

"If a vehicle is pursuing me, then I'm not paranoid."

"Is it the yellow car?"

"No, and it isn't the brown Malibu, either. It's a Crown Vic."

"I thought Crown Vics were the exclusive province of cops and taxi drivers."

"Used to be. You don't see that many of them anymore."

"Does that mean something?"

"Just that it's the sort of car a person might pick so as not to be noticed by anybody."

"But you noticed it."

"I'm not just anybody. I have a keen eye and a very good bullshit detector, and a Crown Vic in Malibu is very much bullshit."

Teddy made a left turn into the parking lot across the street, then left again past the supermarket and another left back into the street.

"Is he still there?" Sally asked.

"Gimme a minute," Teddy replied. "There he is."

"You mean he followed you around the parking lot?"

"That's what I mean. He fell for it." Teddy looked ahead at the traffic light on the Pacific Coast Highway: it turned yellow. He floored the car and made a left turn under the light just as it turned red. "Now," he said, "let's see if he runs the light."

Sally looked over her shoulder.

"Don't do that—he can see you doing that."

"He stopped at the light," Sally said.

Teddy summoned the 520 horsepower at his disposal and was half a mile ahead by the time the light changed. He turned off the headlights.

"Billy, I can't see anything," Sally said, alarmed. "What are you doing?"

"I'm denying him a set of taillights to follow," Teddy said. "Don't worry, I can see. Enough, anyway." As he approached his house he shifted down twice, to avoid using the brakes, then as he made the sharp turn off the highway he began pressing the remote button on his rearview mirror. His garage door opened; Teddy pulled in and pressed the button again to close the door quickly. He made a mental note to himself to remove the light-bulb in the garage.

THE BEAR SWORE. "Where the fuck did he go?" he asked himself aloud. He stopped and checked the glove compartment for his notebook, then looked up the address and compared it to the house number where he sat. He made a U-turn and drove back until he found the address. No lights in the house. "Shit!"

He noted the time; he'd just tell the Russian that he followed them home.

"WHY WON'T YOU let me turn any lights on?" Sally asked.

"For the same reason I turned off my headlights," Teddy replied. "I can see well enough to get you a nightcap, though." He made his way to the bar and poured them both a brandy. "Why don't we take this into the bedroom?" he asked.

She laughed. "I guess we can feel our way."

"I would enjoy that."

*   *   *

BEAR DROVE BACK to the trailer park and banged on the Russian's door.

"Come in, Bear!"

Bear went in and tossed the man the keys to the Crown Vic. "They're down for the night," he said, "at ten-forty PM."

"Good."

"Why is it important?" Bear asked.

"We're establishing their pattern," the Russian answered. "What time they leave and come home every day. That way we'll know where they are when we want to take them."

"Oh, yeah, that makes sense. Okay if I go home now?"

"Yeah, pick up the Malibu and be within sight of their house at seven-thirty tomorrow morning."

Bear sighed. "Okay, if that's what you need."

"It's what Dax needs," the Russian said.

"BILLY," SALLY SAID in the dark as they lay, naked, on the bed, "how long is this going to go on?"

"As long as they want it to," Teddy said.

"Is 'they' Dax?"

"I expect so. Do you think you can stand it?"

"How long?"

"Until they make their move."

"What move?"

"They're following us for a reason. Sooner or later we'll find out why, and then I'll deal with it."

"Deal with it the way you dealt with the guy in Santa Fe?"

"Whatever is necessary," Teddy said.

THE FOLLOWING MORNING after breakfast, Teddy handed Sally his car keys.

"You want me to drive?"

"Yes, and don't be in a hurry. I'll follow a little later in the Mercedes convertible."

Sally rolled her eyes but headed for the garage. Teddy went and stood at the front door, looking out at the highway through the small window. He saw Sally back out of the garage and pull into traffic. Less than half a minute later, a brown Chevy Malibu passed. "Aha!" Teddy said, then headed for the garage.

A minute later he was headed down the highway, passing cars whenever he could, until he was behind the brown Malibu. The figure at the wheel, he noted, was very large and had thick, curly black hair. Sally stopped at the traffic light at Sunset, and the Malibu pulled up three cars behind her in the left-turn lane.

Teddy stayed right on him, then pulled up and stopped about two inches from the Malibu's passenger door. The driver turned and stared at him, and Teddy took an iPhone picture of the man, then he aimed an imaginary pistol at him and pulled the trigger, grinning at the big man.

The light changed, and Teddy turned left behind him onto Sunset and glued himself to the Malibu's bumper. He stayed there, crowding him, and he could see the man angrily looking in his rearview mirror. Traffic stopped at the Stone Canyon intersection. The man took another look at him in the mirror, then made a jerky right turn and ran the red light, toward UCLA.

Teddy waved bye-bye. "I expect I'll see you again," he said.

32

BEAR PULLED UP at the Russian's trailer, got out, and hammered on the door.

"What?" the Russian yelled.

"It's Bear."

"Come in!"

Bear walked in in time to see the Russian put away the snub-nosed .38 that he kept in his desk drawer.

"What the fuck you doing here?"

"They made me."

"What do you mean, 'they made you'?"

"They took two cars to work. I followed the first one,

and the second one followed me. The guy pulled up next to me and took my picture. I lost him on Sunset."

"He took your fucking picture?"

"Yeah, with his cell phone. I was in traffic—what did you want me to do, shoot him?"

"I rather you had shot yourself," the Russian said disgustedly. He picked up the phone and dialed a number.

DAX ANSWERED. "YEAH?"

"You know who this is?"

"Yeah."

"Bad news. Bear followed them, as usual, but the guy took a second car, pulled up next to him at a light, and took his picture."

"Took his picture?" Dax bellowed.

"With a cell phone. What are your instructions?"

"First, shoot Bear, then shoot yourself."

"We need Bear for later, and the guy did not take my picture."

"Well, he already knows what you look like from Santa Fe, doesn't he?"

"I was in a disguise," the Russian said. "He don't know me."

"Okay, then you don't have to shoot yourself. Put somebody else on following them."

"I am running out of cars," the Russian said. "What you want them followed for? They shouldn't see us again until we take them. Then it don't matter if they know Bear. We know where to find them when we want them."

"You have a point," Dax admitted.

"When you want to take them?"

"Soon. I'll call you." He hung up.

BAXTER'S INTERCOM BUZZED. "It's Chita. Carlos Rivera from before is here. You want to see him?"

"Not really, but I'm not going to duck him. Send him in."

RIVERA STOOD AND watched Chita look at him while she talked to Baxter. She was really something, this one.

She hung up. "Okay, he'll see you." She gave him a nice smile.

"Did you know that if you married me, you'd have the same name as that great dancer? Chita Rivera?"

She smiled again. "I saw her once. Go in, hurry."

Rivera heard the lock on the office door click, and he went in.

"Detective Rivera," Baxter said, rising and shaking his hand. "What can I do for you?"

Rivera sat down. "Mr. Baxter, I want you to know you have nothing to worry about."

"Sergeant, I have ten thousand things to worry about, and that's just today. Which one are you referring to?"

"In my investigation I have learned that an employee of yours was attacked in Santa Fe and seriously injured."

Baxter's smile disappeared. "I don't know what you're talking about."

Rivera made a placating motion with his hand. "It's all right. For all practical purposes, I don't know about it either. It happened in another jurisdiction, so it didn't happen. We'll keep everything quiet and between us. I just want you to know that you're not in danger."

"In danger from what?"

"From the man who injured your employee. We have you under surveillance, so if this Barnett guy makes a move, we'll have an excuse to grab him."

"You have *me* under surveillance?"

"Don't worry, you'll never see us, but for the time being, we'll know where you are at every moment of the night and day."

"Now listen . . ."

Rivera stood up and made the placating motion again. "Don't worry, there will be no official record of this, it's just between you and me. Thank you for your time, Mr. Baxter." He turned and walked out of the room while Baxter was still sputtering.

Rivera stopped at Chita's desk and leaned over. "I think you and I should have dinner," he said. "Someplace nice."

"What a good idea," she said. "When?"

"Tonight?"

"I gave you my information last night," she said. "What time?"

"I'll pick you up at seven."

"See you then."

Rivera left the office and joined Joe Rossi in the car. "Mission accomplished," he said.

"Which one, Baxter or the girl?"

"Both," Rivera said. "Drive."

"Where?"

"What do I care? Let's get some lunch. You pick a place, I'll buy."

"Anyplace?"

"Within reason," Rivera said. "I'm taking Chita to dinner tonight, so don't go crazy."

"A burger is good for me," Rossi said, putting the car in gear. "Hey, is that the Porsche 969 over there?" He pointed at the executive parking lot as they passed.

"That's it," Rivera said. "I put a tracker on it earlier. The result of movement will be on my laptop or iPhone."

"Good idea. Why don't we go over there and put a dent in it."

"That's a great idea, Joe, but not yet. Right now we've got Baxter thinking he's under twenty-four-hour surveillance. That's good enough for now."

"Is that what you told him? All we've got is you and me, you know."

"I know that and you know that, but Baxter doesn't."

"I like your style, Carlos," Rossi said.

"Lucky for me, so does Chita, I think."

"Careful, Carlos, she looks like the marrying kind."

"I already suggested to her that she ought to do that."

"You're kidding!"

Rivera shrugged. "What the hell, my ex-wife's alimony payments ran out last month. I'm free as a bird, and my salary is all mine."

"That's a dangerous position to be in," Rossi said. "Don't make any mistakes."

"I don't plan to," Rivera said.

33

CHITA ROMERO SAT in the passenger seat of Carlos Rivera's car and sniffed. "It has that new-car smell," she said.

"It ought to," Carlos replied, "I bought it this afternoon, not long after I saw you at the studio."

"I like the leather," she said.

"So do I."

"What kind of car is it? I mean, it looks familiar, but I don't know it."

"It's North Korean," Carlos replied with a straight face.

"You mean you would buy a car from that fat . . . Wait a minute."

Carlos laughed. "The North Koreans don't manufacture cars," he said. "Just nuclear missiles. I was thinking of buying one of those, too."

She laughed. "You're funny, Carlos, I never know what you're going to say."

"Read my lips," he said, "and from up close."

"You're bad."

"Now you've nailed me."

THEY SETTLED INTO a corner table of the garden behind an Italian restaurant and ordered drinks.

"How come you're coming to see Dax Baxter so much?" Chita asked.

"Twice is much?"

"It's twice as many as most people do. He's not the most popular guy in town."

"That's putting it mildly," Carlos replied, sipping his margarita. "You wouldn't believe some of the things I've found out about him since I've been working this case, and I've only been on it for three days."

"What case?"

"His stolen car. We sit up and take notice when there's an eight-hundred-thousand-dollar theft in our jurisdiction."

"Listen," she said, looking around, "there's something you should know."

"All ears."

"His car wasn't stolen."

Carlos widened his eyes to the max. "No!"

She laughed. "I take it you knew that."

"I figured it out about ten seconds after I started talking to him the first time. I considered arresting him for making a false report, but he began to interest me."

"Why?" she asked.

"Well, who would be stupid enough to pull that kind of stunt?"

"Dax would, if he thinks he can get away with it."

"Do you know what kind of guy you're working for?"

"Do you know what kind of money I make?"

Carlos laughed. "Probably more than a detective sergeant on the BHPD."

"Probably," she said.

"How long have you worked for him?"

"A little over two years. I was working for another exec who got canned, and Personnel sent me to see him. He liked what he saw."

"Oho, I'll bet he did!"

"Don't worry, looking is as far as he got. But he likes having a Latina on display outside his office. It makes him look like an equal opportunity employer."

"Is he?"

"Sort of, but that's because he can pay Latinos and blacks less than whites."

"You make him sound like such a sweet guy."

"He's the most volatile human being I've ever known," she said. "Anything can set him off."

They ordered dinner. "Do you know much about him?" Carlos asked.

"I know just about *everything* about him," she replied smugly.

"So you know about the Russian?"

"Where did you hear about the Russian?" she asked.

"It's my job to hear about things."

"Are you going to arrest him for that?"

"For what?"

"You know."

"Maybe. You tell me yours, and I'll tell you mine."

She shook her head. "You, first."

"The Russian is a killer for hire."

She looked uncomfortable. "I don't know about that."

"You told me you know everything about him."

"I know the Russian works for him sometimes, but I don't know what he does."

"Now you do."

"Then why haven't you arrested Dax and the Russian?"

Carlos shook his head. "It didn't happen in my jurisdiction. That's Santa Fe's problem. Also, I couldn't prove it all if I tried."

"Have you tried?"

He shrugged. "Maybe I took a stab at it."

"And you couldn't find anything?"

"Maybe I haven't finished."

He was getting close to the point where he would have to decide whether to trust her. He decided not to. "Right now, I've got him under surveillance twenty-four hours a day—for his own protection, of course."

"He's in danger?"

"The guy he tried to have killed by the Russian may try to get even."

She thought about that, then shook her head. "I know Billy Barnett a little," she said. "He offered me a job in his office when my boss got fired, so I had an interview. I liked him a lot, and it's a really interesting production company, but then Dax offered me half again as much money. I've got a little girl in Catholic school, and the money makes that possible."

"You were married?"

"I still am," she said.

Carlos looked around the restaurant. "I hope he's not the jealous type."

She laughed. "He is, but he's afraid of cops. Also, my lawyer tells me we'll be divorced in a couple of weeks. We've been trying to get him to pay for the school, and he's agreed to pay half. That's good enough for me."

"How old is your daughter?"

"Six. She's in the first grade."

"I'll bet she's gorgeous," he said. "Like her mother."

"People say she's the spitting image," Chita said. "You like kids?"

"Yes, I do, but I didn't want any with my ex-wife, so I took precautions."

Chita frowned. "What kind of precautions?"

"I stopped screwing her after the first year, told her the Viagra didn't work."

"You took Viagra?"

"Nope."

She laughed aloud. "And what was her reaction to that?"

"She took a lover, thereby relieving me of the duty of servicing her needs. Now, fortunately, she's married to the guy."

"That's convenient."

"It saves on alimony payments," he said. "I celebrated by buying the new car."

Dinner came and they dined. Afterward, when they were on dessert wine, he popped the question.

"So," he said, "tell me everything you know about Dax Baxter."

34

TEDDY AND SALLY departed Centurion Studios at the end of the day. He checked his rearview mirror.

"Anybody following us?" she asked.

"Not that I can see, not so far. It takes a while to spot a tail, unless it's something really noticeable, like the yellow car, the first time."

"Billy, are we in danger?"

"I think we scared them off, but I think it's best to behave as if we're being followed."

"How do I do that?" she asked.

"Leave it to me, and don't worry about it."

"Should I go back to Santa Fe?"

"No. If somebody means us ill, you'll be safer with me than back in Santa Fe."

"We could both go back there and live in my house."

"I have a job here—no, a career. Come to think of it, so do you."

"I've only been at it for a few days."

"I know, but you like it, and everybody at the shop likes you, too. Also, you're making better money than you could make in Santa Fe."

"I can't argue with that."

"And I'm making a *lot* more money than I could make in Santa Fe."

"Should I carry a gun?" she asked.

"Do you know how to use one?"

"Yes, my daddy taught me to shoot when I was a kid."

"Do you have a license to carry in Los Angeles County?"

"No."

"Then you'd be at risk for being arrested here, and I don't think you'd enjoy the accommodations."

"It might be worth the risk, if I could defend myself."

Teddy turned onto the Pacific Coast Highway. "Let me explain something to you," he said.

"Go ahead, the more I know the better."

"Maybe not, but I want you to know this much. If you should ever shoot someone, for any reason, your life will get worse in a hurry, and it will never be the same again. It doesn't matter if it's self-defense."

"Why not? Self-defense is legal, isn't it?"

"Yes, but you'd have to prove that you fired in fear of losing your life. You'd need an expensive lawyer to help you do that, and you'd need witnesses. Of course, if you were lucky and killed the son of a bitch, the most important witness against you would be dead, but then you might face a murder charge, and there's all sorts of other kinds of evidence—ballistic, blood spatter, powder traces."

"And if all of that supported my story, would I be all right?"

"Maybe, but things would never be the same. You'd be all over the newspapers, attracting the attention of people you don't want to know—paparazzi, TV reality shows, and worst of all, crazy people who'd turn up at your door wanting either to shoot you or you to shoot them."

"Why would they want me to shoot them?"

"Because they're crazy. And even if you satisfied the DA that you fired in self-defense, he's still going to charge you with illegally carrying a gun, and you would have no defense against that."

"Billy, are you carrying a gun?"

"As I recall, you frisked me this morning."

"That was in bed. You could still be armed."

"I'm not carrying a gun."

"Do you intend to?"

"Only if I feel that it's necessary. But I have a license to do so. Depend on me to do your shooting for you. You can be a witness in my defense."

"Are you carrying some other kind of weapon?"

"Sweetheart, there are always weapons at hand, if you know how to use them."

"What kind of weapons?"

"A chair, a fireplace poker, a broom handle, an umbrella, a rolled-up newspaper."

"How is a rolled-up newspaper a weapon?"

"Tightly rolled, it's like a thick stick. You can poke somebody in the eye with it, hit him in the solar plexus, or just smash him upside the head. It's unlikely to knock him unconscious, but you'll stun him and give yourself time to find a way to kill him."

"You've given this a lot of thought," she said.

"There was a time when I hardly thought of anything else. That's how I was trained. Once it's sunk in, the knowledge is always there, it doesn't go away."

"I'm starting to feel safer," she said.

"Would you like me to give you some self-defense training?"

"Yes, I think I would."

"Then, this weekend, we'll devote a little time to that."

DAX BAXTER LEFT HIS OFFICE a little later than usual and pointed the Porsche toward home. Somewhere well behind him, a car flashed its headlights, and he was suddenly tense. Was it a signal to somebody up ahead, somebody waiting with a sniper's rifle?

He switched off his headlights and made a sudden turn into a residential street, shifting down to slow the car without braking. He pulled into a driveway behind a row of trees and stopped. A moment later, a car drove past, then turned into a driveway a few doors down. Somebody coming home from work, or somebody looking to kill him?

A porch light went on, and a man stepped outside his front door. Dax quickly backed up and drove back the way he had come. At the intersection, he looked carefully in both directions, then pulled into the road, turning his lights on again. Lights appeared again in his rearview mirror. By the time he got home he was a nervous wreck.

He opened the steel garage door, drove inside, and pressed a button that operated a turntable, rotating the car 180 degrees. He let himself into the house, grabbed a skateboard by the door and pushed off. In a twenty-one-thousand-square-foot, one-bedroom house, it got him around faster than walking. He rolled into his study and poured himself a stiff scotch, not bothering with ice. He took two big gulps and sank into a chair, waiting for the booze to find its way to his fear. It took no more than a minute.

He settled back into his chair, resting the glass on the leather arm. Warmth coursed through him, and confidence. He closed his eyes. And took a deep breath.

This was crazy, he thought. If anybody was following him, it would be the cops. If he was under twenty-four-hour surveillance, what did he have to worry about? He laughed at himself.

DAX JERKED AWAKE. There had been a noise. The digital clock across the room said that it was just after midnight. What was that noise? He eased from his chair, went to a cabinet, opened his safe and took out a loaded 9mm pistol, pumping a round into the chamber and flipping off the safety. He went back to the living room and looked intently around the darkened room. The noise came again, louder this time, making him jump.

It was the ice machine, making ice.

35

CARLOS RIVERA WAS at his desk the following morning when his phone rang. "Rivera," he said.

"Sergeant, this is Dax Baxter."

"Good morning, Mr. Baxter."

"I just wanted to check with you—were your people watching me last night?"

"Let me check my team's field reports. They just came in." Carlos put the man on hold, opened his laptop, and found the GPS file. He pressed the line button again. "Mr. Baxter?"

"I'm still here."

"I'm sorry for the delay. Here's the report. You departed your office at six-forty PM yesterday and drove in the direction of your home, but you made a detour along the way. You turned left into a residential street and entered the driveway of a house. You remained there for four minutes, then drove back to the main road and continued your journey home, arriving at seven twenty-six PM. This morning, you left your house at eight forty-five and drove to your office, arriving at nine thirty-two. You're still there."

"Your men are to be complimented, Sergeant. Please give them my thanks for their attention."

"You're very welcome, Mr. Baxter."

"How long will this surveillance continue?"

"Until we've apprehended a suspect."

"No matter how long it takes?"

"Oh, it shouldn't take all that long, Mr. Baxter. Our average time for apprehension after surveillance is a little under six weeks."

"Six weeks?"

"That's the average, sir. It could take less time, but usually not less than four or five weeks. Sometimes it takes longer, but never more than eleven weeks, in our experience."

"Thank you," Baxter said weakly.

"Oh, Mr. Baxter, I'm sure you own more than one vehicle. Would you please let me know if you plan to take another car somewhere, so I can notify my team?"

"Yes, of course," Baxter said, and hung up.

"That was beautiful," Joe Rossi said, laughing. "I was listening on the extension. How'd your date go last night?"

"Just great. I think I'm in love."

"Easy, Carlos, any guy who's no longer paying alimony is vulnerable."

"Funny, I like feeling vulnerable," Carlos replied.

TEDDY AND SALLY had finished lunch and were lying on the deck, taking the sun.

"Whatever happened to my self-defense training?" Sally asked.

"Is now soon enough?" Teddy asked.

"Sure."

"Come into the living room." He opened the sliding door and they stepped into the air-conditioning. He went into the kitchen, came back with a table knife, and handed it to her. "All right, there are two basic attacks—swinging and jabbing. Take a swing at me."

"But I might hurt you."

"You won't. Go ahead."

She swung the knife toward him; he struck the inside of her wrist with the edge of his hand, and the knife flew away.

"Ow!" she said.

"I'm sorry. Let's do everything at half speed."

"Why didn't you jump back?" she asked.

"Never jump back, he'll just keep coming until you're against a wall. Step into his swing. That shortens his arc and gives you a chance to hit him with your other hand."

"Hit him where?"

"If you're dealing with a man, who may be bigger and stronger than you, hit him squarely in the nose, as hard as you can. You'll break the cartilage, stun him, and blood will pour out. Trust me, everybody hates the sight of his own blood. Then run."

"What if there's nowhere to run, if I'm trapped?"

"Then, before he can recover, find something with some weight to it and strike him in the temple. Like the little bronze sculpture on the coffee table. That would render him unconscious, maybe even kill him."

"But I don't want to kill him."

"Why not? He's already tried to kill you. Don't hold back and let him regain the advantage of his height and weight."

"But you said I should never kill anybody."

"I said you should never use a gun to kill anybody. If a man has attacked you with a knife, everyone's sympathy—the police, the DA, the court—will be with you. You're a defenseless woman who acted in desperation to save your life. A woman with a gun is not defenseless and not so sympathetic."

He walked her around the room and showed her objects that could be used as weapons: a paperweight, a heavy crystal bowl, a letter opener from the desk. "This has a sharp point, but not a sharp blade. How would you use it against an opponent?"

"With the pointy end," she replied.

"Where?"

"In the heart?"

"The heart can be difficult to find when you're under attack. It has a rib cage to protect it, and you might not get a second thrust. Stab him in the throat, here, or here." He pointed to the Adam's apple and the jugular. "Anywhere in the neck is going to hurt like hell and bleed a lot. Stab him more than once, if you can. If he's close to you, stab him in the eye. That will stop anybody."

"Ugh," she said.

"When your life is in danger you can't afford to be squeamish. Get mad at him, that will help." He took her into the kitchen. "You'll notice that the knives are not in a drawer," he said, "but in a wooden block, with their handles exposed. If you're under attack, you don't have time to remember which drawers the knives are in and search the drawer. And when you choose your weapon, don't take the big chef's knife—it's unwieldy. You can kill a man with any knife there, even a three-inch paring knife. Keep them all sharp. A dull knife is of little use, whether you're attacking a man or a tomato."

He led her back into the living room and faced her. "Now, we're both unarmed, but he has height, weight, and strength on you. Don't wait to defend an attack—attack!"

"In the nose?"

"Sure, but that may not be available, and it's defensible, if he's quick. So is the crotch, which is greatly overrated as a place to attack, unless you're wearing heavy shoes and have an open target—from behind is best, that's where his balls are."

"So where?"

"The shin is tempting, if you're wearing the right shoes, but the knee is much better. If you're wearing heels, your only shot is his foot, and his shoe will help protect him. But his knee has no protection. The kneecap is a painful place to be kicked and may be disabling, but a kick inside the knee outward with your instep will, first of all, knock him down, because the knee will collapse, and if you kick hard enough he won't be able to stand on it."

THEY WORKED FOR another hour, increasing their speed. "You're doing well," he said. "That's enough for today. You deserve a reward. What would you like?"

"Anything I want?" she asked, putting her arms around him.

"Anything," he said.

She told him, and she got it.

36

STONE AND ANA were having breakfast in bed. She was speaking on her cell to the prospective buyer of a large property in Santa Fe. "No, I'm out of town," she was saying, "but my associate, Carolyn, will pick you up at your hotel at ten AM and take you to see the house. You may, if you wish, speak to me at any time while you're viewing the place. Carolyn has a phone with a video link to mine, so we can meet face-to-face. Enjoy!" She hung up, just as the butler came into the room and handed Stone an envelope. "Just hand-delivered from the hotel manager, Mr. Barrington," he said.

Stone opened the envelope and found an application for the hotel's private club inside, complete with credit information and a photograph of a man he'd never seen before. He showed it to Ana. "Is this Dax Baxter?"

"Yes, it is. Why do you have his photograph?"

"He wants to join our private club, which gives access to all of our facilities to locals who are not guests in the hotel."

"And you get to approve or disapprove?"

"It happens when an applicant has a reputation for poor behavior or a bad credit record. According to his credit report, Baxter has both—has been sued half a dozen times by restaurants or clubs for nonpayment. A note from the manager says that he typically offers to pay less than what he owes."

"That doesn't surprise me," Ana said. "I ran a credit report on him when he was house hunting, to see if he was a good mortgage applicant, and he wasn't. Fortunately, he paid cash for the house."

There were two boxes at the bottom of the letter, and Stone checked the one marked "Decline," and signed it.

"Smart move," she said. "He's trouble, especially if he owes you money." She picked up a copy of *Architectural Digest* from the bed, opened it to a spread, and handed it to Stone. "You'd think that anyone who lives like this could pay his bills on time. I've heard on the real estate grapevine that he stiffed the interior designer for her work on his house, and she had to settle for half her fee to avoid going to court against him. He would have seen to it that her legal costs would have been more than her fee."

Stone flipped through the pages devoted to the house. "God, it's twenty-one thousand square feet, and it has only one bedroom!"

"Oh, that's just the main house. It has a guesthouse and staff quarters, too. I could find a buyer for it in a week, if it came on the market. There are lots of filthy rich out there."

"This guy gives filthy rich a bad name." Stone buzzed the butler and gave him the application. "Please send this back to the manager, pronto."

"Yes, sir." The man disappeared.

LATER THAT MORNING, Dax Baxter sat at his desk, flipping through his e-mail. He was confronted with a photograph of himself, the application he had completed for membership in the Arrington Club, and a covering letter:

> *Dear Mr. Baxter,*
>
> *Attached please find your application for membership in the Arrington Club, which, I regret to inform you, has been declined by the chairman of our board of directors. State law requires me to give a reason for the declining of a credit application; in your case, your credit record reveals a history of late and/or nonpayment of restaurant and club bills, and of legal action against you for such practices.*

It was signed by the hotel manager.

*   *   *

"**THE CHAIRMAN OF** their fucking board!!!?" Baxter screamed, sweeping his computer monitor off his desk. Then he looked up to find Chita Romero standing in his doorway. "What the fuck do you want?" he demanded.

"I have the production file you asked for," she replied calmly.

"Then put it on my desk and get out!"

She did so and closed the door behind her.

OUTSIDE, AS SHE SAT DOWN at her desk, a colleague asked, "What was it this time?"

"He screamed something about the chairman of the board," Chita said. "What does that mean?"

"Was he on his computer?"

"Yes, and he knocked the screen off his desk."

"Let's see what's in his e-mail," she said, and tapped some keys. "Ah," she said, "here it is. The chairman of the board of the Arrington Hotels has rejected his application for membership in their club—personally, it seems. They cite a poor credit record."

"How many times has he been sued?" Chita asked.

"I don't have that many fingers and toes."

Chita laughed, and just at the moment Baxter opened his office door. "Get a tech guy in here to fix my computer. It's broken again."

Chita picked up a phone. "Yes, sir, right away."

He slammed the door.

"Tech support," a young man's voice said.

"Sammy, you'd better get up here in a hurry. He's broken his computer again. And if I were you, I'd bring a new monitor."

"On my way," Sammy said. He was there in five minutes, with a new monitor on his cart.

Chita buzzed Baxter.

"What?"

"The technician is here to fix your computer."

"Send him in."

"Yes, sir." She hung up and nodded at the young man. "Good luck," she said.

Ten minutes later, the tech left the office, with the smashed monitor on his cart.

"Thank you, Sammy," Chita said. Her phone buzzed. "Yes, sir?"

"I want you to do a little research," Baxter said.

"Of course, sir."

"Somebody named Stone Barrington is chairman of the board of the Arrington Hotel Group. I want to know everything about him, and I mean, *everything*."

"Yes, sir," she replied. "Grace," she said to the woman next to her, "pull a Dun & Bradstreet report on a Stone Barrington, chairman of Arrington Hotels."

"Sure," Grace said.

Chita started in on Google, and in five minutes she had an inch-high stack of paper on her desk. "Got it?" she asked Grace.

Grace handed her the D&B report. "This guy is very well heeled," she said, "and he's a widower. Introduce me, will you?"

Chita laughed and reached for a file folder. She made

a label for it and put the printouts inside. "Here we go," she said. She got up, knocked, and handed the folder to Baxter. "Here's everything we've got," she said. "For anything more, we'd have to hire a detective agency."

She set the folder on his desk and got out. Half an hour later, he buzzed her. "Yes, sir?"

"Call that guy, what's his name, the private eye?"

"Cupie Dalton?" she asked. "Dalton & Vittorio?"

"That's the one. Tell him I want him in my office *now*."

37

CUPIE DALTON SAT in a reclining chair in his office on Venice Beach and gazed out the window at a group of girls in bikinis playing volleyball. Why hadn't girls dressed like that for volleyball when he was still young enough to play? It wasn't fair.

Cupie, who had gained his nickname for his resemblance to a doll of the same name, was ex-LAPD, and in the years since his retirement he had run his little agency with a partner named Vittorio, an Apache Indian based in Santa Fe. Between the two of them, they could cover just about anything. His phone rang, and a recording picked up.

"Good day, Dalton & Vittorio. How may I help you?" Her voice was low and British-accented. He had met her in a bar on the beach.

"I'm calling for Dax Baxter," a woman said. "May I speak to Cupie Dalton, please?"

"One moment," the recording said, and the phone next to Cupie's chair rang, as it was programmed to do. "This is Cupie Dalton," he said.

"Hi, Cupie, it's Chita, in Dax Baxter's office. He has some work for you, and he wants you here pronto. Are you up for that?"

Cupie sighed. He wasn't, but business had been slow. "Sure. I'll be there in forty-five minutes."

"Faster?"

"It takes that long to drive from Venice. I don't have a helicopter at my disposal."

"Okay, hit the road."

Cupie hung up, got into the jacket of his catalog-bought seersucker suit, and went out back to his garage in the alley.

FORTY MINUTES LATER Cupie parked in a guest spot at Standard Studios; his other five minutes were used up waiting for the elevator, in which he snugged up his necktie while ascending.

He waved at Chita and she picked up the phone and announced him, then waved him through. Without slowing down, Cupie walked through the door.

"Siddown, Cupie," Baxter said.

Cupie, like most people who'd worked for Baxter,

loathed him, but he put on his best smile. "Hi, Dax. How's it going?"

"Not great. I want to know everything there is to know about a guy."

"Who's the guy?"

"His name is Stone Barrington. Ever heard of him?"

"Sure," Cupie said with confidence. He'd done lots of work for Ed Eagle, and sometimes Barrington had been involved. "He's a New York lawyer with Woodman & Weld, a top firm, and he's the chairman of the Arrington Hotel Group. His late wife, Arrington, was the widow of Vance Calder, the movie star."

"I'm impressed, Cupie. How'd you know that? I've never heard of the guy."

"I know a little about a lot of people," Cupie replied, "and everything about a chosen few. What's your angle on this, Dax?"

"What do you mean by that?" Baxter replied with a snarl.

"I mean, do you want to go into business with Barrington or just ruin his day? There's a spectrum, you know."

"Well, I don't want to go into business with him," Baxter said. He tossed a thick file folder across the desk. "And don't try to fob off a whole bunch of Google stuff on me—it's all in there."

"Okay, an in-depth investigation into him is going to cost you twenty grand, ten up front. I've got expenses."

"How long?"

"Couple of weeks, if you want accuracy."

"I want accuracy," Baxter said, "and I want it in three days."

"That'll run you twenty-five grand, twelve-five up front."

Baxter glared at him for a moment, then picked up a phone. "Tell Gladys to cut a check to Cupie for twelve thousand, five hundred dollars."

"Oh," Cupie said, raising a finger. "I'm going to need cash. There are palms to be crossed." He didn't want to sit around waiting for the check to clear.

"Never mind the check," Baxter said. "Tell her to draw it from Accounting with a check on my personal business account. They can clear it with me." He hung up and addressed Cupie. "I'll tell you what I really want," he said.

Cupie spread his hands. "I'm at your service, Dax."

"I want some information that, if it were widely known, would wreck his business dealings and make his life not worth living."

"Is that all?" Cupie asked. He took a folded, three-page contract from his pocket, filled in the amount, and handed it across the desk.

Baxter signed it without reading it, a sign that he didn't care if he got sued, and tossed it back at Cupie.

Cupie tucked it away. "Couple of things," Cupie said. "One, if I'm lucky enough to come up with the kind of dirt you want, this is the kind of guy who's not going to take it lying down. Two, his best friend in the world is the police commissioner of New York City, who has all of law enforcement everywhere on speed dial."

"I don't give a shit whether he takes it lying down or in the ass," Baxter said, "and I don't give a shit who his friends are."

There was a knock at the door, and Gladys walked in with a thick envelope and placed it on Baxter's desk. He flipped it across the shiny surface toward Cupie, who, after a glance inside to be sure the sum wasn't in Bulgarian levs, made it disappear.

"See you in three days," Baxter said, "and it better be good."

Cupie picked up the Google folder and made his escape. "You have a good one," he called over his shoulder, as the door slammed behind him.

BACK IN HIS CAR Cupie laughed out loud. He couldn't believe he had scored twelve-five off the biggest cheapskate and deadbeat in town, using nothing more than a whisper of a promise. He knew without even thinking about it that any skeletons in Stone Barrington's closet were female and beautiful and likely had good things to say about him. He wondered if Stone was in town. He called the Arrington and asked, and the extension rang.

"Mr. Barrington's residence," a smooth voice said.

"Tell him it's Cupie Dalton calling and that I know something he doesn't."

A moment later, the phone was picked up. "Cupie? How the hell are you?"

"I'm just great, Stone, and if you buy me lunch, I'll tell you something that you don't know yet, but that will vastly amuse you."

"Sure, Cupie, I'll leave your name at the gate. They'll direct you from there. How long?"

"Half an hour."

"See you then."

Cupie whistled a little tune all the way to the Arrington.

38

THEY MET OUT at the pool, where Stone was wearing a robe, and Ana was swimming laps. Cupie looked much the same, Stone thought, watching him fanning himself with his straw hat.

The butler approached. "What can we get you?" Stone asked.

"Gin and tonic, mostly gin," Cupie replied. "Warm day, isn't it?"

"Take off your jacket, Cupie, and cool down."

Cupie did so. "Thanks, I needed that."

"We're having lobster salad for lunch. That okay with you?"

"Fine, just fine." Cupie took a long pull on his drink, sat back, and sighed.

"What's Vittorio up to these days?" Stone asked.

"Oh, you know Vittorio—he's sitting on a mesa in New Mexico, contemplating the sunrise, or the sunset, or whatever. Work still brings us together, but if he tried to live on Venice Beach, he'd wither and die."

"I expect he would."

"I guess you'd like to know what I know," Cupie said.

"How much is it going to cost me?" Stone asked.

"When you know all and have had a chance to act on it, I will leave my fee entirely to your generosity, Stone."

"I'll hope for the best."

"All right," Cupie said, "I have just come from the office of one Dax Baxter, a movie producer of some repute, not all of it good. Ring a bell?"

"Unfortunately, yes. He sicced a hit man, known as the Russian, on a friend of mine recently."

"My condolences to you and your friend's family."

"Unnecessary," Stone replied. "Save them for the Russian."

Cupie's eyebrows shot up. "Your friend offed the Russian?"

"Close, but not quite. The Russian came after him with a knife, and my friend put him in the hospital for several days."

"Out of professional curiosity, may I know the extent of his injuries?"

"He would have cut the man's leg off, if the shinbone hadn't gotten in the way."

Cupie blinked. "I'm sorry to hear it."

"Sorry?"

"Not for the Russian, for your friend. The only thing worse than having the Russian trying to kill you would be having tried to kill the Russian and failed."

"The man is of a vengeful nature, then?"

"He's the last man on earth I'd want to have a grudge against me—except, maybe, your friend. Would you like me to arrange some personal security for him?"

"I think he's already demonstrated the lack of a need," Stone replied. "The Russian is the one who's limping. Now, what's all this about Dax Baxter?"

"Ah, I almost forgot. Apparently, you have somehow offended Mr. Baxter. Do you have any idea how?"

"Well, when he applied for membership in the Arrington Club, I signed the rejection. That was this very morning."

"And he knows that?"

"I expect so."

"So, you've humiliated him?"

"Not unless he tells all his friends. We didn't publish the letter."

"All Dax's friends would fit into a phone booth, if such still existed," Cupie said. "May I ask how you delivered the rejection letter?"

"By e-mail, I believe."

"That's good, because it isn't lying on his desk where his staff could read it."

"What do I care?"

"Well, if somebody who is acquainted with the gossip industry saw the letter, it might soon find itself in the wrong mailbox."

"Not my problem," Stone said.

"Dax's office called me this morning and told me to get my ass to his office in a hurry."

"Does that happen a lot?"

"Only when there's nobody else he could call. Anyway, I went over there and he threw a thick Google printout at me— all about you—and hired me to find out something that could ruin you. He's paying twenty-five grand, half in advance."

"Well, I wish I could help you, Cupie, but I don't know of anything that could allow Dax Baxter to ruin me."

Their lobster salads arrived; Ana joined them and was introduced.

"Cupie, here, is an ace private eye," Stone said to her, "and he has just been telling me that Dax Baxter has hired him to ruin me because of the rejection letter I signed."

"Ruin you? How's he going to do that?"

"I've just been trying to think of a way, so that Cupie can collect the other half of his fee, but so far, nothing."

"Ana," Cupie said, "perhaps you know some dirty little secret of Stone's that you could share with me?"

"Well," she said, "I ran a check on him recently, and he appears to be as clean as a hound's tooth."

Stone put down his fork and swallowed. "*You* ran a check on *me*?"

"Of course, darling. I don't go jetting off to L.A. with a man I don't know everything about. It's not good for a girl's rep."

"And it's how I stay in business," Cupie said, handing her a business card. "I'm at your service at all times."

"Since I have been unable to assist Cupie," Stone said to her, "perhaps your investigation turned up something damning."

"I'm afraid not," she said to Cupie. "As I said, as clean as a hound's tooth."

"That's very disappointing," Cupie replied, then he brightened. "Here's a thought," he said. "We think of something so obviously untrue that no one would ever believe it. I give that to Dax, he circulates it, then you sue him for defamation and nail him to the wall."

"That is an absolutely terrible idea, Cupie," Stone said. "If you do that, half the people who read or hear this 'obviously untrue' thing that no one will believe, will believe it, and my sterling character will forever be besmirched."

"Well, there is that," Cupie said.

"Cupie," Stone said, "I'm afraid my contribution to your Dax-generated enterprise is going to have to begin and end with lunch."

"And a very fine lunch it has been," Cupie replied, putting down his fork and sipping his Puligny-Montrachet. "I consider it a good use of my time."

"For which Dax is paying," Stone said, "not I."

"I cede you that point," Cupie said. "Billing will not occur."

"I hear that Mr. Baxter has a reputation for being reluctant to pay his debts," Stone said.

"A well-earned reputation," Cupie said. "I compensated for that by doubling my fee and getting half up front in cash."

"Then you will both be happy," Stone said. "You will have been paid, and Dax will believe he has screwed you."

"A happy circumstance, is it not?" Cupie said, beaming. He shook hands, thanked Stone for the lunch, and departed.

39

THE RUSSIAN SAT watching *60 Minutes* on TV, when Bear performed his usual hammering on the door. "Come in, Bear!" he shouted.

Bear came in, puffing a little. "What's so urgent?" he asked.

"Tonight's the night," the Russian said. "Billy Barnett and his girl having dinner up the beach from his house."

"How do you know that?"

"You are not only person working for me, Bear—others, too. We will be there when they leave restaurant. No moon tonight, pretty dark parking lot. We take the van."

"Okay, I'm in," Bear said. "I want that girl."

"Not until Dax is there," the Russian said. "He want very much to see you in action."

"Okay," Bear said.

The Russian picked up a cane, one heavier than his usual. "You drive," he said, tossing Bear the keys.

TEDDY AND SALLY had had what Easterners call a "shore dinner," deep fried, with a bottle of good California Chardonnay.

"I think I'm relaxed again," Sally said. "Life is back to normal."

"You go ahead and relax," Teddy said.

"You're not relaxed, are you?" she asked.

"Not yet," he replied.

"Is there a gun under the jacket?"

Teddy shook his head. "No, not necessary."

"If you say so."

Teddy asked for the check and paid it. They both used the restroom on the way out.

It was a cool, beach evening; the sun had gone, and there was a breeze. Teddy used the remote to find the car in the dark, crowded lot. Its taillights came on with a beep. They were walking past a gray van when something bit Teddy on the neck. He slapped at it and discovered that whatever it was was embedded in his flesh. He had just a moment to figure it out, then he collapsed onto the pavement. The last thing he heard was Sally crying his name.

* * *

THE RUSSIAN PUT his cane, which contained a dart gun, back in the van. He knew they would be out for at least an hour, so he didn't worry. Half an hour later they arrived at Dax's old house in the Hollywood Hills. They pulled into the garage and Bear unloaded their cargo.

The Russian bound Teddy's hands and feet with duct tape and dumped him to one side, then Bear took Sally over to a Ping-Pong table against the other wall, laid her on it, and stripped her.

The Russian came over with some cord. "How you want her?"

"Facedown," Bear said. "Legs off the end of the table, so she can bend in the middle."

The Russian ran the cord from her hands to the double legs in the center of the table, while Bear adjusted her position.

"There," Bear said. "I want her now."

"I told you," the Russian said, "not until Dax gets here. He wants to watch, and he may even want to help."

"I don't need no help," Bear said.

The Russian used a throwaway cell phone to dial an identical one.

DAX WAS WATCHING TV when he heard the phone ring in the next room. He ran for it. "Hello," he said breathlessly.

"You know who this is?" the Russian asked.

"Of course I know who it is. Why are you calling? I told you not to use this phone until—"

"You told me to call when I got them," the Russian said.

Dax's heart leaped. "You've got them? Already?"

"That's what I say."

"Where?"

"At the other place, you know."

"Jesus," Dax said, "the cops are all over me. I can't come now."

"The cops what?"

"They've been watching me to protect me. They've got a bug on the Porsche."

"What about the other car?"

"Of course." Dax had not been thinking clearly. "I'll be there in an hour or so. I want to be sure I'm not followed."

"Take your time, they not going anywhere." He hung up.

"Dax will be a while," the Russian said.

"Can I start entertaining the girl?" Bear asked.

"You know not. Not without Dax. He pays, you know. He don't pay you for your pleasure. Take the load off, relax awhile." There was a TV in the garage; the Russian turned it on, and they dragged a couple of old chairs in front of it and settled in.

THE FIRST THING Teddy knew was the sound of the TV. He opened his eyes and saw Sally across the room, tied to a Ping-Pong table, still out. The same dart would have affected her for longer, because of her lighter body weight.

Teddy breathed deeply, trying to clear his head, but otherwise, he did not move. He heard someone get up, walk, and open a refrigerator. "You want beer?" a voice asked.

That, Teddy knew, was the Russian.

"Yeah," another voice replied. Two beer cans could be heard popping.

Teddy was lying on his stomach in a dimly lit space, his feet and hands bound. He did his best to stretch the tape binding his hands, but it didn't help much.

Teddy heard two voices laugh together as his captors watched TV. The other voice was deeper. It was the man whose photograph he had taken, the hairy one. He could not see them, so he didn't know if they could see him. They laughed again at the TV.

Teddy knew he would have been searched for weapons, but he knew something they didn't. Slowly, quietly, he raised his feet toward his back. His feet did not quite reach his hands. He moved his legs several times, stretching his thigh muscles. He managed to get a finger inside one of his loafers and hold it there, while he relaxed his legs for a moment. Now he could pull his legs toward his hands, but not yet far enough. He got two fingers inside the loafer and pulled it off his heel, so that now, only his toe was inside the shoe. He took a few breaths then made an all-out effort to pull the shoe off his foot, and in so doing, managed to bump into the wall, making a noise.

"You hear something?" the deep voice asked. "Listen."

The sound of the TV was muted, and all was quiet.

"Nothing. You nervous?"

"No, I just thought I heard something. I guess it's nothing."

"They both still out," the Russian said.

Teddy waited for them to become absorbed in the TV again. When they laughed, he took hold of his shoe with one hand, and with the other, pressed a slightly raised place on the heel, then he grasped the heel and pulled. It came away in his hand.

He grasped half the heel, which was now a handle; at the other end was a three-inch, double-sided blade, very sharp.

Teddy's knives were always very sharp.

40

D AX SWITCHED OFF the garage lights, got into the Bentley Mulsanne, and opened the door. He drove down the driveway to the street and stopped, looking both ways. Nothing. He accelerated carefully, avoiding the racetrack roar that the V-12 engine made when punched, and turned onto the main road.

He was surprised at how much traffic there was. He kept seeing cars in his rearview mirror that might have lights on top. He drove for half an hour, then pulled into a driveway and called the Russian.

"Yes?" the Russian said.

"This is going to take some time, there's a lot of traffic, and I've got to be careful."

"Bear and I want to fuck her," the Russian said.

"All right, but leave her in good enough shape for me, and above all, don't finish them until I'm there." He hung up.

TEDDY HAD LISTENED to the Russian's end of the conversation while he used the knife to cut the tape on his ankles and hands. It was hard to do without wounding himself.

"Dax is delayed," he heard the Russian say. "He says we can fuck her, but not to tear her up. He wants to be here to finish her."

Teddy finished with the tape, then he took off his other shoe and retracted another knife. He heard the Russian and the one called Bear taking their clothes off, then a light was switched on over the Ping-Pong table. Good, he thought. That would blind them to him in the shadows. He got to his feet and waited.

The Russian and the Bear, both naked now, approached the table.

"Me, first," the Bear said. "I'm ready."

Teddy had never seen anything like the man's penis. He had to be quick now. The Russian stood with his back to Teddy, watching the table. Sally was moaning, trying to talk—the first sounds she had made. Teddy walked up behind the Russian in his bare feet, noiselessly, and tapped him on the shoulder. The Russian spun around, and before he could react further, Teddy threw an arm over his shoulder, to keep him from backing up, then inserted the knife into the man's belly, just above the pubic hair.

The Russian struggled, but Teddy held him close as he drew the knife quickly up his belly, all the way to the sternum. Then he let the man go.

The Russian staggered back a step or two, making a squealing noise and hugging himself, trying to hold his intestines in. The Bear stood transfixed for a moment, then grabbed the Russian and lowered him to the floor. It was not until he stood up again that Teddy had his full attention.

"I'm going to cut that thing off," Teddy said.

The Bear made a move toward him, and Teddy punched him twice in the solar plexus with his left hand, which held the other knife. The Bear looked at him, astonished. Blood gushed from the two wounds, spilling onto the Russian, mingling with the other man's blood. He collapsed.

Then Teddy did what he had said he was going to do.

DAX FINALLY CONVINCED himself that he was unpursued, then headed for the Hollywood Hills.

TEDDY CUT SALLY FREE, held her for a moment, then helped her find her clothes. While she was dressing, he went to a sink in the corner and cleaned himself up, then he found his shoes and reinserted the two knives into the loafers.

He wiped down anything they had touched.

Sally was calm and still a little groggy. "You've got blood on your shirt and pants," she said. The whole time she had not looked at the two butchered men.

Teddy took a cell phone from the TV table, then found a raincoat on a peg next to the garage door and put it on. "Let's go," he said. She came to him, he pressed the garage door button to open it, she walked outside, then he pressed it again and ducked under it before it could close.

They walked to the end of the driveway and looked around. The neighborhood was deserted.

"Where are we going to go?" she asked.

"Downhill," he replied. "All roads lead to Sunset Boulevard. We'll find a cab." He took her hand, and they started downhill.

DAX APPROACHED THE HOUSE from the uphill side, and as he turned into the driveway, his headlights flashed on two people half a block down the hill, as they turned a corner. "Pedestrians!" he said aloud to himself. "They could get arrested for that around here."

He got out of the car, tapped a code into a keypad next to the garage, and one of the two doors opened. He walked inside and, for a moment, couldn't understand what he was seeing. The Ping-Pong table was flooded in light, and next to it, in a heap, were two bodies. There was blood everywhere.

"Where are you?" he screamed. "I told you not to kill them before I got here. Then he looked again and saw that both bodies were naked men, one of them missing something important.

Dax ran to the back wall and threw up into the utility sink there. Twice. Finally, he stopped vomiting, splashed some water on his face, and washed off the soles of his shoes. He went to the other side of the garage, skirting the pond of blood, went outside, and closed the garage door. He was shaking uncontrollably. He got into the car and sat, taking deep breaths until he got ahold of himself. Had the two men killed each other?

Then, as his mind cleared, he realized that Billy Barnett had killed them both, and horribly. For the first time he began to grasp what kind of man this was, one he had tried to murder twice.

He drove back to his house carefully, not speeding, stopping for every light.

TEDDY AND SALLY retrieved their car from the restaurant parking lot and drove home. Inside the house, he put his clothes into the washing machine and turned it on, then he got into a robe and went back to the living room. "Would you like a drink?" he asked Sally.

"Yes, please."

He handed it to her then sat down beside her. "Are you all right?"

"Astonishingly, yes," she said. "My head has cleared. Did they drug me?"

"Yes, and me, too. I was careless."

"All the way back here I thought about it, and I realize that you had to do what you did. There was really no other way. They would have just kept coming, wouldn't they?"

"They were very confident," Teddy replied. "Too confident, really."

The sun was rising now, and light was pouring into the room. "I'll make us some breakfast," he said. "We have to go to work in a couple of hours. Everything has to be normal."

"I understand," she said.

Teddy went into the kitchen and put on the coffee. Then he took the cell phone he had found in the garage and dialed the last number that had called.

DAX BAXTER SAT, collapsed in a chair in his study, numb, with a large drink. He had to get his brain working again. He was lifted off his chair by the buzz of the cell phone in his shirt pocket. He took it out and looked at it as if it were a cobra. Finally he pressed the button, but said nothing.

"The smart move," Billy Barnett said, "would be to kill yourself now. Eat a gun, run a hot bath and cut your wrists—remember, lengthwise, not across. Go any way you like, because when I find you—and I will, when you least expect it—you won't like the way things end."

He hung up, leaving Dax Baxter staring into the dawning sky.

41

CHITA ROMERO HAD just stepped out of the shower when her phone rang. Who would call this early? "Hello?"

"This is Dax. Got a pencil?"

"Just a moment." She found one.

"I want you to call my pilot and tell him to get weather and fuel and file for Santa Fe, departure in ninety minutes."

She thought he sounded a little shaky. "Got it. Are you all right, Dax?"

"Yes. Call the Santa Fe caretaker and tell him to get

the housekeeper over there and clean, then leave my car at Signature Aviation at the airport."

"Got it. Anything else?"

"Call Cupie Dalton and tell him I want the four toughest security men he can find, two of them to fly with me, the other two tomorrow, at the latest, in Santa Fe."

"Got it."

"I want my phones answered at Standard and routed to Santa Fe. Nobody is to know I've left town."

"Got it."

"I'll call you for messages when I get there." He hung up.

Chita made the calls, then was getting dressed when the phone rang; she was expecting Dax again. "Yes?"

"It's Carlos. How about dinner tonight?"

"You're on. Say, something has spooked Dax. He's leaving for Santa Fe this morning, and he doesn't want anybody to know he's gone."

"Interesting," Carlos replied. "Seven o'clock?"

"See you then."

AT EIGHT AM the contract cleaning lady let herself into Dax's Hollywood Hills house. She had been there for an hour before she went into the garage for some bleach. She switched on the lights and stood stock-still while she tried to figure out what she was looking at.

SHORTLY AFTER NINE AM, a 911 operator answered a call. The woman gave her name and address. "There's a woman in the house next door screaming bloody murder," she said.

"Who lives there?"

"Nobody, I think. It used to belong to some movie guy. She's still screaming—you better get somebody over there."

"They're on their way," the operator said.

A PATROL CAR pulled into the Hollywood Hills driveway, and the cop got out and rang the bell. He heard a scream from inside, so he drew his weapon, backed up a step, and launched a kick at the door. The jamb splintered and the door flew open, revealing a woman sitting on the floor, screaming hoarsely.

He got her calmed down a little. "Are you alone in the house?" She nodded, then thought better of it and shook her head. "In the garage," she said, pointing.

The cop found the door open; he stuck his head inside and yelled, "LAPD! Show yourselves!" Then he saw the heap beside the Ping-Pong table. He moved cautiously into the garage, cleared the area, then stood looking at the two corpses.

His body radio sputtered. "Bravo Three, come back."

He keyed the mike. "This is Bravo Three. I'm on-site at the nine-one-one. I need homicide detectives, a crime-scene unit, and the ME. I've got two corpses, male, naked. One of them is . . . incomplete."

In minutes, everybody was there. The detectives did their work, then turned the garage over to the ME and the crime-scene people. Then they went into the kitchen, where the maid was sitting, drinking tea.

"You feeling better, ma'am?" one of them asked her.

She nodded. "I can't talk very good," she said.

He sat down and produced his notebook. "Who owns the house?"

"I don't know. I never see anybody here." She gave him a card with her service's number, and he called.

"I don't know who owns it," her manager said. "We've had the contract for five, six years, and we get a check from a bank out of town."

His partner came into the room. "Tax records say the place is owned by a Delaware corporation."

"Let's talk to the neighbors," the senior man said. They split up and he went to the house where the 911 call had originated. The woman there offered him coffee, which he accepted.

"Do you know who owns the house?" he asked the woman.

"It used to be owned by some Hollywood big shot, but he left several years ago. I never saw a real estate sign there, so maybe he still owns it."

"Let's try again for a name."

"It had an *X* in it, that's all I remember." She picked up a copy of the *L.A. Times* and opened it to the arts section. "There," she said, pointing at a full-page movie ad. "That's it."

The ad began: "A DAX BAXTER PRODUCTION."

CHITA LOOKED UP to see two obvious cops approaching her desk. Her first thought was, something's happened to Carlos, but she was wrong.

The two men showed badges and introduced themselves. "We'd like to see Mr. Dax Baxter," the taller one said.

"I'm sorry, he's not in."

"What time do you expect him?"

"I'm not sure," she lied. Dax had told her he didn't want anyone to know he was out of town.

"Can you tell me if Mr. Baxter owns a house in the Hollywood Hills?" He gave her the address.

"No, he lives up on Mulholland Drive," she replied.

"Has he ever owned the Hollywood Hills house?"

"I've worked here for two years, and I've never heard that address mentioned."

"Miss, where can we find Mr. Baxter?"

She thought it over for a minute. "He's out of town," she said finally.

"Where?"

"In New Mexico."

"Where in New Mexico?"

"Santa Fe." She looked at her watch. "He should be there by now."

"He left this morning?"

"Yes, from Burbank, in a private jet. About eight o'clock."

"I'm going to need an address and a phone number."

She checked her computer and wrote down both for them.

"Right," the detective said. "And, miss?"

"Yes?"

"I'm going to have to ask you not to let him know we're coming."

She looked surprised.

"I know he pays your salary, but this is a very serious matter, and we wouldn't want him to change locations again. Do you understand?"

Chita nodded, and they left.

Grace, who had heard everything from her adjoining desk, said, "I'm certainly not going to call him, and I don't think you should either."

"I'm with you on that," Chita said.

THE TWO DETECTIVES got into their car. "I'd better call the boss and see if he'll authorize the King Air."

"You think we should call the Santa Fe cops?" his partner asked.

"Not just yet," the senior man replied.

42

CARLOS RIVERA FINISHED his day at half past five and got into his jacket. As he passed the Violent Crimes squad, the lieutenant flagged him down.

"You still interested in Dax Baxter?" he asked.

"Sure," Carlos replied. "You got something?"

"I was just having a chat with a buddy at LAPD Homicide, and they've got something."

"Is Baxter dead?"

"No, but there was a double homicide last night at a house he owns in the Hollywood Hills."

"I thought he lived on Mulholland."

"He used to live in the subject house, but it's been empty for some years."

"Who are the victims?"

"I didn't get that far in our conversation before he had to hang up."

"What's the detective's name?"

"Bob Jensen, with an *e*."

"Thanks, Lieutenant, I'll check it out." On the way to his car he called the detective, whose shift had ended. He checked his watch. What the hell, he had time to get to the morgue before he had to pick up Chita. He drove over there, parked, went inside, and asked for the ME.

"He's doing a couple of autopsies," the woman at the desk said. "You can go in room one, if you're not squeamish."

"Thanks," he said. He knew where room one was, and he went there. He looked through the round windows in the swinging door and saw a large man hunched over a table. He could see the soles of two pairs of feet facing him. He opened the door a foot. "Hey, Doc, it's Carlos Rivera from Beverly Hills PD. May I join you?"

"If you're not squeamish. I don't want you vomiting in here."

"No problem," Carlos replied, and walked over to him, between the two tables. He got a good look at both corpses, and for a moment he thought he was going to embarrass himself, but he got over it. "You got IDs yet?"

The ME pointed at a clipboard hanging at the end of the table. "One of 'em has a Russian name," he said.

Carlos picked up the clipboard, looked at the two

mug shots, and read the sheets on both men. "The Russian doesn't have any convictions, but he's a well-known hit man."

"Well," the ME said, "he ran into a better hit man. That incision looks a lot like one of mine." He pointed with the large scalpel in his hand.

"Very impressive," Carlos said. "The other guy seems to be missing something."

"Yeah. Over there on the desk, in a steel pan. Take a look."

Carlos walked over to the desk and viewed the object. "Holy shit," he muttered.

"That's pretty much what everybody who's seen it said," the ME replied.

Carlos walked back to where the ME stood.

"How did he die?"

"Are you kidding? From blood loss, of course. He also had two knife wounds in the heart. Short blade, razor sharp. Both of these guys bled out, and they didn't have very long to think about it."

Carlos looked at his watch. "Well, if you'll excuse me, I'm running late for dinner."

"Good luck with that," the ME replied.

"Yeah, I think I'll need a drink first." Carlos left and headed for Chita's apartment.

CARLOS NEEDED TWO drinks before he could think about food.

"Anything wrong?" Chita asked.

"You don't want to know," he replied.

"If you say so. Two cops showed up at the office around noon, looking for Dax," she said.

"LAPD Homicide?"

"How'd you know?"

"There was a double homicide at a house Dax owns in the Hollywood Hills."

"They mentioned the house. They didn't mention a double homicide, just said it was serious."

"Did they talk to Dax?"

"Dax called me at the crack of dawn this morning and started issuing orders—get his jet ready, fuel for Santa Fe, don't tell anybody where he is."

"Did you tell the two detectives?"

"Damned right I did. I'm not covering for Dax, not with the cops."

"Good girl."

"Dax sounded funny," she said, "rattled, maybe."

"I expect he had just come from his old house."

"You think he murdered two people?"

"No, I think he had occasion to view the bodies. So did I—that was what ruined my appetite."

Chita raised a hand. "No further details, please."

"Agreed."

"Do you think the cops went to Santa Fe, looking for Dax?"

"I expect so," he replied.

"You think Dax is in jail?"

"If he was, who would he call?"

"His lawyer, I guess. He'd call me if he wanted anything done in his absence, and he didn't do that."

"My guess is, he hasn't been arrested. For that, they'd have to be able to put him at the house. Is Dax the kind of guy who'd pull a knife on somebody?"

"I think Dax Baxter is the biggest coward I've ever met. He's a bully, but he backs down in a hurry."

"He didn't kill the two guys. One of them was a cold-blooded hit man, and the other—well, he worked for the hit man."

"That sounds like the sort of men he might hire to do his dirty work," she said.

"You think he's capable of having somebody murdered?"

"In a fit of anger, yes. And he's capable of staying angry for long periods—days, sometimes."

They ordered dinner, and Carlos pulled out his cell phone. "Excuse me, I want to check something." He pulled up the surveillance app. "The Porsche is still in his garage," he said. "Did he have another car?"

"Yes, a Bentley sedan. I've had it serviced for him."

"Might he drive it to the airport?"

"More likely, he would call a car service. I could check, if you like." Her cell phone rang, and she got it out of her bag. "It's Dax," she said. "Hello?" She listened for a moment. "First thing," she said, then hung up. "He left his briefcase in his office, and he wants me to FedEx it to him tomorrow morning."

"Chita," Carlos said, "do you think I could have a look in that briefcase before you send it?"

She shrugged. "Right after dessert," she said.

43

STONE WAS HAVING a before-dinner drink with Ana, when his cell rang: Cupie. "Hello, Cupie."

"How you doin', Stone?"

"I'm knee deep in bourbon, so pretty good."

"I've got some news on Dax."

"What news?"

"He got out of town early this morning, but not before one of his people called me and asked for four rough, tough security guards."

"Did you supply them?"

"I did. Two flew out with him and two met him in Santa Fe. These guys break heads, on request."

"You have any background on why he left town?"

"Well, yeah. An old buddy of mine still works Homicide at LAPD. There was a double homicide at a vacant house Dax owns in the Hollywood Hills."

"Anybody anyone knows?"

"One of them was a hit man known as the Russian."

"Him, even I have heard of. How did they die?"

"Badly, by the blade."

"Let me understand," Stone said. "Dax's hit man, who's said to be invincible, was knifed by somebody?"

"I don't think Dax could handle that himself."

"So what's going on?"

"Beats me, but Dax was pretty wired, according to his secretary."

"Well, that's fascinating, Cupie," Stone said. "I wouldn't mind hearing more, if it comes to you."

"Sure thing. Have a nice evening."

Ana looked at Stone curiously. "Anything wrong?"

"Not with me," Stone said. "Excuse me a second." He got up and walked into another room, then called Billy Barnett.

"Hi, Stone."

"Hi, Billy. Just a little heads-up. I came by a piece of information, and I'd rather not talk about how. Also, this call to you was just catching up, okay?"

"Whatever you say, Stone."

"There was a double homicide last night at a house owned by Dax Baxter, and he left for Santa Fe this morning in the company of heavy security."

"Anything else?"

"Nope. Nice not talking to you." Stone hung up and went back to the study and Ana.

"You know," she said, "I'm enjoying myself here enormously, but I have to show my face in Santa Fe soon, or my clients will think I'm drying out somewhere."

Stone laughed. "I like having you here, but if you have to go, I'll get somebody to fly you home in my plane."

"We could extend this little tryst for a while if you came with me."

"Well, I have to get back to New York soon, and I could use a couple of days in Santa Fe. Maybe I'll fly you myself."

"That would be lovely."

"And maybe after you've shown your face in Santa Fe, you'd like to spend some time in New York."

"It's a thought," she said.

The butler brought dinner in on a rolling table and set it up.

CHITA GOT THEM past the guard at the gate, saying Dax needed something from his office. She let them into the building, and they went upstairs. "You want lights or no lights?" she asked Carlos.

"Just the desk lamp," he said, sliding into Dax's chair. "Not a bad office. I admired it when I was here."

"Dax hires good people, then renegotiates when the bill comes. People rarely work for him twice." She got the briefcase from the credenza behind the desk and set it down before him.

Carlos looked at the locks. "I don't suppose you know the combination?"

She looked at the numbers. "You're in luck—he didn't lock it."

Carlos opened the case and found a steno pad on top of some papers. He went quickly through them—contracts, correspondence, the budget for a film—he went back to the steno pad.

"He takes notes on that," she said, "whatever he needs to remember."

Carlos leafed backward through the pages, assuming they were chronological. He found phone numbers, doodles, an address or two. Further back in time he came across an address and phone number that interested him. The number was an L.A. cell, but the address was a high-end trailer park on Pacific Coast Highway, on the way to Malibu. There was no name, just one initial: *R*. He wrote it down. There was a key ring in the case, too. He held it up for Chita. "Do you know what these keys are for?"

"Nope. They look like house keys."

"I wish I had some wax to take impressions."

"I wish I could help you."

He took a sheet of Dax's stationery from a drawer, placed each of the three keys on it and traced their outline. "This'll have to do," he said. "I don't suppose you have the combination to his safe? There must be one here somewhere."

She walked over to a wall and pulled on a picture, which, hinged, covered a wall safe with a digital key pad. "What will you give me for the combination?"

"My heart and soul," he said, "but you already have those."

She smiled, tapped in a code, and the door beeped and swung open.

Carlos got up and removed a penlight from his pocket

and shone it into the safe. "Much cash," he said, "several thousand dollars."

"He hates ATMs," Chita replied. "I get him five grand at a time from the bank, and he uses the money as needed."

"Gun," Carlos said, holding it up with a finger through the trigger guard. "Walther PPK, stainless steel, loaded."

"He has a permit for it, city and state."

"I'll bet it's not the only one he has," Carlos remarked. He flipped through the remainder of the safe's contents. "Nothing remarkable. Okay, get me out of here before we're arrested."

She put the steno pad and the keys back into the briefcase, closed it, and put it back inside the credenza.

"Aren't you going to send it to him?" Carlos asked.

"I'll do it from here tomorrow morning," she said. "It's what he would expect, so I'll use an office waybill."

They locked up and walked back to his car. "You've never been to my place," he said.

"No, I haven't."

"I think now would be a good time."

She smiled. "So do I."

44

AT THE END of a very long day, the two homicide detectives, Jensen and Reeves, who were investigating the murders at Dax Baxter's house, got into their car in the garage in the basement of the building. As they did a man dressed in black stepped from behind a concrete column, held out a black pistol equipped with a silencer, and shot Reeves in the head through the window. Then he pointed the gun at Jensen, in the passenger seat, fired twice, then put one more into Reeves.

Jensen slumped in his seat, but he was still alive, even though he was not thinking very clearly. He fumbled for the radio's microphone, clipped to the dash, then keyed it. "Mayday, mayday," he said into it. "Two officers down in police garage." Then he passed out.

CARLOS RIVERA WAS just turning into the parking lot at his building when his police radio came alive. He stopped and listened.

"How do you understand that gobbledygook?" Chita asked.

Carlos translated: two officers down in a police garage; help on the way.

"In a *police* garage?" Chita asked. "That's bold. Do you need to go there?"

"Outside my jurisdiction," Carlos said. "I'm where I need to be." He parked and took her to his apartment.

STONE WAS HAVING a brandy in bed with Ana when his cell phone rang. He looked at it, then picked it up. "It better be good at this hour, Cupie."

"I'll be brief," Cupie replied. "News has reached me on one of my grapevines that the two detectives investigating the homicides at Dax Baxter's house were shot in the garage at their building. One of them is dead, the other is critical. Happened half an hour ago."

"Any suspects?"

"None so far, but you've gotta think that it might be whoever killed the two guys at Dax Baxter's house."

"Thanks, Cupie." Stone hung up, walked into the bathroom, closed the door, and called Billy Barnett.

"Hello?"

"You know who this is?"

"I do."

"Where are you?"

"At home."

"How long have you been there?"

"Since about seven. We had dinner here."

"Two cops investigating the Dax homicides have been shot in their car, in a police building, one is dead."

Silence, then: "Weird," Teddy said.

"Some think that whoever killed the two at Dax's house may have shot the two cops. Maybe he thought they had some evidence implicating him."

"That would not be my first guess," Teddy said.

"Do you have a first guess?"

"No. Just not who they think it is."

"Right." Stone hung up. So Billy didn't do it, unless he was lying, and he had never known the man to lie. He went back to bed. "Sorry about that," he said.

"Anything important?"

"I don't know, maybe."

CARLOS PUT THE cop shootings out of his mind and concentrated on Chita. It took about ten minutes, then they both came, Chita first. She rolled on top of him. "Don't go to sleep," she said.

"I'm not sleepy," Carlos replied.

"Sex renders men unconscious," she said.

"Not me, not now."

"I'm happy to hear it."

They rested for a few minutes then did it again.

*   *   *

TEDDY AND SALLY finished the dishes and put them away.

"You're very quiet," she said.

"Something strange happened."

"What?"

"The two detectives investigating the events at Baxter's house have been shot in their car."

"When did it happen?"

"This evening, I think."

She thought about that. "We've been here all evening."

"How'd you like a little trip to Santa Fe for the weekend?" Teddy asked.

"Weekend? It's a two-day drive."

"I can borrow Peter's Mustang."

"You want to go on horseback?"

Teddy laughed. "Sorry, a Mustang is a small Cessna Jet. The flight's not much more than an hour."

"Sure. I'd like to pick up a few things at home, anyway."

"Good."

"Billy, you're not going to go after Dax, are you?"

"I doubt it. I would like to talk to him, though."

"I've got the phone number at his house there. You could call him from here," Sally said.

"It's going to be a nice weekend," Teddy replied. "Let's go to Santa Fe."

"Whatever you say," she said.

Teddy laughed. "I love the sound of that. You can say that to me anytime."

*   *   *

STONE AND ANA lay in bed, sweating, after another round of enthusiastic sex. "I've been thinking," he said.

"About sex?"

"I'm all thought out about that, for the evening, anyway. I was thinking maybe I'll fly you to Santa Fe and spend a couple of days, then we'll go on to New York for a while."

"Haven't we had this conversation before?"

"That wasn't a conversation, that was a decision, based on our earlier conversation."

"Ah, yes," she said, "I remember it well. I think that, in two or three days, I can reestablish myself with my colleagues and clients as alive and working in Santa Fe. And it's been a long time since I was in New York."

"It will be my pleasure to reacquaint you with the city," Stone said, kissing her. "Now let's get some sleep so that I'll be in shape to fly tomorrow."

45

CARLOS RIVERA WALKED into the station feeling refreshed and renewed, and confident that he and Chita Romero might have a future. As he passed the Violent Crimes squad, Lieutenant Goodwin waved him over.

"Morning, Carlos."

"Morning, Lieutenant."

"Did you hear about the two detectives from LAPD Homicide?"

"Yes, sir, I heard it on the radio last night, but I didn't get any details."

"They had just gotten into their car in the garage when somebody put two slugs into each of them."

Carlos winced.

"Reeves is dead, but Jensen survived."

"How's he doing?"

"Awake and talking. He was awful lucky that the slugs were .22s and not something heavier. They think he's going to make it."

"I'm glad to hear it," Carlos said.

"They're trying to connect it with the perp in the double at Dax Baxter's place the other night."

"I don't get that. Did Jensen get a look at the shooter?"

Goodwin shook his head. "Just a black blur, that's all."

"Why would the perp in the Baxter case want to kill the detectives investigating it? Did they have enough evidence to hang it on somebody?"

"Not a thing," Goodwin said. "Tell me, Carlos, how are you enjoying Vehicle Theft these days?"

"Less and less every day," Carlos replied.

"How'd you like a crack at Homicide?"

"I'd like that very much," Carlos said, grinning.

Goodwin looked around his squad. "I don't have anybody to partner with you right now—we've barely got our noses above water. You want to work alone?"

"How about my current partner, Joe Rossi?" Carlos asked. "He's a very smart cop."

"Yeah, he's been around long enough. Maybe a gray head on the squad wouldn't be a bad idea. Let me talk to the captain, and I'll get back to you."

"Yes, sir," Carlos said. "You can tell the captain that car thefts are trending downward, and we're underworked." He continued to his desk. Rossi was working a crossword puzzle. "Hey, Joe."

"Yeah?"

"How'd you like a move to Homicide?"

"At my age? Fat chance."

"I just had a chat with Lieutenant Goodwin." He looked up and saw Goodwin walking toward the captain's office. "It's not as crazy as it sounds."

"Well, I'm spending most of my time around here doing crosswords," Rossi said. "It would make a nice change."

Rivera's phone rang. "Sergeant Rivera. . . . Yes, sir." He hung up. "We're wanted in the captain's office."

"Both of us?"

"Both of us. Get your jacket on." They walked across the floor and knocked on Captain Fitzhugh's door.

"Come in."

Carlos opened the door; the two senior officers were seated at the captain's conference table.

"Take a seat, Carlos, Joe," the captain said.

They took a seat.

"We've got us a situation here," the captain said. "Homicide is underwater, and you've got time on your hands. Goodwin, here, has asked for you two. How would that suit you?"

"Very well indeed, Captain," Carlos said, and Joe was nodding rapidly.

"All right, we'll get your desks moved over there today."

"Something else," Goodwin said. "LAPD is short-handed in Homicide, what with Reeves and Jensen being out. They've asked us for some help, and since all my people have active cases right now, and you're the new guys, I'm going to send you over there and let you do what you can for them. They need another team, so you're on loan. Get over there and ask for Sergeant Ortega, Jensen's number two, and he'll put you to work. By the time you get back, we'll have your desks moved."

"Yes, sir." The two cops got up, saluted, and headed out.

AT THE LAPD they found Ortega, looking harassed. "You're Rivera and Rossi?" he asked.

"Carlos and Joe," Rivera said.

"You'll have to share a desk, until I can get Reeves's stuff out of there." He handed them a folder. "Here's the case file on the double homicide. Have you heard anything about it?"

"I happened to be at the morgue and the ME showed me the corpses. Very messy."

"You could say that," Orgeta replied. "We're looking for a connection between that and the shootings of Reeves and Jensen." He handed them another folder. "Concentrate on that."

"Right, Sarge." The two detectives found chairs and pulled them up to the desk. They went carefully through the two case files. A couple of hours later, Ortega wandered over. "You get through the files?"

"Yes, Sarge," Rivera said. "As far as we can tell, the only connection between the two cases is that Reeves and Jensen were working the double homicide. There's no connecting evidence to their shooting."

"Well, now you know as much about these two cases as anybody else around here," Ortega said. "I can't spare anybody else, so tomorrow morning, I want you to fly to Santa Fe and interview Dax Baxter about the homicides

at his property, and see if he'll spit up a connection between the two cases."

"Yes, sir."

"There's no direct flight to Santa Fe, so in order to
avoid overnight expenses, I've ordered a King Air from
the LAPD flight department. You're to be at Burbank
Airport at eight AM tomorrow. They'll take you there, you
do the interview, and return in the afternoon. We've made
an appointment with Baxter for you." He handed them a
slip of paper. "Here's the address. Cab it there and back
to the airport."

"Got it, Sarge," Rivera said. Ortega left them.

"I've never been to Santa Fe," Rossi said.

"I spent a weekend there a couple of years ago."

"What's it like?"

"Nice, you'll like it. It's a pity we can't make an overnight of it."

"That's my luck weighing you down," Rossi said.

"You want to know what I think about connecting
these two cases?" Rivera said.

"Okay."

"I think they've got fuck-all to do with each other.
Once we get Baxter out of the way, I think we're going
to find that this cop shooting is connected to another
case entirely, maybe some old case."

"I can't argue with you on that," Rossi said.

46

STONE AND ANA arrived at Santa Monica Airport and, almost immediately, ran into Billy Barnett in the lobby at Atlantic Aviation.

Stone and Teddy shook hands. "Headed somewhere?" Stone asked.

"We're going to Santa Fe for the weekend. Sally wants to get a few things from her house, so I borrowed your old Mustang from Peter."

"Maybe we'll see you there," Stone said. "Call me, if you've got any dead time."

"Will do," Teddy said. Sally joined him, and they walked out onto the ramp where the Mustang awaited.

Stone and Ana took off a few minutes later. As they landed in Santa Fe, Stone saw the Mustang being towed off the ramp. As he taxied in, a black car pulled onto the ramp to meet them. Half an hour later they were at Ana's house, and she was calling clients and employees.

CARLOS RIVERA AND JOE ROSSI used the GPS on their rental car to locate Dax Baxter's address. As they pulled into the drive, two large men came out of the house, and each opened a door for the detectives.

"Who are you?" one of them asked.

"We're Detectives Rivera and Rossi, BH—rather, LAPD. We have an appointment with Mr. Baxter."

The two men led them into the house, installed them on a sofa in the large living room, then went and stood by the door across the room.

Dax Baxter came in and shook their hands. They showed their badges. "What can I do for you, gentlemen?" he asked. "We'll have some coffee in a minute."

"We're here in connection with the double homicide at your house, Mr. Baxter," Carlos said. "We—"

"Hold on a minute," Baxter said, raising a warning hand. "What did you say happened at my house?"

"A double homicide," Rivera said.

"When?"

"The night before last."

"I was home that evening, and no such thing happened."

"I beg your pardon, Mr. Baxter, not at your home on

Mulholland Drive. I'm referring to a property you own in the Hollywood Hills."

"I do own a house there, but it's been empty since I moved out four years ago. A cleaning service keeps it neat, but it's all locked up."

"And you've been told nothing about what happened there?"

"No, your office called mine and made this appointment, but nobody mentioned homicide. What happened?"

Carlos opened his briefcase and showed him photographs of the two men. "The one on the left is a Russian, called Dimitri Kasov, the other is named Richard Krauss. Do you know them?"

Baxter looked at the photographs and shook his head. "Neither of them. They were murdered at my house?"

"Yes, in the garage. Both were knifed in a rather gory fashion."

"Who the hell are they, and what were they doing in my house?"

"Kasov has a reputation as a hired killer, and Krauss worked for him. We don't know what they were doing in your house or how they got in. Your cleaning lady discovered the bodies."

Coffee arrived, and a maid poured it for them. Baxter sat back in his chair and sipped. "This is a joke, right? Somebody put you up to this?"

"It's not a joke, Mr. Baxter. Have you ever had reason to want somebody killed?"

"Four or five times a week, when I'm filming," Baxter

replied. "It's like that. But I've never had any reason to hire a professional killer."

"Do you have any idea how they got access to your property?" Rossi asked.

"I don't know—maybe there's a key under the doormat. This whole business is just crazy."

"Are you acquainted with a film producer named Billy Barnett?"

"Him I know. When I was shooting here in Santa Fe a few weeks ago, he was hired as a production assistant, under an assumed name—Ted Shirley."

"Why under an assumed name?"

"Beats me. Turned out, the fellow was very good at his job. He saved me a considerable amount of money when we ran into problems on the shoot."

"Do you have any reason to wish him harm?"

"Certainly not. I just told you, he saved me money. I gave him a bonus at the end of shooting."

"Is your wife's name Geraldine Baxter?"

"Yes."

"Where is she at the present time?"

"We are estranged. She's been in a clinic for treatment of an addiction problem for several weeks."

"Are you aware that she ran down a pedestrian in Beverly Hills while driving under the influence?"

"Yes, I know about that. She had some sort of attack. No charges were brought against her."

"Did you know that the woman she ran down was the wife of Billy Barnett? Betsy Barnett?"

Baxter looked shocked. "I'm sorry, I didn't remember her name. I never made that connection."

"Do you understand why Billy Barnett might have some sort of grudge against you?"

"Why? I didn't run over his wife, and he never mentioned the incident to me when I met him."

"You never felt that he might be a danger to you?"

"Never. How is he connected to these homicides?"

"We have no evidence that he is, but we'll be talking to him."

"Well, gentlemen," Baxter said, "if you ever get this worked out, please let me know the details. It sounds as though it would make an interesting movie. Is there anything else I can do for you?"

"Mr. Baxter," Rossi said, "why do you have bodyguards here in your own home?"

"Over the years, I've disagreed with various people—artistic differences, you might say. I don't wish to be disturbed."

"Do you have security personnel at your home on Mulholland Drive?" Rivera asked.

"No."

"Then why in Santa Fe?"

Baxter appeared to be searching for a reason. "I gave a wrap party at my house when we finished filming in Santa Fe, and two people got into a fight on my patio. One of them was hospitalized, the other left."

"Who were they, and what was the fight about?"

"I'm not sure I was ever told their names, and I have no idea why they were fighting. I found the incident disturbing, though—thus, the security."

"When do you plan to return to Los Angeles, Mr. Baxter?"

"I haven't decided. I'll be working here with a writer, developing my next picture. It depends on how that goes—days, weeks, whatever it takes." Baxter stood up. "Now, if there's nothing further, gentlemen, I have to go to work."

They thanked him for his time, then left.

"HOW MUCH OF that did you buy?" Rossi asked as they got into their car.

"Not much," Rivera replied. "His surprise about the homicides seemed genuine enough, but he began to flounder as we progressed. Have we got a phone number for Barnett?"

Rossi checked the homicide file. "Yes, looks like a cell number."

"Call him, maybe we can see him after we get back this afternoon."

Rossi rang the number. "Hello, is that Mr. Billy Barnett? . . . My name is Rossi. I'm a detective with the LAPD. My partner and I would like to speak to you for a few minutes late this afternoon, if you're available." He got out a pen. "Thank you. May I have the address?" He wrote something down. "Is that in Malibu? . . . Oh, we're in Santa Fe, too. How about in half an hour? See you then." He hung up. "There's a stroke of luck. Barnett is in Santa Fe. I'll put the address in the GPS."

"What a coincidence," Rivera said. "I hate coincidence."

47

RIVERA AND ROSSI found the address: a small adobe house in the Eastside section of Santa Fe. Billy Barnett opened the door.

"What's the LAPD doing in Santa Fe?" Teddy asked, waving them to a seat.

"We could ask you the same question," Rivera replied.

"My girlfriend owns this house. She's been living with me in Malibu, and she wanted to pick up some of her things, so we decided to make a weekend of it."

"Did you drive?"

"No, we borrowed a friend's airplane."

"And we borrowed the LAPD's airplane," Rossi said.

"You haven't told me why you are in Santa Fe," Teddy said.

"We came to question a Mr. Dax Baxter, whom I believe you know," Rivera said.

"I do," Teddy said with a grimace.

"Not your favorite person, I gather."

"Not anybody's favorite person," Teddy replied. "Though I do have to thank him for introducing me to my girlfriend. We both worked on a film of his here."

"I believe you're also acquainted with a Dimitri Kasov," Rivera said.

Teddy shook his head. "Doesn't ring a bell."

"It's our understanding that you and Mr. Kasov had a conversation during which knives were employed."

"Ah, is *that* his name?"

"It is."

"It wasn't a very long conversation," Teddy said. "No introductions were made."

"When you met Mr. Kasov at Mr. Baxter's house, were you anticipating an attack?"

"I was given a warning before the party."

"Who warned you?"

"A member of the film crew told me that Baxter had hired a Russian to kill me. I went to see Baxter about it, and he denied it, but I was wary when I went to his house."

"So you were carrying a knife?"

"It was a legal one, five-inch, fixed blade."

"How did you happen to know how to use it?"

"I was given some instruction in self-defense when I was a young man in the service." He didn't mention which service.

"Had you any occasion to hone those skills in the years since?"

"No. Fists, a couple of times, no knives."

"Would you describe yourself as a combative man, Mr. Barnett?"

"I am a peaceable person, who has, on widely separated occasions, had cause to defend myself. I expect you gentlemen have, as well."

"Mr. Barnett, I believe you recently lost your wife."

"That is so. She was run down by a drunk driver in Beverly Hills."

"I recall the case," Rivera said. "Do you know the name of the person who ran her down?"

"I suppose I was told, but I don't remember it. I've made a great effort to put that event behind me."

"Was she prosecuted?"

"I don't believe so. I was told that she had some sort of medical episode, blacked out."

"Are you aware that she is the wife of Dax Baxter?"

Barnett looked at him for a long moment. "I was not."

"So you don't bear a grudge against Mr. Baxter?"

"Why would I do that? He didn't run down my wife."

"Is it possible that Mr. Baxter believed that you had a grudge against him, and that you planned to harm him?"

"I don't know, he didn't mention it on the occasion when we met. Incidentally, that was the only occasion on which we met."

"Do you know whether Mr. Baxter has paranoid tendencies?"

A woman's voice behind them said, "I can answer that."

"Come in, Sally," Teddy said. "These are Detectives Rivera and Rossi. Gentlemen, this is Sally Ryder, whose home this is."

"How do you do," Rivera replied. "You were saying, Ms. Ryder?"

"Dax Baxter was well known among the film crew to be a paranoiac. He had a very thin skin, and he employed two large men to protect him on the set."

"Protect him from who or what?"

"Who knows?"

"Mr. Barnett," Rossi said, "do you think it's possible that Mr. Baxter sent Mr. Kasov to see you a second time?"

"I'm under the impression that the Russian gentleman was hospitalized after our encounter, and I think it's unlikely that he would be well enough for another such encounter."

"I don't think you need worry about him," Rivera said. "He was murdered the night before last at a house owned by Dax Baxter."

Teddy shrugged. "Well, I suppose that is a hazard associated with the man's trade. Did Baxter kill him? He doesn't seem like the type, frankly."

"That remains undetermined at this time. When he was killed, Mr. Kasov was in the company of another man, his employee, whose name was Richard Krauss. Do you know him?"

"No, I've never heard of him."

"He was a rather large man. Perhaps Mr. Kasov felt he would make up for his own temporary disability."

Teddy shrugged. "I have no such knowledge."

"Mr. Barnett," Rivera said, "is it possible that Mr. Baxter sent Mr. Kasov and Mr. Krauss to kill you, and that you were again required to defend yourself?"

"When did you say these killings occurred?"

"The night before last," Rivera said.

"Sally and I had dinner after work at a restaurant about a mile from my house. We came home after that and remained there for the rest of the evening."

"That is so," Sally echoed.

"And if Mr. Baxter still wants to kill me, he's beyond paranoid, he's crazy."

The doorbell rang, and Sally went to answer it, and a couple came in. "Gentlemen," she said to the detectives, "this is Stone Barrington."

"And this is Ana Bounine," Stone said. "Billy Barnett and Sally Ryder."

"Stone," Teddy said, "these gentlemen are Detectives Rivera and Rossi from Los Angeles."

"Billy," Stone said, "do you need an attorney?"

Teddy laughed. "No, I don't think so." He turned to the detectives. "Gentlemen, we have plans for dinner, so if there's nothing else . . ."

"Nothing else at this time," Rivera said.

Stone spoke up. "Have you come all the way from L.A. to speak to Mr. Barnett?"

"No, we came to speak to someone else. Mr. Barnett just happened to be in town."

"May I ask who you came to speak to?"

"It was Dax Baxter," Teddy said. "Apparently they think Baxter is trying to kill me."

"From what I've heard of Mr. Baxter," Stone said, "I wouldn't be surprised."

"We've been hearing that a lot," Rivera said. "Thank you for your time, Mr. Barnett. Perhaps we'll talk another time, in Los Angeles."

"Anytime," Teddy said. "You can reach me at Centurion Studios. And good luck in your investigation."

The detectives left, and Teddy got everyone a drink.

"You sure you don't need a lawyer, Billy?" Stone asked.

"Sounds to me that Dax Baxter is the one who needs the lawyer," Teddy said.

48

THEY HAD DINNER at Geronimo, on Canyon Road, and dined on tenderloin of elk and a fine cabernet. After dinner, the women excused themselves.

"Billy, what's going on with the cops?" Stone asked.

"You may remember that I was attacked by a man at Dax Baxter's wrap party a few weeks ago?"

"Ah, yes. The Russian."

"One and the same. The detectives came to Santa Fe to interview Baxter, then they phoned me. Since I was here, they came to see me, too."

"What is their theory of the case?" Stone asked.

"They seem to have two notions. One, that Dax killed

them or hired someone to; the other that Dax hired them to kill me, and that I defended myself."

"I'm reliably informed that they were both knifed in a particularly gory fashion."

"As I said to the cops, a hazard of their trade."

"Do you have an alibi for that time?"

"They said it was the night before last. Sally and I had dinner at a local restaurant. I suppose I have a credit card receipt somewhere. We went home and stayed there."

"I'm relieved to hear it."

"I guess I'm relieved that they weren't killed at a time when I didn't have an alibi."

"Here come the ladies," Stone said. "Don't mention this to Ana, she'll hear about it soon enough on her personal grapevine, which is extensive."

TEDDY AND SALLY were in bed by eleven; Teddy dressed and left the house before midnight, while she slept soundly. He found a sharp boning knife in her kitchen and took her binoculars from a peg in the living room.

He drove out to Tano Road, and using the dashboard GPS map, found a road roughly parallel to Dax's. He parked the car in someone's driveway and stood facing Dax's house, about a hundred yards away. He leaned on a fender and viewed the property through the binoculars.

There was perimeter lighting, so he had a good view. Two men stood on a porch near the front door, and as they waited, a car drove up and two other men got out. All four were tall and beefy. They exchanged a few words, then the first pair walked away from the main house to a guesthouse, and Teddy saw lights come on there. The replacement shift went inside. With four guards on the property, it seemed like an unpromising time for him to visit Dax. Teddy got back into the car, and before he could turn on his lights, another car drove past him with its headlights off. Very dark out here, he thought; no place to drive without lights.

He got out of the car and walked down to the road. The other car had parked perhaps twenty yards away, at the roadside. The door opened, illuminating the interior, and Teddy got a good look at the man's back. He had a completely bald head and, while not particularly tall, looked muscular, dressed in tight-fitting black clothes. He was wearing a leather shoulder holster, but Teddy couldn't see the weapon. The car door closed, and the man stood next to it, using binoculars to look at Dax's house.

Well, Teddy said to himself, that makes two of us.

Then the man left the road and, using a small flashlight, began making his way down the hill toward the Baxter residence. Teddy got his binoculars and watched the man's progress. It occurred to him that he looked like someone Teddy had seen before, but he couldn't get a look at the man's face.

The man reached Dax's road and stopped, clearly casing the house. He walked down the road for fifty yards or so, while Teddy kept him in sight with his binoculars. Finally, he crossed the road and, staying outside the perimeter lighting, made his way around the house and disappeared.

Teddy wondered if there was some sort of perimeter

alarm. He hadn't heard anything, so probably not. Lights went off at the rear of the house, and everything got quiet.

DAX BAXTER HAD taken a sleeping pill and was becoming groggy. He switched off the lights, got into bed, and settled in for the night. He didn't know how long he had been asleep when he was awakened by pressure on his neck, and something sharp against his skin.

"Wake up," a man's low voice said. Then he was slapped twice, bringing him to consciousness.

"Do you know who I am?" the man asked.

"No," Baxter replied. "But you'd better leave. There are armed guards in the house."

"Not very good ones," the man replied, switching on a reading light and turning it on its gooseneck so that it illuminated Dax's face and made it impossible to see the man's face. "My name is Kasov. Does that sound familiar?"

"Dimitri?" Dax asked, confused.

"Dimitri is dead," the man said. "My name is Sergei, and I am his brother, younger by one year. Did you kill my brother, or order him killed?"

"No, no," Dax said. "I hired Dimitri to kill a man called Billy Barnett. It was Barnett who killed him and the other man, Krauss. He also may have shot two police detectives."

Sergei shook his head. "I killed the two cops. Dimitri always told me that if anybody ever killed him it would be the cops, so when I heard, I got angry and killed a couple of cops. Who is this Billy Barnett?"

"He is a man who wishes me dead," Dax replied.

"If this Barnett could kill Dimitri with a knife, then you are in great danger."

"That's why the guards are here."

"Where is this Barnett?"

"He lives in Malibu, in Los Angeles."

"What is his address?"

Dax gave it to him from memory. "He works at Centurion Studios."

"The movies? Like you?"

"Yes, but at a different studio. How did you find me?"

"You are an amateur. I can find you anywhere. You might remember that."

"I want to hire you," Dax said. "I will give you one hundred thousand dollars to kill Billy Barnett and his girlfriend, Sally Ryder, who lives with him. I don't care how you do it, as long as it can't be traced to me."

"Your interests seem to coincide with mine," Sergei said. "Give me fifty thousand now."

"I have twenty-five thousand in the house, but I can see that you get more."

"Give it to me."

Dax got slowly out of bed, went into his dressing room and opened the safe. He stuffed the money into a laundry bag and handed it to the man. "How can I get in touch with you?"

The man handed him a cell phone. "Press one to dial me, and leave a message. I will call back on this phone."

"Good," Dax said. "When can you do it?"

"First, you will give me the other twenty-five thousand, then I will kill both of them, and you will pay me the other fifty thousand, yes?"

"Yes," Dax said. "I'll arrange to have the other twenty-five thousand delivered anywhere you say in L.A."

"I will tell you where."

"One other thing," Dax said.

"Yes?"

"Before you kill them, tell them you're from me. And kill the girl first, while he watches."

"Go back to bed," the man said, then he left the room.

Dax got back into bed and waited for the pill to work.

TEDDY WATCHED AS the man appeared from around the corner of the house, then made his way back to his car. He turned around and drove back toward Santa Fe, this time with his headlights on, the dash lights revealing his face.

Now Teddy knew why he looked familiar. He bore a strong resemblance to Kasov—a familial resemblance, perhaps. There seemed to be only one reason why the man would seek out Dax's Santa Fe house, then visit him in the middle of the night. He had a very strong intuition that Dax Baxter was now dead.

He started the car and drove back to Sally's house.

49

TEDDY AWOKE TO the smell of bacon and coffee, and shortly, Sally came into the bedroom with a tray. They propped themselves up in bed and watched the morning news show.

"I woke up sometime after midnight and you were gone," Sally said.

"I took a stroll."

She looked at him askance. "Really?"

Teddy smiled and kissed her on the forehead. "Nothing to worry about."

"Frankly, I thought you'd gone to Dax Baxter's house and killed him."

Teddy just laughed. He switched to the local news, but Baxter's name was not mentioned.

"I'm going to walk over to La Fonda and get us a *New York Times*," she said. "Can I bring you anything?"

"Maybe the Santa Fe paper, as well."

"Okay."

She left and he tried the Albuquerque stations: still no mention of Baxter. The man had four guards in or around the house; surely one of them would have discovered his body by this time.

Sally came back after a few minutes with the papers, and he read the *Santa Fe New Mexican* first. No mention, but they had probably gone to press after dinner sometime, so they wouldn't have the story until tomorrow.

"I saw Hal Palmer at the hotel," she said. "You remember, the writer on Dax's Western?"

"Sure, I remember him."

"He's here to work with Dax on the screenplay for his new film—expects to be here for at least a couple of weeks."

"Better him than me," Teddy said.

While Sally cleaned up the breakfast dishes, Teddy turned on the radio and tried a couple of stations. Nothing. Something was wrong, here: the guards would have discovered Baxter's body and called the police, and somebody at the police department would have leaked the news. Then he had a chilling thought. Dax was not dead.

If the man had gone there to kill him, he must have blamed Dax for Kasov's death. But Dax must have talked him out of it—probably bought him off. It's what Dax would have done. What's more, he would have told the man that Billy Barnett was Kasov's killer. Moreover, he would have tried to hire the man to kill him.

Teddy realized he had made a big mistake the night before. He didn't kill Baxter because he believed him already dead, and he had missed an opportunity to follow the killer and deal with him, as well.

Sally came back into the bedroom. "Sweetheart," he said, "did you mention to Hal Palmer that I'm in Santa Fe, too?"

"I believe your name came up. Hal said to say hi to you."

Hi, indeed, Teddy thought. As soon as Hal Palmer was in Dax's company he might very well mention that he and Sally were in town, and that would put the fear of God into Dax. Shortly, he would have even more security in place.

STONE ANSWERED HIS cell phone over breakfast at Ana's. "Hello?"

"Hi, Stone, it's Billy."

"Good morning, Billy."

"I want to ask a favor of you."

"Of course."

"Can you arrange for Sally and me to stay at the Arrington for a few days? I want to have my house painted, and I don't want to be there for that."

"I can do better than that, Billy. You and Sally can use my house on the grounds. There's a staff there, and they'll take good care of you."

"That's very kind of you," Teddy said.

Stone gave him directions to the house. "I'll let the staff know and arrange for security passes for the grounds. When will you arrive?"

"Tonight."

"They'll be expecting you."

Teddy thanked him again and hung up. He got dressed and found Sally. "We have to fly back this afternoon, but I've arranged a little vacation for us in L.A. We won't be going back to the house for a few days."

"Where will we be staying?"

"That will be a surprise," Teddy said.

CARLOS RIVERA PICKED up Joe Rossi at his house.

"Where are we headed?" Joe asked.

"In the direction of Malibu," Carlos replied. "Do you know a clever locksmith?"

"Sure, in Santa Monica."

"Is he good enough to make some keys from tracings?"

"I don't see why not," Joe said.

They drove to the shop in Santa Monica and found the locksmith. "I want a couple of keys made," Carlos explained to the man, "but I don't have the originals. I made a tracing of them, though." He showed him the drawings he had made.

"Sure, I can do that," he said. "It'll take me an hour or so, because it's all handwork, it's not like duplicating an existing key."

They left the tracings with him and found a place for breakfast nearby. "Okay," Joe said when they had ordered. "You want to tell me what this is about?"

"I wish I could, but I don't know."

"Make sense, Carlos."

"Okay, I had an opportunity to get into Dax Baxter's briefcase, and I found some keys there, and I traced them."

"What are they keys to?"

"Beats me. I guess we'll have to try every lock in L.A."

"Okay, why are we headed toward Malibu?"

"Dimitri Kasov lived in that trailer park on your right, past Sunset."

"Up on the hill?"

"Right. I'd like for us to take a look at it. We won't need a warrant, it's an extension of the crime scene, and the owner is dead."

"And what do you hope to find?"

"I don't know."

"Jesus, for a cop, you don't know anything, do you?"

"Don't you like surprises, Joe?"

"Only on my birthday."

THEY PICKED UP the keys and drove out to the Pacific Coast Highway. The trailer park was not a run-of-the-mill place: people had landscaped their plots, and many of the cars parked there were expensive—BMWs and Mercedeses. Carlos checked his notes for the address, and they pulled into a little yard, where half a dozen cars were parked.

"Jeez," Joe said, "the yellow one is a '71 Pontiac GTO. That would be worth some money at auction."

"You can mention that to Kasov's heirs, if such exist."

They got out of the car and approached the entrance to the trailer, which was a big Airstream.

"I saw something move inside," Joe said. "Maybe Kasov does have heirs."

There was a doorbell, and they rang it.

50

JOE WAS GETTING IMPATIENT. "Why don't you just kick it in?" he asked.

"You said you saw somebody in there. What if it's a burglar? What if he's armed?"

"Suddenly, you're a pessimist," Joe said. "Why don't you try the keys?"

"What keys?" Carlos knocked loudly. "Police! Open up!"

"The ones you just had made. They came from Dax's briefcase—maybe he owns the trailer."

Carlos looked at the two keys and held up one. "This is a Yale key, and that's a Yale lock."

"Then they were made for each other," Joe said. "Try it."

Carlos inserted the key and tried to turn it. Nothing.

"Jiggle it at little, he said it might be rough."

Carlos jiggled it and pulled out the key just a hair. The lock turned.

Joe pulled his weapon. "Me, first," he said, opening the door. As he did, the glass in the door exploded and Joe fell inside, blood coming from his neck.

Carlos drew his weapon and dropped to one knee, then peered around the door. There was a *pfft* noise, and something struck the doorjamb above his head. He held his pistol out and sprayed the interior of the trailer, then he heard a door slam at the other end. He checked Joe's pulse. He was moving and had clamped a hand to his neck. He stepped over Joe and ran toward the other end of the trailer, where he found a rear door flapping in the breeze. He stuck his head out and saw no one. He went back to Joe. "Are you alive?"

"It seems so," Joe replied, sitting up, his hand still holding his neck. Carlos moved his hand and found a neat wound, oozing blood. He put his handkerchief there. "Hold this in place, and keep pressure on it." He got out his cell phone.

"Don't call nine-one-one," Joe said. "I don't want an ambulance and all that. Just drive me to the nearest emergency room."

"You're sure?"

"It was a .22. I'm sure I'm not mortally wounded."

"Okay." Carlos got him outside, then closed the door and locked it with his key, then he kicked it open. "Let's go," he said.

Carlos helped Joe to the car, left the trailer park, and drove back toward Sunset.

"UCLA," Joe said. "There's a hospital there."

"Right." They were at the ER entrance in minutes. "Don't you move, Joe, I'm going to get some help." He went inside and stepped up to the desk.

"Fill out this form," the woman behind it said.

"I'm a police officer," he said, showing his badge. "I've got a cop outside in the car with a gunshot wound."

She picked up a phone and pressed a button. "Code one at the ER entrance," she said, then hung up. An orderly came through the swinging doors. "Where is he?"

"Just outside, in the car," Carlos said.

Joe walked in, holding the handkerchief to his neck. "Where do you want me?" he asked.

THEY MADE CARLOS wait outside the treatment room for nearly half an hour before an impossibly young girl in scrubs came out. "Detective Rivera?"

"That's me."

"I'm Dr. Reiner." She held up a plastic zipper bag containing what appeared to be a .22 caliber short slug. "I thought you might want this for a souvenir."

Carlos put it in his pocket. "Where's my partner?"

"Right here," Joe said, walking through the door with a bandage on his neck.

"He didn't need to go to surgery. The bullet was just under his skin. Good thing it wasn't a .38 or a 9mm. He's got a couple of stitches, and he's had an injection of an antibiotic and a prescription for a pain pill. Take him home and force him to rest." She walked away.

"So?" Joe said. "Let's get out of here." Back in the car he said, "It was a .22 with a silencer. Let's get it to ballistics."

"That's what our two predecessors were shot with. Check on the silencer. I heard the second shot." He made a U-turn and headed for LAPD headquarters.

An hour later they stood in a lab and looked at a large computer screen that had photos of two bullets. "The top one came out of your partner," the technician said. "The bottom one came out of Reeves."

"Send your report to the captain," Carlos said, then turned to Joe. "Do you want me to take you home and put you to bed?"

"I'll outlast you," Joe said.

"Let's go back to that trailer. I want to see it without the reception committee."

Back in the car, Carlos said, "You're a tough old bird."

"High school football," Joe replied.

"What are you talking about?"

"I had a coach who was a nut on every team member being fit. He particularly worried about spinal injuries, so we had to do this exercise every day where you lay on your back and dug in your heels, arching your back until all that was touching the ground was your heels and the top of your head. Then he yelled at you to keep pushing, until your neck bent back and your nose touched the ground."

"That's impossible," Carlos said.

"It was on the first day, and the second, but on the third day I made my nose touch the ground. We did that every day for the rest of the season, and we all developed necks like bulls. That's why my shirt size is eighteen and a half inches today. I have to order my shirts off the Internet. I thought all that muscle might come in handy in a car wreck or something, but I never thought it would stop a bullet."

THEY ARRIVED BACK at the trailer, and this time Carlos went in first, his weapon drawn. He cleared the place. "Neat as a pin," he said.

Joe sat down on the sofa. "You check the desk. I'm gonna rest, like the kid doctor said."

Carlos began rifling the drawers and held up a checkbook. He leafed through the index. "Balance of a hundred and thirteen grand," he said.

"Somebody's been paying him big for something," Joe replied. "What's his name?"

"Dimitri Kasov."

"The Russian?"

"One and the same."

"Anything else in there?"

"A printout of an investment account," Carlos said, holding up the document. "He's got nearly a million dollars in stocks."

"I would have thought a hit man would deal in cash and bank it offshore," Joe said, "not leave a paper trail a mile wide."

"Maybe he banked offshore, too," Carlos replied. "Maybe this is just the cherry on the sundae, what the IRS sees."

Joe got up from the sofa, walked to the desk, and picked up a framed photo of a woman and two young boys, maybe six and seven. "There's our shooter," he said, pointing to the younger boy. "The older one looks like the Dimitri I saw on the autopsy table."

Carlos looked at the younger boy. "So what's your name, kid?"

Joe pulled the back off the picture frame, took out the photograph, and turned it over. "Stamped Miller Studios," he read. "Then in ink, 'Olga Kasov, Dimitri and Sergei.'"

"You ever heard of a Sergei Kasov?"

"Nah," Joe said, "but I never heard of a Dimitri Kasov until recently."

"We should go see the captain," Carlos said.

51

CARLOS AND JOE sat in Captain Regan's office; Lieutenant Grover, who commanded the LAPD Homicide squad, sat in, too.

"You got the ballistics report?" Carlos asked.

"I did. Now we need to put a name to the bullet."

"I think we've got that," Carlos said, handing him the photograph from Kasov's trailer. "Look at the back."

The captain did, then showed it to Grover.

"The guy in the trailer has to be the younger one, Sergei," Carlos said.

"He's our cop killer," Grover said.

"Pull out all the stops on this Sergei," Regan said. "Do we have a motive for the cop shootings?"

"We've got the connection," Carlos said. "Dimitri and Sergei are brothers. As for the motive . . ."

"It's bizarre that this Sergei would shoot the cops who were investigating his brother's death."

"It certainly is," Carlos agreed. "Maybe he wants to find the killer himself, before the cops can."

"That's thin," Grover said, "but I think it works."

"Do we have a sheet on Sergei?" the captain asked.

"No, sir," Carlos replied. "We tried the FBI database, too. There's nothing on him. Never served in the military, either."

"He's gotta live somewhere," the captain said. "Check the utility databases—everybody has an electric bill."

"Already done, sir. You want an opinion, I think the guy lives in motels and rooming houses and pays cash. He doesn't have any credit cards, either, unless they're in another name. He doesn't own a car registered in the United States. There's no record of a cell phone, either, but he'd need one to do business. How else could his customers get in touch?"

"Good point. How did Dimitri's customers contact him?"

"He had the usual paper trail of a solid citizen—property, utilities, bank account, investment account. He had half a dozen cars registered in his name. He wouldn't be hard to find for anybody who had his name."

"There's another possibility on Sergei," Joe Rossi said. "He could have been living and working in another country—Russia, the Ukraine, Eastern Europe."

"Then check with Interpol," the captain said. "Check with immigration, too, see if he entered the country recently." He handed back the photograph. "See if the FBI can use their software to age the kid. Maybe we'll get something we can circulate."

"We're on it, sir," Carlos replied. The meeting broke up, and he and Joe went to work.

TEDDY SET DOWN the Mustang at Santa Monica Airport as the sun was sinking into the Pacific, then taxied to the hangar, chocked the airplane, and transferred their bags to his car, parked in the hangar.

"So, where are we vacationing?" Sally asked, as they drove out of the hangar, leaving the airplane to be put away by a lineman with a tractor.

"Wait and see," he said. He took the I-10, then the I-405 to Sunset Boulevard, then drove to Stone Canyon Road and turned left, passing the Bel-Air Hotel. A couple of minutes later they were at the gate to the Arrington.

"Ah, yes, Mr. Barnett," the guard said, looking at his driver's license. "They're expecting you at the Barrington cottage. Do you know the way?"

"I do, thanks." He drove up the hill and came to a stop in front of the house.

"Cottage?" Sally asked, looking at the house.

"That's what very rich people call big houses," Teddy said. A butler appeared, introduced himself, and got their things inside and upstairs.

"All the comforts of home," Sally said, looking around their spacious room. "Who does this belong to?"

"Stone Barrington," Teddy said. "We had dinner with him last night, remember?"

"Of course I do. Is there a pool?"

"A very nice one," Teddy replied.

"Do I need a swimsuit?"

"Take a robe, just in case. Once there, you're safe, except from me."

Sally started peeling off clothes.

CARLOS AND JOE sat at a large computer monitor with a split screen. On one side was an Interpol photograph of Sergei Kasov; on the other, the FBI aging of his childhood photo.

"Pretty good software, huh?" Joe said. "Without the hair, he's a ringer for the real guy."

"Born Leningrad, thirty-nine years ago," Carlos read from his sheet. "Educated in a private academy associated with the KGB, then on to their college. A full-fledged agent from the age of twenty-one until the breakup of the Soviet Union, then a freelancer."

"Good training for a killer," Joe replied. He typed the name into the Immigration & Naturalization database. "Entered the country at L.A. International a week ago," he read. "He must have been staying with his brother."

"There's a team out there now, taking apart the trailer."

"He must have gotten the gun from Dimitri. He could be driving one of his cars, too. Run Dimitri's name through the DMV database and see if there's a car missing from his collection."

Joe did some typing. "Here we go—a two-year-old Prius. Lots of those in L.A. I'll add the plates to the APB."

"This guy's not going to last long," Carlos said. "We've got him bracketed, now."

*   *   *

TEDDY AND SALLY had a good dinner in Stone's study and drank some wine. "You sleepy?" she asked him.

"Not yet. You go on to bed, I'll be up in a while." He gave her time to get to sleep, then he went outside, got into the car, and drove out to Malibu. He drove slowly past his house, and a couple of doors down, he saw something he had never seen in his immediate neighborhood: a BMW motorcycle. He drove down to the Village, then turned around and drove back. The motorcycle was gone. He made a U-turn and went back to the restaurant where he and Sally had dined a few nights ago. He parked in their lot, then went into the restaurant and out onto their deck, from which there was access to the beach.

He walked down the beach toward his house. He walked past it, looking for unwanted company, but saw only one couple walking barefoot on the wet sand. Then he doubled back. He pressed a hidden switch under his deck, and a staircase came down. At the bottom he took off his shoes and climbed the stairs. He paused where his head was level with the deck, then stood, watching and listening for any sign of anybody at his property. He saw and heard nothing.

Satisfied, he went up the stairs and let himself in through the sliding door.

CARLOS E-MAILED THE PHOTO and sheet to Regan and Grover. "The picture will help with the APB. All we have to do now is wait for him to be picked up."

52

THE LIVING ROOM was well lit by moonlight, and he stood in a corner shadow while he listened for any sign of movement in the house. He slowly closed the sliding door and waited for another couple of minutes.

Finally, he took a small flashlight from a kitchen drawer and stepped out of the living room into a hallway. He stopped and listened again, then proceeded with caution into the master bedroom, checking the closet. He pushed aside the clothes on the rack and opened the wall safe. He took out some cash, then slipped into a shoulder holster and stuck a small 9mm pistol into that, checking it first for a full magazine. He pumped a round into the chamber, then set the safety, then he chose a lightweight jacket and slipped it on to cover the weapon. He slipped on the loafers holding the two short knives, then stuck an extra couple of pistol magazines in a hip pocket. Teddy wasn't sure why: he had never required more than two rounds to resolve a situation.

Thus fortified, he let himself out the sliding doors, set his other shoes inside, locked up, and went back down to the beach. Still watching the shadows for company, he made his way back to the restaurant and his car. The BMW motorcycle he had seen earlier was in the parking lot, near the road.

He had a good look at the machine, then went back inside the restaurant, stood near the door, and had a look around. It was a fairly busy night and he took time to check the occupants of each table, then turned his attention to the bar. His scan stopped on a leather jacket, worn by a thickly built bald man whose back was turned as he chatted to a woman on the stool beside him.

Teddy walked to the end of the bar and took a seat; the bartender recognized him and started toward him. Teddy held a finger to his lips, and the bartender nodded.

"Evening, sir. Can I get you something?" the bartender said softly.

"Macallan 12 on the rocks," Teddy whispered, and the drink was brought. He checked the mirrors around the bar, but he could not see the man's face; he'd just have to wait for him to turn around. He placed a twenty-dollar bill on the bar in anticipation of his departure and waited. As he did, the woman holding the man's attention said something to him, then got up and walked toward the ladies' room.

Teddy stared at the back of the man's head. Then, slowly the bald head turned toward Teddy and his eyes locked onto him. Both men held their gaze without flinching. Both knew immediately who they were looking at.

Teddy hoisted a foot and slipped a knife from his heel, then he got up and left the restaurant. He waited for the man to follow, but he did not. Teddy walked over to the motorcycle and quickly slashed both tires, then he got into his car and pulled out of the lot. As he did, he checked his rearview mirror and saw the man come out the front door, look around, then walk toward the motorcycle.

"Have fun with that," Teddy said aloud as he drove away.

He got back to the Arrington and was soon in bed beside Sally, who was snoring lightly.

CARLOS AND JOE were working late when the call came in.

"Rivera," he said.

"Detective, this is Dispatch. A patrol car just called in a location for the Prius you're looking for."

"Where is it?"

"In the parking lot of Malibu Village, outside the grocery store."

"Tell them not to touch it but to observe from a distance until I get there," Carlos replied. He hung up. "We've got the Prius," he said to Rossi. "Let's go."

*   *   *

DAX BAXTER GOT out of the limo in his driveway and said good night to his screenwriter, Hal Palmer. "I'll speak to you tomorrow," he said. "Sorry about the abrupt return, but there's something I've got to take care of here."

The car drove away. A car that had been following them pulled into his driveway, and Baxter used his remote to open the garage so the two men could put their car inside. He let them into the house through the garage door to the inside, and checked the alarm box for any attempted entries. None. Then he took the two men to the kitchen. "Make yourselves at home here. Take anything you want from the fridge."

"Thank you, sir," one of them said. "We'll check the house, inside and out, before we do."

Baxter went into his study and poured himself a drink, then he called Chita.

"Hello, boss."

"Hi, I'm back from Santa Fe, and I'll be in tomorrow morning, usual time."

"Got it." They both hung up.

RIVERA AND ROSSI turned into the Malibu Village parking lot and drove slowly around it once, passing the Prius. Farther along, they passed a patrol car backed into an alley between two shops, its lights out, and Rivera flashed his own lights to let them know he was there. He then parked fifty feet from the Prius, facing the market, so they could see the whole area. His cell rang. "Rivera," he said.

"Hey, it's Chita."

"Hey, there," he replied, then covered the phone. "Give me a minute, will you?" he said to Rossi.

"I'll go talk to the uniforms," Rossi replied, and got out of the car.

"You back yet?" she asked.

"Yeah, but I'm working."

"I just got a call from Dax. He's back in town, and he'll be at work tomorrow morning."

"Did he say why he came back so soon?"

"No, but he sounded pretty calm. He was very nervous when I spoke to him before I left. You want dinner here tomorrow night?"

"I'd love to, but let me call you tomorrow afternoon and confirm. We're working a case almost constantly."

"Something to do with Dax?"

"I'll tell you about it when I see you."

"Bye-bye." They hung up.

Rossi got back in the car. "They've been here about forty-five minutes," he said. "They don't know what time the car was parked."

Rivera pointed at the little theater. "Maybe he's taking in a movie," he said.

"Could be."

Dispatch called them on the radio.

"This is Rivera."

"We got another call from Malibu Village," the operator said. "A motorcycle, BMW, reported stolen from the same lot where the Prius is."

"Roger. Over and out." He replaced the microphone.

"You think our boy abandoned the Prius and stole the motorcycle?" Rossi asked.

"Possibly," Rivera said. "Let's take a ride down to Billy Barnett's house. Call the patrol car and ask them to stay on here and to apprehend the driver of the Prius if he turns up."

They got as far as the beach restaurant, when Rossi said, "BMW motorcycle on your right."

They parked and walked over to the machine. "The right plates," Rivera said.

"Well, look at that," Rossi said, pointing. "Two slashed tires."

53

TEDDY WAS NEARLY asleep when he heard his cell phone vibrate. He got out of bed, picked it up, and went into the bathroom, closing the door behind him. "Yes?"

"Mr. Barnett, I'm sorry to disturb you at this time of the evening, but—"

"Who is this?" Teddy asked.

"This is the LAPD, Detective Sergeant Rivera. We spoke in Santa Fe. As I said, I'm sorry to wake you but—"

"I'm going to hang up now," Teddy said.

"Shut up and listen to me!" Rivera said. "Your life is in danger."

Teddy sighed. "All right, tell me something I don't know."

"Are you aware that Dimitri Kasov has a younger brother?"

"Who's Dimitri Kasov?"

"You know goddamned well who he is," Rivera said. "His younger brother, Sergei, shot two LAPD homicide detectives in their car, murdering one of them, and this afternoon he shot my partner."

"Where did this happen?" Teddy asked.

"In an Airstream trailer at a trailer park quite near your house, belonging to Dimitri. So he's in your neighborhood."

"Go on."

"He took a Prius from his brother's place, then drove it to Malibu Village and abandoned it, then stole a BMW motorcycle. We found the motorcycle in a restaurant parking lot near your house with both tires slashed. I think you slashed them."

Teddy said nothing.

"Sergei Kasov was not in the restaurant, and I believe that he may have walked down the beach to your house. Are you at home?"

"No," Teddy replied.

"That's good news. My partner and I would like to enter your house."

"I thought you said your partner was shot this afternoon."

"He was, but he was not seriously wounded. I have two questions for you. One, may I have your permission to enter your house to see if Kasov is there?"

"What's your second question?"

"If I may do that, is there some method by which I can enter your house quietly without a key?"

Teddy thought for a moment. "No, but there is a key concealed near the front door. When I was last there, I forgot to arm the alarm system."

"May I have your permission to enter your house?"

"Oh, all right, you can go inside. The key is in a fake rock, on a pile of rocks about eight feet to the right of the front door. The lock turns very quietly. The front hall leads directly to the living room, which overlooks a deck and the beach. Master bedroom is to the left, open kitchen to the right. A spare room is beyond the kitchen. Got that?"

"Yes, thank you."

"Listen to me, Detective. That man is very dangerous, and you should not go in there without serious backup."

There was no response.

"Detective Rivera?" The man had hung up. "Shit!" Teddy quickly got into some clothes, slipped on his loafers and his shoulder holster, and left the sleeping Sally there. He got into the car and aimed it at Malibu. Traffic was light at this hour: he could make it quickly, if the cops didn't give chase. He left through the main gate and turned into Stone Canyon Road, then floored the car. He had to slow to make the first couple of turns, but after turning onto Sunset Boulevard he drove as fast as he could, running every light. On the straightaways, he was topping a hundred mph.

*   *   *

RIVERA AND ROSSI parked their car three houses down from Billy Barnett's address and walked carefully down the paved road, avoiding the noise of the graveled edges. Rivera found the fake rock containing the key and moved very quietly to the front door. He put his ear to the wood panel and listened for the better part of a minute, then gave Rossi a thumbs-up and put his finger to his lips, which was unnecessary. He carefully inserted the key and slowly turned it, until he felt the bolt retract, then he opened the door a couple of inches and stood still, listening. All he could hear was the waves coming in at the rear of the house.

Both detectives drew their weapons, armed them, and entered the residence.

Rossi waited until they were abreast of the kitchen, then pointed at himself, then to the hallway leading to the master bedroom.

Rivera gave him a thumbs-up, then made a tamping motion with his free hand. *Take it easy.*

Rivera turned and assumed a combat position, aiming down the hallway toward the bedroom. He could just make out Rossi's broad back. Then he heard a muffled thump, and suddenly Rossi was running backward toward him, taking up most of the hallway.

Rivera tried to aim past him but could see nothing. Then Rossi struck him, and he fell backward into the kitchen. As he struggled to get up, he heard another thump, and it was as if someone had punched him hard in the middle of his body. He fell onto his back, his weapon pointing toward the hallway, and got off two rounds.

Then he heard a door open and, a moment later, a garage door opening. A car started and drove away from the house, burning rubber.

TEDDY TURNED FROM SUNSET onto the Pacific Coast Highway and let the Porsche have its head. He passed a couple of cars, then saw one coming toward him in time to get back into the right lane. He saw the star in a Mercedes grille as it passed, going very fast. A moment later he was at his house: the garage door was open and Sally's Mercedes convertible was gone.

Teddy wanted to give chase, but he had to get inside the house. He pulled into the garage and saw that the door into the house was open. He got out of the car, pulled the 9mm semiautomatic from its holster and flung himself into the hallway, stopped by the wall. He stood there for a moment, and he heard a moaning noise. He flipped a light switch and the living room lights came on.

One of the cops, the older one, Rossi, was lying on his back in the hallway, pumping blood through what looked like a knife wound to the chest. He took a step forward and found himself looking down the barrel of a pistol.

"Freeze!" Rivera said weakly. He was sitting on the kitchen floor, his back against a cabinet.

"It's Billy Barnett. Put the gun down."

"Help Rossi," Rivera said.

Teddy grabbed a dish towel from the kitchen counter, knelt beside Rossi, and pressed it to his chest. He picked up Rossi's hand and put it on top of the towel. "Press," he said, then turned back to Rivera.

A small hole in Rivera's shirt trickled blood. "Don't call it in," Rivera said.

"Why not?"

"You're not here, and Sergei is in your car, headed down the PCH. I think he's going to the trailer park, number 601. I fired two rounds, and I may have hit him. I'll give you as much of a head start as I can. Check on Joe."

Teddy went to Rossi and put a hand to his neck, looking for a pulse. The man stopped breathing.

Teddy sagged. He could hardly do chest compressions with that knife wound where it was. It would just pump out more blood. He turned his attention to Rivera.

"He okay?" Rivera asked.

Teddy shook his head.

"Go," Rivera said. "Kill the sonofabitch. And by the way, Baxter is back in L.A., at his house on Mulholland." He gave him the number. "Go," he said again.

Teddy turned, ran for the garage, got the car started, and went back the way he had come. If Kasov had headed for L.A. he was gone. His only chance of catching up to him was the trailer park, if that was where he was going.

54

RIVERA SAT NEXT to his dead partner. He reached out and held his hand. "It was my fault, Joe," he said. "I should have gone in there." He looked at his watch; he had to give Barnett five minutes, anyway. Instead, he found his phone and called Chita.

"Carlos?"

"I'm sorry to wake you."

"I wasn't asleep."

"Listen, I'm not going to make it to dinner."

"That's okay, we'll do it later."

"It'll be a while. I got shot."

"Carlos!"

"Don't worry, I'm going to be okay. An ambulance is on the way now, be here in a minute."

"Where will they take you?"

"I don't know, maybe UCLA hospital."

"I'll be there," she said.

"Gotta run," he replied.

"I'll be there." They both hung up.

Carlos pulled on the cord of the land line until the telephone fell to the floor, then he dialed 911.

"Nine-one-one. What is your emergency?" She sounded very young.

"Two officers down, one stabbed, one gunshot wound." He gave her the address.

"Stay on the line, Officer, while I call it in."

"Okay." He could hear her using the radio.

"They're on the way," she said. "You stay with me. Talk to me."

"What's your name?"

"Emma."

"I'm Carlos."

"Are you bleeding a lot, Carlos?"

"Not a lot. I think it was a .22. Don't worry, I'll make it. What hospital will they take me to?"

"I don't know, but I'll hear after they pick you up."

"Do me a favor—call this cell number." He gave her Chita's cell. "Tell her which hospital I'm going to. She's on the way to UCLA now. I don't want her to go to the wrong hospital."

"How's your partner doing?"

"He didn't make it," Carlos said. "Nothing . . . I could do for him."

"Anybody else I can call for you?"

"No, nobody else. I can hear the ambulance now, so you can go back to work."

"I'll wait until they're with you."

He heard doors slamming and people running. "They're here," he said. "Thanks." He hung up and passed out.

TEDDY MADE THE LEFT turn into the trailer park, then eased off the throttle; he didn't want to make any more noise than necessary. He pulled over to the side of the road, got a small flashlight from the glove compartment, got out of the car, and began trotting up the drive, unholstering the 9mm. Up ahead, he could see the rear of the Mercedes protruding from a driveway, and as he approached it, he saw that the driver's door was open, and the car was still running.

He hoisted a foot and slid a knife out of the heel, holding it in his left hand. The trailer door was open, and a light was on. He heard a man's voice. "Now you listen to me, Baxter," he was saying. "I'm at Dimitri's trailer, and I've taken a bullet. No! Don't call an ambulance! There's a doctor named Schweitzer, near the trailer park. Do you have his number? Call him and get him over here now. Tell him to bring an IV, some Lidocaine and antibiotics. He'll need surgical stuff, have some stitching to do. I'll need blood, type O. You got that?"

Teddy knelt and peeped around the doorjamb. Kasov was sitting at a desk, and he was wearing a shoulder holster with a weapon in it. He could see the silencer protruding from the bottom. Good.

"Don't you worry about Barnett," Kasov was saying.

"He is a dead man. Call Schweitzer!" He hung up, and he was panting.

Teddy stepped through the doorway, pistol out in front of him. "Good evening, Sergei," he said. The man whipped around and got a hand on the butt of his pistol. "No! Don't reach for it! I'll put one in your head."

"You are Barnett," Sergei panted. "I suppose you're going to kill me."

"That would be a great pleasure," Teddy said, "but then I'd have to explain how my bullet got into your head. No, I think I'll just wait for you to bleed out. It won't be long. Are you in pain?"

"Yes," Sergei replied. "What do you think?"

"I'm delighted to hear it. Dimitri died in great pain— bled out, just like you. Do you know why you're panting like that? It's because your body cavity is filling up with your blood, and it's pressing on your lungs."

Sergei made a prolonged groaning noise as he turned the swivel chair so that he was facing Teddy. "Doctor!" he said.

Teddy thought he was asking for a doctor, then he sensed someone standing to his left. He swung the blade in his left hand, not really aiming at anything. There was a scream, and he glanced to his left. A man was standing there with a slash across his face. He dropped a medical bag from his hand.

Sergei got to his feet and staggered toward Teddy, clawing at his holstered weapon. Teddy retreated in small steps; he didn't want to fire and then have to find the bullet. Sergei fell to his knees, then facedown. Blood oozed from around his body. He couldn't see any breathing.

Teddy went to the door and stepped over the doctor's cowering form. "If anybody asks," he said to the man, "my name is Dax Baxter. That's Dax Baxter." He left him there, still alive, and trotted back to his car. He started it, made a U-turn, and got back onto the highway, headed toward Sunset.

No need to speed now, he thought. Just take it easy.

CARLOS CAME TO with the pungent smell of ammonia in his nostrils. He was on a stretcher, being carried out of the house.

"Who did this to you, Detective?" a cop was asking. "Did you know the man?"

"Yes," Carlos said.

"What was that again?"

"Yes."

"Who was he?"

"Sergei," Carlos replied, then passed out again.

55

TEDDY CONSIDERED GOING back to his house and talking to the police, but he thought better of it. He'd leave Sally's car where it was and let the police deal with it. Back on the highway, he turned left and drove up Sunset. At the Arrington's gate he stopped.

"Evening, Mr. Barnett," the guard said. He was wearing a name tag that said Earl.

"Evening, Earl." He handed the man a hundred-dollar bill. "It's unlikely that anyone would ask, but if anyone does, I've been in my bed all night."

"Sure thing, Mr. Barnett. I'll see that the logbook jibes with that."

"Thanks, Earl, and good night." Five minutes later he slid into bed beside Sally.

She snuggled close. "I don't want to know where you've been," she said.

"I haven't been anywhere," Teddy replied, kissing her. "I've been right here beside you all night."

"Of course you have."

TEDDY'S CELL PHONE rang at seven AM. "Hello?" he said sleepily.

"Mr. Barnett?"

"Yes. What time is it?"

"Seven-oh-six," the man said. "I'm sorry to wake you so early, but this is Detective Schwartz of the LAPD. I wanted you to know that there was an incident at your home in Malibu last night. Where are you?"

"I'm staying with a friend in Bel-Air."

"That's just as well. There are still officers at your home. Two police officers were wounded there last night, one of them fatally."

"Who are they?"

"Detectives Carlos Rivera and Joseph Rossi, who is the deceased."

"Detective Rivera called me last night and said he thought there might be an intruder in my house. I told him where to find a key. I'm sorry to hear what happened."

"Detective Rivera is recovering at the UCLA Medical Center. He should be out of the hospital in a couple of days."

"I'm glad to hear it. When will your people have my house cleared?"

"This morning sometime."

"Well, I'm enjoying my friend's place, so I think I'll stay another day or two."

"May I ask where you're staying?"

"My friend has a cottage at the Arrington Hotel."

"I'm sure you'll be very comfortable. May I contact you at this number should I have any questions?"

"Of course. I'd be happy to help in any way I can."

STONE BARRINGTON WAS having breakfast at Ana's house in Santa Fe when his cell rang. "Hello?"

"Hi, Stone, it's Cupie."

"Good morning, Cupie. You're up early."

"I had a worm to catch. Listen, I thought you'd like to know that the heat seems to be off Dax Baxter. He called a few minutes ago and told me to pull my guys off him."

"Did he say what the reason was for his new confidence?"

"He said the guy who was after him is dead."

Stone's stomach lurched. "Good luck to him," he said. "Gotta run."

"See ya, Stone." They both hung up.

Stone immediately called Billy Barnett.

"Hello?"

"Billy?"

"Good morning."

"I'm relieved to hear your voice," Stone said.

"Relieved? Why?"

"I just got a call from a PI I know, and he told me you were dead."

"Let me see," Teddy said. "No, I've still got a pulse. Where did he hear that?"

"From Dax Baxter. He had four men protecting him, and he told my friend to call them off."

"Because I'm dead?"

"That's what he said."

"Listen, Stone, we're really enjoying the house."

"Stay as long as you like, Billy, and take care of yourself."

The two men hung up.

SALLY NUDGED TEDDY. "What was that about your having a pulse?"

"I do," Teddy said. "Why don't you feel around for it, just to be sure."

"Love to," she replied.

CARLOS RIVERA WOKE up with sunlight streaming through a window. Chita was asleep in a reclining chair next to his bed. He reached out and tweaked a toe.

Chita sat up, blinking. "You're awake!"

"And alive, too."

"How do you feel?"

"Surprisingly good. My chest is kind of sore."

"When they told me you had a chest wound, I nearly died," she said.

"It's not as bad as it sounds."

"You know about Joe."

He nodded. "I wasn't careful enough."

There was a knock at the door, and Rivera looked up to find his LAPD and BHPD captains standing there.

"Ah, you're awake," Fitzhugh said.

"Awake and hungry, sir," Rivera replied.

"I'll go get you some breakfast," Chita said, and disappeared into the hallway.

The two men pulled up chairs. "First of all," Fitzhugh said, "we both want you to know how bad we feel about Joe Rossi."

Carlos nodded. "Thank you, sir, both of you. I should have gone in first, but Joe got ahead of me. Any news on the perp?"

"A call came in last night from a Dr. Schweitzer, who had been called to the perp's trailer to treat a gunshot wound. He found Kasov dead—probably your bullet. We're running the ballistics now. Another man was present, who knifed the doctor—non-fatal wound."

"What other man?"

"He told the doctor his name was Dax Baxter. We've got him down at the station now, but he'll be released soon. He had four security guys sitting on him at his house, and they backed him up, said he never left. Any idea who else the guy could be?"

"No, sir."

"We were thinking, maybe, the owner of the Malibu house where you and Rossi were found. Kasov had stolen his car to make his getaway."

"Barnett? No, sir, I don't think so. We thought Sergei Kasov might be in his house. We found a stolen motorcycle abandoned nearby. I called Barnett, and he told me where to find a key."

"Where was he when you spoke?"

"At the Arrington Hotel, in Bel-Air."

"Well, he's still there with his girlfriend, and, according to her, as well as the security log, he hasn't left the property since arriving there yesterday."

"Any other suspects?"

"None."

"What kind of a doctor responds to a gunshot victim in a private home without calling nine-one-one?"

"We're looking into the good doctor. He was very well equipped to treat the victim, but he didn't get there fast enough."

"Well, I'm not unhappy that Kasov is dead, and I hope it was my bullet."

They chatted for a moment longer, then left.

Chita came back with a nurse who bore eggs and bacon. She looked at her watch. "I'd better get to work. You going to be okay?"

"You don't have to rush. I hear Dax is going to be late." He explained what had happened.

"Well, in that case," she said, "I'll beat him to Burbank." She kissed him and left.

Rivera finished his eggs, then fell asleep again. He really hoped it was his bullet that killed Kasov.

56

DAX DROVE FROM the police station back to his house, showered and changed clothes, then drove to his office.

"Morning, boss," Chita said brightly. "Good trip to Santa Fe?"

"Very good," Dax replied. "Hal Palmer is coming in at noon to work on a screenplay with me. Order us a good lunch from the commissary."

"Okay, boss."

*   *   *

TEDDY GOT A call from the LAPD later in the morning, saying that a Mercedes convertible registered in his name that had been reported stolen had been found at a trailer park on the Pacific Coast Highway, undamaged. He was told where he could recover it. He hung up. "They found your car," he said.

"I didn't know it was lost."

"I forgot to tell you. Somebody stole it last night. We'll pick it up later today at the police pound." He called the office and told them he would be out a couple more days. "If anyone calls, say that I'm not at work and you don't know when to expect me."

RIVERA GOT A CALL from Captain Fitzhugh later in the morning. "You'll be happy to know that the bullet found in Kasov matches your gun's ballistics on file."

"Thank you, sir, that's good news."

"The LAPD is very impressed with you, Carlos."

"Oh?"

"Well, in a matter of days you solved the shooting of their two detectives and shot their assailant. It was intimated to me that if you'd like to go work over there, they'd be glad to have you."

"That's very flattering, sir."

"On the other hand, Lieutenant Goodwin is up for retirement in a few months, and if you'd like to continue working here, I'd be disposed to promoting you to head of the squad."

"That sounds great, sir."

"Then you'd better start studying for the lieutenant's exam, which happens in three months."

"I'll do that, sir."

"When they release you, take a week and rest up. There'll be an inspector's funeral for Joe Rossi next week. I'll let you know the day and time."

"Thank you, sir." They hung up.

DAX BAXTER SAT at his desk. For some reason, he didn't feel as relieved as he thought he should. He Googled Centurion Studios and called the Barrington unit. "Billy Barnett, please," he said to the woman who answered.

"I'm afraid Mr. Barnett is not working today," she said, "and we don't know when he'll be in. May I take a message?"

Baxter hung up. He felt better now.

TEDDY AND SALLY drove to the LAPD pound and rescued her car, then Sally said she'd like to do some shopping, and they'd meet back at the Arrington in time for drinks. Teddy watched her drive away, then drove up to Mulholland Drive. He found Dax's house, a very large establishment, nestled on the mountainside, overlooking the city. He parked along the drive and took a stroll, taking with him a pair of binoculars from his glove compartment.

There were people there: servants, workmen, a pool guy, but he got the lay of the land. There was the large house with an attached garage, then two outer buildings that looked like guesthouses, or maybe servants' quarters.

He found a deer trail that led down from the road to the property and disturbed a large rattlesnake there.

As the sun approached the horizon, people began leaving the Baxter property, and soon the place was deserted. Teddy walked down to the house and toured the perimeter. High up on a wall he found the junction box installed by the security company. It was nice of them to label it so visibly, he thought. He found a workman's ladder and climbed up to it. Twenty minutes of careful work with his Swiss Army knife and he had the system rigged. When Baxter entered his code, the system would shut down and not come up again.

Using a pair of lock picks he had made from a hacksaw blade and tucked away in his wallet, he picked the lock of a rear door to the house and had a look around. He found the master suite and went into the dressing room and took a pair of socks from a drawer, drawing one onto each hand, then he searched the master bedroom until he found a loaded 9mm semiautomatic pistol in a bedside drawer. There was a round in the chamber, and the hammer was back. Dax wasn't taking any chances. He replaced the weapon exactly as he had found it, returned the socks to their drawer, and let himself out again.

BACK AT THE ARRINGTON he went into the kitchen of the cottage and found a pair of rubber dishwashing gloves under the sink, along with a box of large garbage bags. He tucked both items behind a book in the library, and he was having a swim when Sally arrived home, bearing shopping bags, and joined him.

"What's going to happen now?" she asked.

"We're going to take a couple of days off, then go back to work," Teddy replied.

"I take it I'm not supposed to ask."

"You shouldn't ask, if you think you wouldn't like the answer."

"Once the Dax thing is over, then you'll be done? We can live normal lives then?"

"When Dax is no longer our concern, we won't have a care in the world."

"I'll look forward to that," she said.

"I'll look forward to it, too," Teddy said.

"Have you always been like this?"

"Like what?"

"Concerned with revenge?"

"I'm not concerned with revenge in the least—only with our safety, particularly yours."

"I'm glad."

"It was careless of me to allow us to be taken so easily last time," Teddy said. "I'll see that it doesn't happen again."

"Why do I have the feeling this isn't finished?" she asked.

Teddy laughed and kissed her. "Once in a while, a woman's intuition works overtime and comes up with the improbable."

"Mine doesn't do that," she said. "I'm practically psychic."

"Sweetheart," he said, "switch it off for a little while— we'll both be happier."

57

AFTER TWO DAYS in bed, Carlos Rivera was released from the hospital, and Chita was there to meet him. She drove him to his apartment, and she sent him inside, then brought her luggage in, along with a shopping bag belonging to Carlos.

"I'm moving in with you," she said, "until you're all well."

"That's good with me," he said, kissing her.

"And no sex until the doctor says it's okay."

Carlos took her hand and led her into the bedroom. "The bullet struck my sternum, then stopped. No internal damage. The doctor has already said it's okay."

"He really said that?" she asked.

"He certainly did," Carlos said, working on her buttons.

DAX WORKED ALL afternoon with the writer, eliminating scenes and demanding new ones; adding lines to the male star's role and eliminating many from his costar. They had a drink at five, then continued for another couple of hours.

"That's it, Hal," Dax said, finally. "We've got a script. I'll get it printed out and distributed in the morning." He reached into a desk drawer, withdrew an envelope, and handed it to Palmer. "Here's your final check, along with a bonus."

Palmer thanked him profusely. "I gotta say, Dax," Palmer said, "you really know how to shape a script. I'm learning a lot from you."

"A lot of people could learn a lot from me," Dax replied, "but you're the only one listening."

"It's their loss," Palmer said.

They had another drink, and Palmer pocketed his check and went home.

CHITA MADE CARLOS DINNER. "What's in the shopping bag?" she asked. "The heavy one," she said, pointing.

"The study materials for the lieutenant's exam," he replied.

"You have to take an exam to be a lieutenant?"

"You certainly do, and it's a big one. My captain says he's going to promote me to the head of Violent Crimes when my boss retires in a few months, but I have to make lieutenant before that can happen."

"Then you'll get a raise?"

"Certainly."

"I'm due for a raise pretty soon, too. Another producer on the lot has asked me a couple of times to come work for him, but I've hesitated."

"You like working for Dax Baxter that much?"

"It's not that, it's just that Dax would view the move as disloyal, and he could make trouble for me on the lot. He's nothing if not vindictive."

"Tell him you've got a cop boyfriend with a mean streak," Carlos said, and she laughed.

STONE AND ANA were having dinner in Santa Fe, at El Nido, near her house. "Listen," she said, "this has been wonderful, but I'm not going to be able to come back to New York with you."

"Why not?" He was disappointed.

"Have you noticed that I've been on the phone, nonstop, since we got here?"

"I had noticed that," Stone said.

"Well, that's what happens when I'm out of town for longer than a day or two—my clients get mad at me because I'm not available, and my staff goes nuts trying to placate them and keep the gravy train moving."

"Did you ever consider that you might work too hard?"

"I have considered that, deeply, and after a couple more good years I'm going to sell the company and pack it in."

"Do you think you'd be happy doing nothing?"

"I wouldn't be doing nothing, I'd just be doing less. I'll have to consult with whoever buys me out, because I'm the company's prime asset, but that I can do on the phone. Then I'll come to New York."

"Sounds like a long wait," Stone said.

"The price of success," Ana said.

TEDDY LAY ON his back and stared at the ceiling. He was nearly done, he reckoned. This one more thing to do, and he could relax and enjoy the movie business again.

Keeping people from killing him and protecting Sally was hard work, and he was tired of it. The thing about that kind of tired, he remembered—it makes you sloppy, and he couldn't afford sloppiness. He ran through what he had to do again, to be sure there were no slipups. What he had to do was harder than just eliminating somebody. He had to do it so finally, so definitively that no one would come looking for him, no one would be looking for anybody to hold responsible.

He could leave no tracks.

58

DAX BAXTER DROVE HOME, exhausted. He put his car in the garage, then let himself into the house, entering the alarm code. To his surprise, instead of giving him an "accept" reply, it just went dark. He was about to call the alarm company when it came on again. Power glitch, he said to himself. He warmed up the dinner the cook had left for him and ate, then went into his bedroom and undressed for bed. He called Chita's cell number.

"Yes, boss?" she said quickly.

"Listen," he said, "tomorrow morning, print out the script that's on my computer and distribute it to production, set design, costumes, and all the other usuals."

"You sound tired, boss."

"I'm exhausted and depressed. I always feel this way when a script is finished. I'm not going to come in tomorrow, I'm just going to sleep, probably all day. I'll turn off the phones, including my cell."

"See you Monday, then?"

"Right. I'll feel better when I have some production problems to deal with. Good night." He hung up and fell into bed.

"He sounded terrible," Chita said. "I don't think I've ever heard him so down."

"I guess that's the price for his kind of success," Carlos said.

"He's not going in tomorrow. I can sleep late, if you like. You don't have to go to the office, do you?"

"I've pretty much been ordered not to," Carlos replied.

"How are you feeling?"

"A little tired. The doctor told me I might feel this way for a few days. Hospitalitis, I guess. My body doesn't believe I'm out of their clutches yet."

"Well, we'll have to see what we can do to distract you. We've got the whole weekend ahead of us."

TEDDY FAY CALLED his housekeeper. "The police have been at the house," he said, "and I'm sure they left a mess—tape all over the place, maybe some stains on the carpet. Do the best you can with all that, and we'll be home sometime over the weekend." She said she would, and he hung up.

The butler brought them dinner, and they got into bed and watched a movie. Sally fell asleep in the middle, as she often did. Teddy looked at his watch. He couldn't leave for another couple of hours, and he knew he wouldn't sleep.

AT TWO AM he got out of bed, dressed, and went downstairs to Stone's study. He removed a couple of books from their shelf and removed the items he'd placed there earlier and put them into a plastic duffel.

He left the house and walked to a spot along the fence where he knew there was a gap in the security camera coverage; he tossed his bag over the fence, then climbed over.

He walked down a path to Stone Canyon Road, down the hill for a few yards, then into an employee parking lot for the Bel-Air Hotel. He found a nineties-era, anonymous-looking car and took a minute or two to hotwire it. Then he backed out of the parking space and turned down Stone Canyon to Sunset, then up Beverly Glen Boulevard, all the way to Mulholland Drive.

The night was amazingly clear for L.A., and he saw more stars than usual. The city was a riotous grid of lights, stretching to the Pacific. He'd always loved the sight. He stopped at the Stone Canyon overlook for a while to enjoy the view and to check traffic. He saw two cars, then, for the next half hour, no traffic at all. He started the car and drove until he could see the security lights of Dax Baxter's house.

He drove a bit farther, then made a U-turn and parked

behind some scrub. He checked his pistol for a full clip, pumped a round into the chamber and engaged the safety, then he got out of the car and, using a penlight, walked until he came to the deer path down the mountain. He made his way slowly down the mountainside, and halfway down, he heard a rattlesnake, probably the one he had heard before on the path. He thought about catching it and taking it to Dax as a kind of gift, but the police probably would suspect that someone put the snake inside the house.

He continued down the steep path, until he came to the security perimeter. He knew that he wouldn't set off any alarms or cameras because he had already disabled them at the security box. Still, he walked the perimeter, checking the house for anyone still up and about, but saw no one. He found the ladder he had used before and set it up so that he could reach the control box quickly on his return.

He slipped out of his shoes, went to the rear door he had entered earlier, and let himself into the house. Then, in his thick, cotton athletic socks he padded here and there in the house to be sure he was alone with Dax.

Satisfied, he stopped outside Dax's bedroom and removed the trash bag from his duffel. With his Swiss Army knife, he cut a twelve-inch hole in the bottom for his head and two others for his arms, then pulled it over his head. He tied a handkerchief around his neck, so that he could pull it up to cover most of his face.

Thus prepared, he walked into Dax Baxter's bedroom.

59

TEDDY STOOD SILENTLY and watched the figure in bed. Baxter's chest rose and fell rhythmically, and he emitted an occasional snore. Teddy pulled up his handkerchief mask and walked over to the bedside. He pulled on his rubber gloves and slowly opened the bedside drawer, revealing the pistol.

Teddy picked up the weapon, slid back the slide far enough to be sure there was still a round in the chamber, then flicked off the safety and held the gun to Dax's temple. He didn't wake up—probably had taken a sleeping pill. He reached out with his free hand and pinched the man's nostrils shut. Dax sucked in a breath through his mouth and opened his eyes.

"Hello, Dax," Teddy said. "Remember me? Your wife killed my wife, then you covered it up. Welcome to hell." Teddy saw recognition in his eyes. He squeezed the trigger.

Dax's body twitched; blood and brain matter sprayed everywhere—over the adjacent pillow, around the bed, and back toward Teddy. Teddy picked up Dax's empty hand, put a gloved finger into the blood on the pillow and flicked it onto the hand, then he dropped the pistol onto the floor and let Dax's hand dangle over it.

Teddy made sure that none of the blood had splattered onto his socks, then he backed away from the bed and took a look around. Everything seemed to be in an order the police would find plausible. He went into the bathroom and rinsed the blood from his face, handkerchief, garbage bag, and gloves, walked back to the rear door, opened it with a clean glove, stepped outside, then shed the garbage bag and stuffed it into his duffel. He pulled off the handkerchief, then checked the doorstep for splatter and, finding none, put the handkerchief into the duffel.

He took a few deep breaths, then slipped his feet into his loafers and walked around the house to where the ladder leaned against it. Carefully, clenching his penlight in his teeth, he climbed up, restored the security box wiring to its original state, then closed it, returned the ladder to its usual place, shed the gloves, and put them into the duffel.

He made his way around the house, found the deer trail, and started up the mountainside. He was approaching the road when he heard a distant rumble growing closer. Two Harleys roared around a bend, and he ducked to the ground to avoid their headlamps. He lay there and suddenly, something struck his leg sharply like a punch. Only then did he hear the rattle and feel the sharp fangs in his left calf.

He made a grab for the snake and caught it a few inches below the head, then he grabbed it with both hands and squeezed with all his might. The animal writhed, and it was very strong; he got his legs around it to hold it still, then increased the pressure on the neck with both hands. Nearly a minute elapsed before the creature went limp.

Teddy got to his feet, hoisted his trouser leg and inspected the wound, then he went into the duffel, removed the spattered handkerchief, and used it to make a tourniquet around his leg, below the knee and not too tight. He knew the venom, if the snake had not struck a vein, would move upward in the tissue just under the skin. He checked his watch: two thirty-five. He had to move fast.

He grabbed the snake and the duffel, got back to the car, tossed the duffel onto the front seat and the snake onto the passenger floor, then started the car and drove away. Twenty minutes later he turned into the Bel-Air employees' parking lot, put it into its original parking space, and returned the ignition wiring to its original state. He grabbed the duffel and the snake and got out of the car, glancing at his watch. Nearly twenty-five minutes since the snakebite, and the pain and burning were very bad.

He got across the road and trotted up the path along

the fence until he came to the place where he had crossed before. He slung the duffel over the fence, but the snake was harder to deal with. It was about five feet long, thick and heavy, several pounds. He grasped it near the rattles, swung it around his head a couple of times and flung it over the fence. It hung up on the top.

With some difficulty, Teddy climbed over the fence, freeing the snake as he went. On the other side he stopped to rest for a moment, then made his way back toward the cottage. On the drive back he had formulated a plan, and now he executed it.

He dropped the dead snake near the pool, next to a chaise, where he had left his robe that afternoon, then he stripped off his clothes, went into the house, through the kitchen, into the laundry room. He emptied his pockets, stripped and stuffed his clothes into the washing machine, along with the garbage bag, gloves, and handkerchief, then turned on the cold water and started it, no soap.

He took his phone and trotted back to the pool area, slipping into his robe, then he called 911. His leg was swelling badly and throbbing, and he noticed that his lips were feeling numb.

"Nine-one-one. What is your emergency?"

"I've been bitten by a large rattlesnake, and I can't walk on my leg. I need an ambulance and anti-venom immediately." He gave her his name and the address of the hotel. "I'll let security at the gate know to let the ambulance in." He hung up, called the gate on the house phone on the table beside his chaise and gave them instructions. He hobbled to the pool, jumped in and made sure his body and hair were free of blood and debris, then he toweled off and called Sally's cell phone. She took three rings to answer.

"Yes, Billy?"

"I'm down by the pool," he said. "I've been bitten by a rattlesnake, badly. I've called an ambulance, and it's on its way. Get dressed, and grab some clothes for me. I'm naked."

"I'll be right there." She hung up.

Teddy got into his robe and tied it, then sat down on the chaise, leaned over the side and vomited; he was having some difficulty breathing. His cell phone rang.

"Yes?" he panted.

"Mr. Barnett?"

"Yes."

"The ambulance was delayed. They had to pick up the anti-venom from a hospital, but they're about five minutes out now. How're you doing?"

"Pain, nausea, difficulty breathing," he said.

"I'll stay on the line with you."

"No, my girlfriend is here. You can't help." He hung up and checked the time. Fifty-five minutes since the snake struck him.

Sally came running from the house, clutching his clothes, and knelt next to the chair. "Are you all right?" she asked, helping him into his underwear and trousers.

"I'm in considerable pain," he said.

"You're panting—are you having trouble breathing?"

"Yes."

"Then don't talk, just breathe." She looked at his leg. "Oh, God," she said, "it's twice its usual size."

*　　　*　　　*

THREE MINUTES LATER, the ambulance pulled up at the cottage, and Sally shouted for them. Two EMTs ran over with a stretcher.

"Anti-venom?" Teddy asked.

"Got it right here," the man replied; he was filling a syringe.

"He's in a lot of pain," Sally said to him.

"Let's get him into the wagon," he said to his partner.

"Bring the snake," Teddy managed to say. "Sally, follow in your car." Then he passed out.

60

CARLOS WAS AWAKENED by his ringing telephone. He glanced at his watch as he picked it up: just after ten; he had needed the sleep. "Hello?"

"It's Regan, downtown." The LAPD captain. "How are you feeling, Carlos?"

"Much better, sir. I had a very good night."

"If you're not up to this, tell me."

"What's up, sir?"

"We had a mass shooting in an East L.A. club last night, at least four dead and several wounded. Everybody in Homicide has pitched in, so nobody from the squad is available."

"How can I help?"

"Dax Baxter is dead. A housekeeper found him a few minutes ago, single gunshot to the head, very likely a suicide. I need a homicide detective there to confirm the details and manage the crime-scene people. Do you feel up to doing that?"

"Yes, sir, of course."

Regan gave him the address. "You'll be on your own. I'll send a crime-scene team as soon as they can shake somebody loose from the other scene."

"I'm on my way, sir."

"Don't break your neck. Baxter isn't going anywhere, and the housekeeper has been told to stay out of the bedroom."

"Got it, sir." He hung up and found Chita staring at him. "Are you really going out?"

"I have to, there's a big shooting in East L.A. and everybody else is working that."

"I'll fix you some breakfast."

"Just a muffin and coffee while I shower. And, Chita?"

"Yes?"

"You might want to call your office. Dax Baxter apparently killed himself last night."

"Well," she said, "he said last night that he was depressed."

CHITA CALLED HER OFFICE and broke the news to Gloria. "You tell the others. There's a new script ready on Dax's computer. His last instructions to me were to print and distribute it to the whole list of people, and he's already given the writer his check. I'll be there in an hour or two." She hung up and went to get Carlos's breakfast.

CARLOS DRANK A SECOND CUP of coffee en route; he made good time to Mulholland Drive. He parked, got out of the car, and rang the doorbell. A uniformed maid opened it, looking distraught. He showed her his badge. "Take me to his bedroom, please."

He was astonished at the size of the place. He saw a skateboard in a corner and figured that was how Baxter got around it. The maid pointed at the bedroom door. "There."

"You go back to the kitchen and make yourself some coffee. Make a big pot—there are other cops on the way."

She walked away and left him standing at the bedroom door. He opened it and walked to the foot of the bed. He could see a hole in Baxter's temple, and when he walked around the bed he saw an even bigger hole. Crime scene would have to find the bullet. He walked back around the bed and could see nothing that didn't point to suicide. The gun was where it should be, and there were blood spatters, blowback, on it.

The doorbell rang, and a moment later a young Asian man was standing at the foot of the bed.

"Anybody else?" Carlos asked.

"I'm all they've got. There was a big shooting last night."

"I heard," Carlos said. "Do a quick walk-around and see if you see anything that contradicts a self-inflicted gunshot wound."

The tech set down a large bag and did so. "Looks pretty straightforward to me," he said.

"Okay, you get started. I'll go interview the maid."

THE TWO OF THEM sat at a kitchen table, drinking coffee.

"Name?" Carlos asked.

"Anita Escobar."

"Nationality?"

"Born in Mexico, a U.S. citizen for the last seven years."

"Tell me what happened this morning."

"I came to work. I thought Mr. Baxter was at work, so I went into the bedroom to get the sheets and towels. I found him like that, and I called nine-one-one."

"That's it?"

"Yes, nothing else."

"What time was that?"

"Eight forty-five, maybe. I thought you'd get here faster."

"It's a very busy morning for the LAPD." He wrote down her address and phone number. "We'll want you to come downtown and dictate a statement to a stenographer, then sign it."

"That's all I have to do?"

"It's possible somebody from the coroner's office will want to ask you some questions, but everything seems pretty straightforward."

"He offed himself?"

Carlos nodded "He offed himself. Any idea why he might have done that?"

She shrugged. "He was an unhappy man. I worked here three years, and he was unhappy all that time."

Carlos made a note of that. He went into the living room, sat down, and called Chita.

"Hello, there. Everything okay?"

"As much as a suicide can be okay."

"How did he do it?"

"Gunshot to the temple. A bedside drawer was open, so that's probably where he kept the gun. What's happening there?"

"Everybody's shocked, but not exactly surprised. When I spoke to him yesterday he said he was depressed, that he was always depressed when he finished a script. He worked with a writer yesterday. You might want to speak to him." She gave him the name and number. "Will you be there all day?"

"I'm about done, but I'll have to go back to the office and write my report. I should be home in time for dinner."

"I'll be waiting," she said. "I found a key under a flower pot."

"Just keep it," he said. "I love you."

"I love you, too," she whispered.

He hung up and found the tech standing there. "I'm done," he said. "A wagon is on the way. They'll pronounce him and get him to the morgue. I didn't find anything to change my opinion of the circumstances."

"There's coffee in the kitchen," Carlos said. Suddenly, he was tired, but he still had to go downtown, and he had another stop to make.

61

TEDDY WOKE UP feeling terrible.

Sally was sitting in a chair beside the bed. "How do you feel?"

"Dead of a rattlesnake bite."

"I'll get the doctor. Don't die while I'm gone." She came back with a surprisingly mature physician.

"My name is Springer," the man said. "I guess I've treated a dozen or so snakebites, but you're the first victim who brought the snake with him. A very impressive animal. How do you feel?"

"Like shit," Teddy said.

"I'm not surprised. When they wheeled you in, you

looked like a man who'd gone untreated for more than an hour after an attack."

"I'm a little fuzzy on the timeline," Teddy said. "Will I live?"

"Yes. The anti-venom did its work. You're going to continue to feel like shit for a while. I don't know if you know this, but the chances of dying from a snakebite in this country are just about zero."

"That's very comforting."

"Still, you came about as close as anybody ever does, I think. A snake that size could pump a lot of venom in a very short time. How did you kill the thing?"

"With my hands," Teddy said. "It was all I had. Listen, I need to be back at work on Monday."

"Good luck with that," the doctor said, "but if you want to get released from this joint, you'd better start getting better, and fast. It's bad publicity for a patient to walk out of here and then die. Our board wouldn't like it."

"Doctor," Teddy said, "you put whatever you need to in my chart, but early Monday morning, maybe sooner, I'm taking a hike."

The doctor threw up his hands. "I'll alert the media." He walked out.

Someone else passed the doctor on the way in. "Good morning, Mr. Barnett," Carlos Rivera said. "The gate guard at the Arrington told me I might find you here."

"Welcome to my torture chamber," Teddy said.

"I thought you might like to know that last night, Dax Baxter died."

Teddy tried to look surprised. "Really? Did an actor or a director do it?"

"Mr. Baxter saved them the trouble," Carlos replied. "It was suggested that I speak to you, but you seem to have a very good alibi. I saw the snake downstairs. They have it in a jar in the ER."

"I hope they're charging for viewings," Teddy said.

"I just wanted to see that you're recovering, and I can see you are."

"Thank you, Detective."

"I've got to run. I have a report to file, 'Death by self-inflicted gunshot.' If I don't see you again, good luck to you."

"Thank you," Teddy replied, and the detective left.

Sally came and put her head on his chest. "Never a dull moment with you," she said.

"You're not the first to tell me that," Teddy replied.

AUTHOR'S NOTE

I am happy to hear from readers, but you should know that if you write to me in care of my publisher, three to six months will pass before I receive your letter, and when it finally arrives it will be one among many, and I will not be able to reply.

However, if you have access to the Internet, you may visit my website at www.stuartwoods.com, where there is a button for sending me e-mail. So far, I have been able to reply to all my e-mail, and I will continue to try to do so.

If you send me an e-mail and do not receive a reply, it is probably because you are among an alarming number of people who have entered their e-mail address incorrectly in their mail software. I have many of my replies returned as undeliverable.

Remember: e-mail, reply; snail mail, no reply.

When you e-mail, please do not send attachments, as I never open them. They can take twenty minutes to download, and they often contain viruses.

Please do not place me on your mailing lists for funny stories, prayers, political causes, charitable fund-raising, petitions, or sentimental claptrap. I get enough of that from people I already know. Generally speaking, when I get e-mail addressed to a large number of people, I immediately delete it without reading it.

Please do not send me your ideas for a book, as I have a policy of writing only what I myself invent. If you send me story ideas, I will immediately delete them without reading them. If you have a good idea for a book, write it yourself, but I will not be able to advise you on how to get it published. Buy a copy of *Writer's Market* at any bookstore; that will tell you how.

Anyone with a request concerning events or appearances may e-mail it to me or send it to: Publicity Department, Penguin Random House LLC, 375 Hudson Street, New York, NY 10014.

Those ambitious folk who wish to buy film, dramatic, or television rights to my books should contact Matthew Snyder, Creative Artists Agency, 9830 Wilshire Boulevard, Beverly Hills, CA 98212-1825.

Those who wish to make offers for rights of a literary nature should contact Anne Sibbald, Janklow & Nesbit, 445 Park Avenue, New York, NY 10022. (Note: This is not an invitation for you to send her your manuscript or to solicit her to be your agent.)

If you want to know if I will be signing books in your

city, please visit my website, www.stuartwoods.com, where the tour schedule will be published a month or so in advance. If you wish me to do a book signing in your locality, ask your favorite bookseller to contact his Penguin representative or the Penguin publicity department with the request.

If you find typographical or editorial errors in my book and feel an irresistible urge to tell someone, please write to Sara Minnich at Penguin's address above. Do not e-mail your discoveries to me, as I will already have learned about them from others.

A list of my published works appears in the front of this book and on my website. All the novels are still in print in paperback and can be found at or ordered from any bookstore. If you wish to obtain hardcover copies of earlier novels or of the two nonfiction books, a good used-book store or one of the online bookstores can help you find them. Otherwise, you will have to go to a great many garage sales.

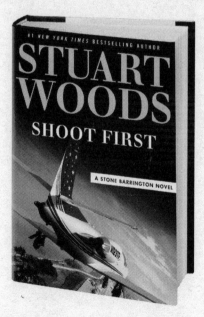

1

STONE BARRINGTON AND his friends Dino and Vivian Bacchetti had just finished a dinner of Caesar salad and Dover sole at Patroon, a favorite restaurant of theirs in the East Forties of New York.

"Oh, by the way," Stone said, "there's a Steele Group board meeting this weekend, and I wondered if you two would like to come?"

"Let me get this straight," Dino said. "You want us to come to a corporate board meeting?"

"Did I mention that it's in Key West?" Stone asked.

"Love to," Dino said.

"Same here," Viv echoed.

"Joan has found a rental house for me, and I'm told it's comfortable, and she's stocked it with food and drink. Why don't we all stay a few days?"

"I can get some time off," Viv said.

"I'll ask my boss," Dino said. Dino was the police commissioner of New York City.

"The mayor?"

"No, me. I asked, and I said, 'Sure, it's okay, stay as long as you like.'"

"You're a very generous boss," Stone said.

"Thank you. I try to cultivate good employee relations."

"I can back him up on that," Viv said. "When I was his employee, he cultivated relations with me."

"I hope he's not that generous with all his employees," Stone said.

"I hope so, too," Viv replied.

"You can both hope," Dino said. "When do we leap off?"

"Saturday morning. Pick me up at ten. We'll be in Key West by four. The board meeting isn't until Friday, but most of us will be playing in a golf tournament on Sunday and Monday."

"Arthur Steele is getting very generous with his directors, isn't he?"

"Oh, once in a while he'll spring for a jaunt. They're all staying at the Casa Marina, the old hotel built by Henry Flagler, the railroad guy who built the Breakers in Palm Beach and others in the early part of the last century."

"So why aren't we staying there?" Dino asked.

"You want to rub elbows with a lot of suits this week-end?"

"We'll stay with you," Dino said. "Should I go armed?"

"I'm not anticipating bandits in the Keys, but suit yourself." Dino always went armed.

THEY WERE WHEELS-UP before noon on Saturday, and Stone's Citation 3 Plus made the flight easily in one leg, no refueling along the way.

At Key West International there was an envelope waiting for Stone at the FBO's front desk, containing house keys and a car key and instructions for operating the house, as well as some history of it. The car turned out to be a metallic white Mercedes S-Class convertible with twenty-eight miles on the odometer. They stowed their luggage in the trunk, and Stone put the top down.

"I hope you like freckles on a girl," Viv said. She was a redhead. "Dino will turn the color of mahogany in about an hour, and I try to keep up."

Stone followed the directions in the envelope; their landmark was a strip club called Bare Assets.

"Sounds like a nice neighborhood," Viv said.

"Can we have drinks there tonight?" Dino asked.

"If we do, it will be the only sex you'll get on this trip," Viv replied.

"They don't have sex there, just looking," Dino protested.

"I'm aware of that, and it's all you'll get. How many bedrooms are there, Stone?"

"Four, I'm told."

"Then you'll have two to choose from, Dino."

"Here's a thought," Dino said, "let's stay home and grill some steaks."

"Good idea," Viv replied.

The house was on a narrow lane between Truman Avenue and the island's cemetery. It had a bricked driveway and a garage and a carport, housing a golf cart, and Stone pulled into the garage. They got out and toured the house.

There was a book-lined study, next to an outdoor courtyard, followed by a dining room, a living room, and another, larger courtyard bordered by a koi pond, and beyond that there was a spa and a sunken swimming pool, all of it surrounded by jungle-like vegetation and flowers.

"Stone," Viv said, "this is spectacular!"

"We haven't seen the guest rooms and the kitchen," Stone said, consulting the note, "and there's a bar/video room. Oh, and that little house over there is the master suite, and we have an outdoor kitchen, bar, dining room, and living room, as well as the indoor ones." He pointed out everything. "From what it says here, I think you two will want the first guest room." They looked at it and approved. The kitchen was next. "Laundry room off the kitchen, in case Dino wants to rinse out his underthings." The next room contained a fully stocked bar and a very large flat-screen TV. They went back to the car, got their luggage, and settled in. "Drinks in half an hour," Stone said. "Outdoor bar."

STONE CHECKED OUT the master suite and found a bedroom, dressing room, and a bath with a large tub. He found a TV remote control on the bedside table, but no set. He pressed the on button and a flat-screen TV rose from a cabinet and filled the wall at the foot of the bed. He could watch the Sunday political shows from there.

EVERYBODY MET IN the outdoor living room, which was covered with an awning, in case of showers. There was no rain, and Stone tended bar, also making a couple of bottles of vodka gimlets and putting them in the freezer. In the process he found steaks and groceries in the outdoor kitchen fridge.

"I could live here," Viv said, settling into a sofa with a gimlet.

"If only it were in New York City," Dino responded, "on top of a tall building, maybe."

"Oh," Stone said, "there's a little house next to the back door that used to be free-standing, but a previous owner moved it over, bolted it to the main house, and made room for the driveway. A caretaker lives there. He keeps the place running and feeds the koi."

As if on cue a large, well-built man appeared and introduced himself as George. "Let me know if you need help with the electronics or anything else," he said, then he declined a drink, excused himself, and returned to his little house.

"There'll be a housekeeper, too, tomorrow morning." Stone looked at another sheet of paper. "The property was originally three small houses on three lots. Somebody bought them all and made them into the property you see now."

"Smart move," Dino said. "And you're playing golf tomorrow?"

"Arthur hustled me into playing in his tournament, and I haven't touched a club for more than a year."

"Then you'll lose," Dino pointed out.

"I think that's what Arthur has in mind," Stone replied.

"Oh," Viv said suddenly, putting a hand to a cheek.

"What?" Stone asked.

"I just had a premonition."

"A premonition of what?"

"I don't know, but something bad."

Dino waved an arm. "Bad? What bad could happen here?"

"As Fats Waller used to say, 'One never knows, do one?'"

2

STONE WAS UP early and found a housekeeper cleaning up their dishes and the grill from the night before. She introduced herself as Anna, then went
back to work.

When she was done with the kitchen, Stone scrambled
himself some eggs, microwaved some bacon, and toasted
a Wolferman's English muffin, the sourdough flavor he
liked. Joan, his secretary, had briefed somebody well.

He left Dino and Viv to sleep as late as they liked, then
he recorded the Sunday political shows on the DVR, got
the golf invitation from his briefcase, and followed the
directions to the golf club. Somebody took his clubs from

the trunk and carried them to the practice tee, and Arthur Steele greeted him there, his nose already sunburned.

"You'll be in my foursome with Arthur Junior and Meg Harmon, both new board members," Arthur said.

"I'd better hit a few to find out if I still can," Stone said.

He teed up a ball and made a big swing with his driver, then watched it slice fifty yards into a swamp. "Nothing's changed," he muttered, and he hit a bucket of balls, working on his swing until it began to straighten out a little.

Arthur Jr. was a clone of his old man, and Meg Harmon was a thirty-five-ish blonde, slim and fit-looking. She, Stone knew, had started a Silicon Valley software company in her early twenties and had recently sold it to a syndicate, with the Steele Group as a partner, for $1.5 billion. She teed up, and her drive went straight for better than two hundred yards. Arthur Jr. was next, and he drove about the same distance, but hooked it into the rough, muttering under his breath. Big Arthur hit one straight for two hundred and fifty yards.

"You've been practicing, Arthur," Stone said. "That's cheating." He teed up and sliced into the rough, but he was long and he still had a shot to the green, if his lie was good.

They were walking back to their carts when Stone heard a single *crack*, and he immediately thought: rifle! A man in the next foursome, waiting to tee off, made a loud noise and was knocked down.

"Everybody on the ground!" Stone shouted as he ran to the man, who had a bleeding shoulder wound. Stone looked around him and from the way the man had fallen, thought the shot had come from a swampy area to his right. He heard a vehicle door slam and gravel spraying beyond the trees. "From over there," he said, getting to his feet.

A club employee came running up. "Call nine-one-one," Stone said, "and tell them a man's down with a gunshot wound. Ask for an ambulance and the police."

Arthur walked over, dusting himself off. "That's Al Harris," he said, nodding at the man on the ground. He knelt. "How are you feeling, Al?" He got a grunt for an answer. "Hang on, help is on the way."

Stone looked around him at everyone's position. From where people had been standing when he heard the shot, he calculated that the shooter could have been aiming at Meg or Arthur, and with a miss, Al Harris had caught the stray bullet. It could, Stone thought, also have been aimed at himself.

THE AMBULANCE ARRIVED first, the hospital being nearby, and two detectives were next by a couple of minutes. Stone greeted them and introduced himself, then he told them his theory of where the shot had come from and where it had been aimed.

"Are you a police officer?" the older of the two men asked.

"Retired detective," Stone replied. "I worked homicide."

"I'm Harry Kaufelt," the man replied. "This is my partner, Moe Cramer. We work anything that comes up. Did you see the shooter or his vehicle?"

"No, but from the sound of the door slamming and the engine, I think it could have been a pickup truck."

Harry got on his radio and reported. "Look for a pickup with a rifle rack. Yeah, yeah, I know, lots of those around. He could be headed north on U.S. 1. Let the sheriff know."

The EMTs were loading Al Harris into their vehicle, and one of them came over to Harry. "He's in shock," the man said.

"Get him taken care of," Harry said. "We'll talk to him later." Then he spoke to Stone again. "And you figure either you or the lady or the gentleman there could have been the target?"

"He only needed a gust of breeze or a jiggle of something to miss one of us and hit Mr. Harris."

"Well, Mr. Barrington . . ."

"Stone, please."

"Well, Stone, we're going to follow your lead on this, because we don't have one ourselves. Moe, you go talk to the other two, and I'll grill Stone, here."

"What would you like to know?" Stone asked.

"You all look as though you're out-of-towners," Harry said. "Where you from?"

"Mr. Steele and I are New Yorkers. The lady is from the West Coast, south of San Francisco somewhere."

"And what brought you all down here?"

"All the people playing are directors of the Steele Group, an insurance company. Mr. Steele is the chairman and CEO. The fellow next to the cart is Arthur Steele Junior."

"You have any reason to think that somebody down here might hold a grudge against any of you?"

"I've visited Key West a few times, but I don't know a lot of people. I've done some business with an attorney named Jack Spottswood."

"Him, we know, and his family. You haven't screwed any of them on some business deal, have you, Stone?"

"No, and if I had, I don't think the Spottswoods would react this way. They're nice people to do business with. And, for what it's worth, I don't think this is local."

"Oh? You think a professional is involved?"

"Are you aware of any contract killers living on your turf?"

"Nope. Our killers are usually drunk or mad at an ex-wife or girlfriend."

"Then that leaves a pro, doesn't it?"

"You may have a point."

"And a pro is going to be a lot harder to catch," Stone said. "He'll have an escape route all planned. You've already covered U.S. 1—that leaves the airport, doesn't it?"

"First call I made, when we got here," Harry said.

"Look for a couple," Stone suggested.

"Why's that?"

"Because the shooter would want to blend in, and he knows you'll be looking for a man traveling alone."

"'Scuse me." Harry got on the radio. "Thanks, Stone, that's a nice insight. Not that I wouldn't have thought of it myself, a couple of hours after they flew out of here. Any other thoughts?"

"I'd check the car rental agencies at the airport, too. I doubt if he took a cab out here."

"I doubt if he rented a pickup truck, too," Harry said, "since nobody rents pickups. A van, maybe."

"He's not getting on a plane with a rifle," Stone said. "Maybe he left it in whatever he rented."

"I think he would think it would take us longer to find it in that swamp," Harry said.

"You have a good point, Harry."

Moe rejoined them. "I got exactly nothing from those folks," he said to Harry.

"Stone, how well do you know those two?"

"I've known Arthur for at least ten years. I met the lady about half an hour ago. I can tell you that she recently sold her software company for one and a half billion dollars."

"Well, that opens up a whole new field of suspects for us, doesn't it?" Harry said. "Ex-partners who feel cheated, ex-lovers or husbands, or anybody who might profit from her death. What town is she from?"

"You'll have to ask her," Stone said. "I don't know that territory."

They both shook Stone's hand and wandered off in the direction of Meg Harmon.

Arthur walked over. "I've canceled play for today," he said. "We'll play tomorrow, if Al isn't too badly hurt. I'll call you."

"Arthur," Stone said, "do you know anybody who might want you dead?"

"Everybody who wasn't happy with his insurance settlement, I guess. That's why we try to err on the side of generosity." He walked off toward the parking lot.

Meg Harmon was walking that way, too.

"Can I give you a lift to the hotel?" Stone asked. "Or even better, join us for lunch at my house."

STUART
WOODS

"Addictive . . . Pick it up at your peril.
You can get hooked."
—*Lincoln Journal Star*

For a complete list of titles and to sign up for our
newsletter, please visit prh.com/StuartWoods